THE MOAI MURDERS: The globe-trotting Lara travels to Easter Island, where ancient mysteries spawn modern-day murder . . .

"Hamilton craftily blends mystery, history, and travelogue."
—*The News & Observer* (Raleigh, NC)

"Fascinating details about the island's history and the Moai."
—*Booklist*

THE MAGYAR VENUS: A suspicious suicide and a twenty-five-thousand-year-old artifact draw Lara to the fascinating city of Budapest . . .

"Lyn Hamilton's archaeological mysteries follow a formula sure to have armchair travelers on the edge of their settees."
—*The New York Times Book Review*

THE THAI AMULET: Broken terra-cotta amulets lead Lara on a search for a missing antiques dealer in Bangkok—where the sights and sounds cloud her judgment . . .

"Lush local color . . . an entertaining tropical tragedy."
—*Kirkus Reviews*

THE ETRUSCAN CHIMERA: An ancient mythical creature rears three of its ugly heads in the form of deception, dishonor, and murderous greed . . .

"A journey that is every bit as magical as the elusive chimera."
—*The New York Times Book Review*

THE AFRICAN QUEST: The sea and shopping take a backseat to murder when Lara leads a tour group to Tunisia . . .

"The exotic world of northern Africa comes vividly alive . . . A strong amateur sleuth tale."
—*Midwest Book Review*

continued . . .

the MOAI MURDERS

LYN HAMILTON

BERKLEY PRIME CRIME, NEW YORK

THE BERKLEY PUBLISHING GROUP
Published by the Penguin Group
Penguin Group (USA) Inc.
375 Hudson Street, New York, New York 10014, USA
Penguin Group (Canada), 90 Eglinton Avenue East, Suite 700, Toronto, Ontario M4P 2Y3, Canada
(a division of Pearson Penguin Canada Inc.)
Penguin Books Ltd., 80 Strand, London WC2R 0RL, England
Penguin Group Ireland, 25 St. Stephen's Green, Dublin 2, Ireland (a division of Penguin Books Ltd.)
Penguin Group (Australia), 250 Camberwell Road, Camberwell, Victoria 3124, Australia
(a division of Pearson Australia Group Pty. Ltd.)
Penguin Books India Pvt. Ltd., 11 Community Centre, Panchsheel Park, New Delhi—110 017, India
Penguin Group (NZ), Cnr. Airborne and Rosedale Roads, Albany, Auckland 1310, New Zealand
(a division of Pearson New Zealand Ltd.)
Penguin Books (South Africa) (Pty.) Ltd., 24 Sturdee Avenue, Rosebank, Johannesburg 2196,
South Africa

Penguin Books Ltd., Registered Offices: 80 Strand, London WC2R 0RL, England

This is a work of fiction. Names, characters, places, and incidents either are the product of the author's imagination or are used fictitiously, and any resemblance to actual persons, living or dead, business establishments, events, or locales is entirely coincidental. The publisher does not have any control over and does not assume any responsibility for author or third-party websites or their content.

THE MOAI MURDERS

A Berkley Prime Crime Book / published by arrangement with the author.

PRINTING HISTORY
Berkley Prime Crime hardcover edition / April 2005
Berkley Prime Crime mass market edition / April 2006

Copyright © 2005 by Lyn Hamilton.
Cover photographs by Luis Casteneda Inc./Getty Images, Peter Hendrie/Getty Images.
Cover design by Richard Hasselberger.
Interior text design by Stacy Irwin.

ISBN: 0-425-20897-4

BERKLEY® PRIME CRIME
Berkley Prime Crime Books are published by The Berkley Publishing Group,
a division of Penguin Group (USA) Inc.,
375 Hudson Street, New York, New York 10014.
The name BERKLEY PRIME CRIME and the BERKLEY PRIME CRIME design
are trademarks belonging to Penguin Group (USA) Inc.

PRINTED IN THE UNITED STATES OF AMERICA

10 9 8 7 6 5 4 3 2 1

Acknowledgments

Many thanks to Edith Pakarati and Bill Howe for showing me their Rapa Nui and to my sister Cheryl for accompanying me there. Readers interested in learning more about this fascinating island can read authors to whom I am indebted—Jo Anne Van Tilburg's wonderful books, including *Easter Island: Archaeology, Ecology and Culture;* John Flenley and Paul Bahn's *The Enigmas of Easter Island; Legends of Easter Island* by F. Sebastian Englert; and of course, Thor Heyerdahl's *Aku-Aku.* This book is dedicated to the charming and resilient people of Rapa Nui.

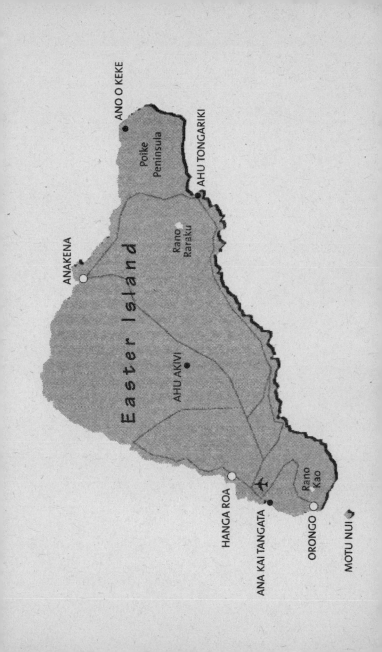

VERI AMO

ANA O KEKE—*It was the third day that the food hadn't come, judging by the cycle of light and darkness seen through the narrow opening in the rock, and Veri Amo could feel the pangs in her stomach growing fierce. The others were hungry, too, of course, but secure in the knowledge that sustenance would come, brought and pushed through to them as it always had been. After all, were they, the Neru, not essential to the coming of the birds? But why had the food not come? That was what Veri Amo wanted to know.*

She could feel her bones already, through the still abundant flesh, and this was not good. For three days they had been forced to eat the skins from the bananas and potatoes brought before, but now even these were gone. Surely they were not forgotten! No, that would not happen. Her father, after all, was the one who brought the food. But where was he? Veri Amo missed her mother, but she had told Veri Amo to be brave, and brave she would be. Was she not, after all, clan Miru, direct descendants of the great Hotu Matu'a, the first ariki mau *at this, the center of the world? Was the king not always chosen from clan Miru?*

It was her brother she missed most of all, Veri Amo thought. He had been taken away in the big ship, and she feared he might never return.

It would be possible to go out, she thought, to slither on her back, head first through the narrow opening, and thence on to the narrow ledge, high above the rolling sea. Then, she could make her way cautiously up the rocky slope. She would enjoy the feel of the wind on her face after all these weeks. But if she did that, then the carefully cultivated pallor would, like the folds of flesh, be gone. She and the other girls, the chosen, had to be pale and corpulent. They would emerge to take part in the ceremonies at Orongo as soon as the birds came.

She wondered if already the wisemen who scanned the heavens for a sign that the birds were near had taken their places at Haka-rongu-manu to await the signal that the sacred first bird's egg had been found. If so, then soon they would be sent for. No, she would wait, with the others, in the darkness. The food would come as it always had.

I

TE-PITO-TE-HENUA—If there is a list kept somewhere of the most common motives for murder, I very much doubt that a disagreement over a potato features very highly on it. Not that this was just any potato, mind you. It was *ipomoea batatas,* the sweet potato, and its existence on a tiny island in the middle of nowhere—a mere mote in the planet's watery eye—has plagued those who care about such things for a very long time. Still, you wouldn't expect anyone to kill over it, no matter what the police said.

For me, the tawdry tale of man and potato, one in which I rather reluctantly played a part, was an object lesson in perspective—both keeping it and losing it. In a way, it ended as it began, with a conscious decision about what is most important, in one case life affirming, in the other, bringing life to an end. More than anything else, I think, the events that unfolded at the center of the world demonstrated the fierce grip that the past holds on us all.

The story began happily enough, with news I'd hardly dared hope for lest in doing so I would jinx the outcome. It came in an unexpected visit to my antique shop by my best friend, Moira Meller. She waited while I rang up a sale and saw another satisfied McClintoch and Swain customer to the door. I was a little apprehensive as I wrapped up the merchandise and chatted away to the customer. Moira had not been well in the past few weeks. She was paler and thinner, and I noticed she sat down while she waited. She looked terrific despite that—her dark brown hair in a very sleek "do," without so much as a gray strand visible, and her makeup was, as usual, perfect. She has to look that way, of course. She owns a spa just down the street, and there are certain expectations about the appearance of a spa owner. Fortunately, these do not apply to an antique dealer, although certain standards must be met. By and large, people do not buy antiques from someone who looks as if they acquired their merchandise by backing a van up to the door of a house while the owners are vacationing at their condo in Palm Beach.

"Guess what?" she said when we were alone at last. "Everything's okay. The tests have all come back clear."

"Oh, Moira," I said, giving her a hug. "I am so happy to hear that!" She sounded remarkably calm about it. I was over the moon.

"Me too," she said. "Another one of those character-building experiences life throws our way from time to time."

"I suppose it does help put things in perspective," I said.

"Funny you should say that," she said. "When I came out of the anesthetic, the first thought I had, other than 'ouch,' that is, was that if I survived this, I was going to make a list of the things I'd put off and another list of those things that I didn't want to do anymore, and I was going to do the former and stop doing the latter."

"I've been feeling the same ever since I heard you had to

have the operation," I said. "I'll tell you now what I wouldn't say before: It was a shock that someone so close was so ill."

"I know," she said. "But now that the doctors have told me I'm fine, I'm not going to forget this. I'm not going back to putting off what I want to do for some indefinite time in the future. You don't know how much time you've got."

"True," I said. "But where to start?"

"Clive isn't here, is he?" she said, looking around.

"No," I replied. "He's off to pick up some stuff for our booth at the antique show at the end of the month."

"I thought I saw his car go by," she said. "There's something I want to discuss with just you."

"There's nobody here," I said. "Not a single customer, either, I regret to say. Discuss whatever you want."

"Easter Island," she said.

"Easter Island?" I said. Somehow this didn't seem to be a topic that required the utmost secrecy.

"Easter Island," she repeated. "It's right at the top of my new life To Do list. I'm going to hug a statue."

"Okay," I said. "That's . . . well, far."

"I don't care how far it is. Ever since I was a kid, I've wanted to go there," she said. "I read all Thor Heyerdahl's books, the one about sailing a raft from South America to Polynesia when everyone said it couldn't be done—*Kon Tiki*, it was called—and then *Aku-Aku,* about his archaeological studies on Easter Island. It was incredibly romantic. I thought he was brave and handsome—a hero, in my eyes. I wanted to be an archaeologist, just like him. It's a far cry, I'll grant you, from the spa owner I actually became."

"A very successful spa owner," I said. "Don't forget that. You get written up in business journals all the time."

"I suppose," she said. "I am proud of what I've done, but I'm not just a spa owner. I have lots of other interests, even if it would be difficult to guess that judging by what I've done in the last ten years. Now I'm going to pursue those other interests for a while, starting with Easter Island. It's on my life list. You know—the pyramids in Egypt, the Parthenon in Athens, the Forum in Rome. But somehow, I didn't get to Easter Island to see those stone statues. I don't know why. Maybe life just got in the way. Now I'm going, so there. Admit it, you've always wanted to go."

"Yes, I have," I said. "It's on my life list, too, but I've never been able to think of a single reason for an antique dealer from Toronto to go there. All my travel is for the shop. I haven't had a trip with no work involved for years."

"I guess they wouldn't let you take one of those giant stone heads home with you," she laughed. "There are probably rules about that."

"Even if there weren't, they're at least fifteen or twenty feet high and weigh several tons," I said. "Rather exorbitant excess baggage charges."

"And a little too large for carry-on," she said. "Isn't there something there that could justify the trip?"

"I expect there are all kinds of treasures," I said. "But nothing I'd be allowed to sell at McClintoch and Swain."

"I guess not," she said. She paused a second or two. "The thing is, Clive is not dealing well with the fact I might have been seriously ill, that I haven't been my usual perky self."

I was tempted to say that Clive Swain wouldn't deal well with a hangnail. I should know. I was married to him for twelve long years, and we were still in business together. On the personal side, however, he was Moira's problem now.

"I'm sure he's just been worried about you, Moira," I said, silently congratulating myself on my tact and diplomacy. "You've had a close call. You can't blame him."

"I suppose not," she said. "So will you?"

"Will I what?"

"Come with me, you dope. I know I could go by myself,

but it would be so much more fun if you'd come, too. Think about it: a fun-only excursion. No work. No men."

"Now there's a subversive thought. When were you thinking of going?"

"Next week."

"Next week!" I thought of the upcoming Antique Fair where Clive and I had booked a large booth. I thought of the shipment arriving any day from Italy. I thought of the backlog of paperwork sitting on my desk. I thought of what was becoming an unending kitchen renovation at home, one that required constant pestering of workmen.

"I'll pay your way," Moira said. "If that's an impediment."

"You will not!" I replied.

"So you'll come?" she said.

"It's a very long trip. Are you sure you're up for it?"

A significant pause greeted my question. Quite right, too. It was a silly thing to ask. If I had had surgery less than three weeks before, I'd still be horizontal, back of hand to forehead, whimpering. Not Moira. She is the most determined person I know. Nothing stops her when she puts her mind to it. I thought of the last several months, of the unpleasant tests, the painful surgery, then the interminable wait for results. I could only imagine what she'd been going through, because through it all she'd never discussed how she felt. This was the first conversation we'd had on the subject. It was too bad, really, because at one time we talked about everything.

"Why not?" I said, decision made. "I've always wanted to hug one of those statues, too." If Clive couldn't deal well with Moira's illness, we would see how well he could deal with the Antique Fair all by himself. It would serve him right for not being more supportive of Moira.

"Thank you," she said. "It means a lot to me."

"We'll have a great time," I said. "We haven't traveled together in years."

"Decades," she agreed. "I wonder what happens to us, all the things we wanted to do, like my being an archaeologist. Instead we sort of fall into some kind of work, the same way we just fall into one relationship or another. It sort of seems right at the time, I guess, but the excitement, the zest for life and its endless possibilities, is lost. Did you always want to be an antique dealer? I suppose you did. You were pretty focused on it when we first met."

"I don't think anybody plans to be an antique dealer when they grow up, Moira," I said. "I was always interested in history, ancient history, really. Anything after 1500 was a bore as far as I was concerned. I didn't want to be a teacher, so I guess I just found something that appealed to an innate interest, and yes, I'm glad I did it. No, I didn't plan it that way. After university I traveled, as did about two-thirds of my graduating class. The difference was they drank their way around the world. I shopped. In fact, I shopped so much I had to sell a lot of the stuff to make room for more."

"A slight exaggeration, I'm sure," she said. "Seriously, though, wasn't there something you wanted to be when you were a little kid?"

"A train conductor," I said. "I thought it would be cool to sit in the back of the train and wave at everybody at the railway crossings. But do I regret not doing it? No."

"You're lucky. I got my MBA because it seemed kind of cool, to use your word, and I opened a spa partly because I did the research and saw an opportunity, but also, in part, because it bugged my parents to no end. They hated the idea of a shopkeeper in the family. Still do, in fact. Not a good reason, I know."

"But you're so good at it," I said. "Don't you get some enjoyment out of it?"

"Sure I do," she said. "And you're right, I've done well by it. I just wonder where I'd be if I'd followed my dream, fol-lowed my bliss, as Joseph Campbell used to say. Would I be here, running my spa and in a relationship with Clive, for example? I don't know."

I said nothing. Having been married to the guy, divorced, and then a hardly disinterested spectator as Clive and my best friend took up with each other, I'd long ago promised myself never to discuss my feelings on that subject. In fact, I'd buried my feelings so deep, I wasn't sure I knew what they were anymore. I had always felt my friendship with Moira hinged on our mutual silence and that, close friends though we were, if we ever got into a discussion about it, one of us was bound to say something that would bring our relationship to an end. I was happy with my partner, Rob Luczka, and even with him, I had made a point of discussing neither my past life with Clive, nor the often conflicting emotions I had felt about Clive and Moira together.

"What do you want me to do about the arrangements for Easter Island?" I said. "Shall I get the tickets? Given I have enough points to get me to Mars and back, why don't I see what I can do?"

"I am going on, aren't I?" Moira said. "You're quite right to change the subject. Blame it on the anesthetic. The surgeon told me it would be months before it worked its way out of my system. I will try not to be so maudlin from now on. But if I learned one thing from the experience, it was that it's a mistake to wait to do something, because you may find you missed your chance. *Carpe diem*—seize the day. That's my motto from now on. I'm going to Easter Island, and if I have to sneak out in the middle of the night when no one is looking, I'm hugging one of those things."

"You aren't having a midlife crisis right here in my store, are you?" I said.

"Maybe," she said.

"Okay," I said. "Just so I know."

"I'll get over it," she said.

"I'm not sure how Clive is going to feel about this," I said with a very slight, almost imperceptible twinge of guilt.

"Leave Clive to me," she said.

Easter Island has to be one of the remotest places on earth. While my European ancestors were busy thinking that if they sailed out too far they'd fall off the edge of the world, other ancient mariners crossed thousands of miles of empty ocean, apparently routinely. And, some of them, by chance or by design, found the island, risked being crushed to death in the wicked surf that pounds the shore incessantly, and stayed. The kind of journey they must have had, I cannot imagine. It was nerve-wracking enough on an airplane—more than five hours and about 2,400 miles straight out into the Pacific from Santiago, Chile, looking for a small triangle of land only twenty-five miles long from tip to tip. If you missed it, there were almost 1,200 miles of water before you came to the next dot on the ocean's surface—Easter Island's nearest inhabited neighbor, the infamous Pitcairn Island. They named this part of the Pacific the Desolate Zone for a reason, one it's best not to think too much about while you're sitting on Lan Chile flight 841.

Easter Island is, in fact, very far away from everywhere, especially home. I'd spent way too many hours in the air, Toronto to Sao Paulo, Sao Paulo to Santiago, then on across thousands of miles of water. Moira, through it all, was perky as anything. She'd spent the air time sleeping, which would have been a sensible thing for me to do, if I were capable of such a thing. "There has to be some advantage to having had surgery three and a half weeks ago," she said, somewhere over the Caribbean. "I believe I could sleep sitting up on a camel."

"I almost envy you that," I said. "Except for the stitches."

"I don't know about you, but I am really out of date," she said, tapping the guidebook she'd been reading on and off between naps. "Did you know they now call Easter Island, Rapa Nui?"

"I think I heard that somewhere," I said. "Really, though, my knowledge of the place is limited to the odd documentary on TV."

"Rapa Nui," she repeated. "Two words and it's the place. Run together as one word, it's the language they speak. It can also refer to the people. Did you know the people on the island came from Polynesia somewhere around sixteen hundred years ago and lived there in isolation for almost fourteen hundred years? That's amazing, isn't it? I guess that's why those statues aren't found anywhere else but there. What are you reading by the way?"

"A camera manual," I said. "Rob gave me a lovely little digital camera before we left. I'm supposed to bring back lots of pictures. He said it was all automatic, I just have to point the thing and push the button, but the manual is about an inch thick. I've been through it twice, and so far all I've managed to figure out is how to put the strap on it. Third time lucky, I'm thinking."

"That was nice of Rob," she said. "Keep reading, because I want a picture of myself with those statutes."

"Don't make me nervous," I said. "Actually this camera was a peace-offering of sorts. I asked Rob if he would mind keeping an eye on my kitchen renovation while I was away, and he said, in something of a huff, that if I insisted on having my own place I would have to deal with my own kitchen renovation. But then he felt bad and went out and bought me this camera for what he has taken to calling the only vacation I've had in my life. Not true. I'm sure I had one once before. I just can't recall when or where."

She laughed. "You could move in together."

"Don't you start," I said.

"We're going to have fun," she said, somewhere over Brazil. "Look at this. There's something called the Rapa Nui Moai Congress on while we're there." She pointed to the in-flight magazine.

"What or who is a moe-eye?" I said. "Or is it what or who are moe-eye?"

"I think that's the name of those giant stone carvings. We're going to hug moai," she said, spelling the word for me. "And, if I have read this correctly, nouns are the same in both the singular and plural. You have to grasp which is intended from the context."

"I see," I said.

"The congress is being held at our hotel," she said. "According to this, experts from around the world are coming to Rapa Nui for the meeting. There will be lectures and field trips and everything. Maybe we could crash some of the sessions. It's the first three days we're there, so we could learn about everything and then go see it for ourselves."

"I hope they're not noisy," I said.

"You really are a poop. Admit it," she said. "It sounds exciting."

"I think most of those academic conferences are really boring," I said. "So-called experts droning on about some tiny theory they have."

She patted my arm. "Thank you for coming with me," she said. "I know the timing wasn't ideal, and I want you to know I really appreciate it."

"This camera manual is making me crabby," I said. "Or maybe it's more that just before I left Rob told me he's thinking of retiring. He just kind of sprang it on me as I was packing."

"He's a bit young for that, isn't he?" she said.

"Not really. He went into the RCMP right out of school. They have a new early retirement package, so he's thinking about it."

"That's okay, isn't it?" she said.

"What's he going to do for the rest of his life? Follow me around?"

"Ah ha," she said. "Now we're getting down to it."

"He did threaten, I mean *suggest,* that he could come with me on my buying trips, but really, they're work. I told him he'd be bored if he came with me."

"What did he say to that?"

"Something along the lines of *Bored in Paris? Bored in Tuscany? Mexico? I don't think so.*"

"He has a point. Maybe he just wants to do something else now, just like me. *Carpe diem* and all that."

I thought that was enough Latin for now. "You told me what was on your To Do list, but not what you won't do anymore," I said.

"I'll never eat beets again," she said.

If anybody thought that heading that far into the South Pacific got you palm trees, thatched huts, and sandy beaches—and I may have been one of those people—they'd soon be disabused of that notion. There are trees, but they are sparse, and *lush* is a word that would never enter your mind as you looked around. Instead, the island is all grassy meadows and jagged coastline, volcanic outcrops and little walled gardens, soaring cliffs where the sea has pounded away forever, a lonely place in many ways, where the wind roars all the time, birds swirl and shriek overhead, and dust settles like a second skin on everything, insinuating its way into your nose, your mouth, your pockets, your hair. And everywhere you look there is the empty horizon and endless sea, disorienting in its vastness. Looking around from the parking lot of the tiny airport, I felt as if Moira and I were clinging to a piece of driftwood, a large one to be sure, and could only go where the current would take us. In a way, I wasn't wrong.

Our hotel was just outside Hanga Roa, the main town.
Perhaps I should say it was just outside the only town. The
hotel was a pleasant enough spot, a sprawling low-rise
whitewashed structure with red roof, a drive lined with hibiscus and large cactus, and a view of the ocean from its vantage point atop a cliff that took my breath away. A large
hand-lettered banner was strung across the main entrance:
Iorana, it read, whatever that meant. *Welcome Delegates to the
First Annual Rapa Nui Moai Congress.*

The hotel lobby was open on three sides to the breeze,
with wood columns beautifully carved with birds and animals supporting a thatched roof. It was also something of an
obstacle course. There were cables crisscrossing the floor
that required careful attention if one preferred not to end up
nose to red carpet. People were milling about everywhere,
and given the day's only flight had come in, piles of luggage
dotted the area and there was something of a line at the
check-in counter.

A rather sturdy-looking man with reddish hair and
beard, a pronounced paunch, and denim jeans and shirt
adorned with a red bandana around his neck was standing
just inside the door. "Hey, girls," he said. "*Iorana.* Hello. I
don't suppose one of you would be Hottie Matu'a would
you?"

"What?" we said in unison.

"Oops. I guess not. Sorry. You girls here for the Moai
Congress?"

I braced myself. Nobody calls Moira a girl.

"I'm afraid not," Moira said. "We certainly wish we were,
though. Is there any way of signing up at the door?" My jaw
dropped.

"I dunno," he said. "It was kind of by invitation only. But
for two girls as pretty as you, there should be a way. Maybe
I could speak to the organizers."

This guy is dead meat, I thought.

"Would you mind asking for us?" Moira said, extending her hand. "I'm Moira, and this is my friend Lara."

"It would be a pleasure," he said after holding Moira's hand just a trifle too long. "Hey, Lynda," he added. I still had not recovered the power of speech, so I just smiled as best I could and shook hands.

"She's the quiet one, I see," the man said, inclining his head in my direction. "Cat got your tongue? I'm Dave, Dave Maddox."

"And what's your specialty, Dave?" Moira said.

"I'm in construction," Dave replied. "Condos, mainly. But I've developed an interesting theory on how the moai were moved down from the quarry and then stood upright on the *ahu.* I'm going to be presenting a paper here at the congress. I'm trying to get my hands on the agenda so I'll know exactly when. Hey, Jeff!" he said suddenly, waving at a tall, thin, graying man in a baseball cap, lugging an enormous bag. "Come and meet Moira and Lynda."

"Lara," I muttered. "And what's an ahu?" The man in the baseball cap looked over his shoulder for a second, as if he wondered to whom Dave was shouting, but then, seeing no one else, came over to our little group.

"Jeff's a history teacher from Albuquerque," Dave said. "Knows everything there is to know about *rongorongo.*"

Rongorongo? I thought.

"Fascinating," Moira said.

"Nice to meet you both," Jeff said. "And it's Seth, by the way. Seth Connelly."

"Right. Sorry, Seth. Care for a drink, girls?" Dave said.

"We haven't checked in yet," I said, finding my voice at last. "We'd better do that first. But thanks."

"Back at ya," he said, turning to Moira. "When I've had a chance to talk to the organizers."

"Thanks, Dave," Moira said, giving him her nicest smile. "I hope we can get in, at least to your session. Your work sounds fascinating." I swear she batted her eyelashes.

"Hey, Bob," I heard Dave say as we made our way to the desk.

"So how do you like the new me?" Moira said, as we completed the formalities. "Even if I've used the word *fascinating* way too often since I got off the plane."

"I'm thinking you'll be asked to turn in your Feminists-R-Us membership card," I said.

"It's only a cunning subterfuge," she laughed. "I'm going to get us into this congress. Just you wait and see. Are you hungry? I'm not sure whether I am or not. Jet lag, I guess."

"You didn't eat much on the plane, or planes, that is."

"Could that be because the food was dreadful? Let's get unpacked and cleaned up quickly and then go see if we can persuade somebody to feed us," she said.

The hotel had only about forty rooms, all of them in two annex buildings, designed motel-style with doors that opened to the outside, but with rather pleasant sliding doors at the back, which opened, in our case, onto a stretch of lawn and a view of the coast.

The dining room was what I would call basic, as was the food. The walls were painted utilitarian white, with blue plastic tablecloths over which had been placed white mats, also plastic. To one side was a wall of windows, though, that exhibited the extraordinarily vast blue sea.

A portion of the dining room had been marked off with bamboo screens, and a few minutes after we sat down and ordered, our newfound pal Dave appeared from the other side.

"Here's the drill, girls," Dave said, coming over to our table. "I'm still working on getting you into the sessions, but there's a field trip first thing tomorrow morning—the quarry—and there's two empty seats on our bus. The field trips are extra, and I've said you'll each pay ten bucks. That okay?"

"Okay," we both said.

"Front door, eight AM," he said. I stifled a groan. After two days of flying, I had thought a little sleep-in might be in order.

"I'll get you into my session no matter what," Dave said. "I got a good time on the agenda. Not too early, not too late, not over the cocktail hour. I'm a happy guy. You two girls just wear something pretty, and I'll give you some charts to hand out to everybody at the session. You'll be my little helpers, like. You can do that, right?"

"We'll do our very best, Dave," Moira said.

"My teeth are hurting from clenching them so hard," I said when he was out of earshot.

"Maybe a Dramamine would help," she said. "I took one before we came down."

"Is there a plan?" I said. "Wait! Just a minute! Of course there is. We suck it up until he gets us registered, and then we kill him, right?"

"Right," Moira said.

"I suppose you noticed we're getting up early to go to a quarry," I said.

"I think we should just go with the flow here, Lara," she said. "Savor whatever comes along. It's bound to be fascinating . . . oops, that word again. Let's say *compelling*. Obviously I should have brought a thesaurus."

"You should have if you're going to chat up every guy on the island," I said. "They can't all be fascinating."

We were just finishing our meal when Dave showed up at our table again, this time with a very slight woman with tightly curled gray hair and a tightly clenched jaw to match, in tow.

"This is Babs, the registrar for the conference. Be nice to her, and she'll get you into the conference. Babs, this is Marilyn and Lynda."

"Really, I don't know if I can," Babs said. "I've got it all organized just so, and the count for the meals has been given to the hotel. I mean, if I tried to change it, they might not be happy. And rooms? What will you do for a room?"

"We're staying here," Moira said. "So rooms are not a problem."

"Come on, Babs," Dave said. "You told me earlier there were a couple of cancellations, and I'm sure Maddie and Lesley won't mind if they have to go out for the odd meal. Gotta go, though. I'll leave you girls to work this out. Bye, girls."

"It's Lara," I said, as Dave rushed off to punch someone else's shoulder. "Not Lesley, not Lynda, not Girl. Lara! And this," I said, pointing to my friend, "is Moira."

Babs, who'd up until this moment been looking rather flustered, if not stern, actually cracked a smile. "And I'm Brenda, not Babs. Brenda Butters. Are you sure you really want to come to this conference?"

"No," I said.

"Absolutely," Moira replied.

"A slight difference of opinion, I see."

"I'll do whatever Moira wants to do," I said. "But maybe you should tell us something about the congress first."

"Not much to tell," she said, handing us a registration form and pens. "Everybody here is interested in Rapa Nui. We have some great speakers lined up, real experts, you know, as well as some presentations by what I'd refer to as talented amateurs. Like Dave, for example, even if he can't remember anybody's name to save his life."

"So who is putting this on? Is it a heritage organization of some sort? The Easter Island Foundation or something?"

"No," she replied. "I'm afraid I can't offer you a tax receipt or anything. It's just a group of interested individuals. Some of us are volunteer organizers, and we got some financial support from a film company. They put in some money to help with the advertising and such. Kent Clarke Films, it's called."

"Cute," Moira said. "A reference to Superman, is it?"

"Not exactly, no," Brenda said. "Kent Clarke's the name of the owner. They are filming a documentary about the conference and featuring our keynote speaker, Jasper Robinson."

"Who's he?" I said.

"Jasper Robinson?" Brenda looked aghast. "I'm surprised you haven't heard of him if you're interested in archaeology. He's the fellow who found a very ancient fortress in the Atacama Desert of northern Chile a year or so ago. They did a special on it for television. He confounded all the experts, too, who had already looked where he did, but completely missed the fortress. He does all kinds of things—diving under the polar ice cap, traveling the Silk Road all alone. He's made some amazing discoveries."

"I know the fellow you mean," Moira said. "Didn't he swim across the Straits of Magellan or something?"

"That's him," Brenda said. "Crazy idea if you ask me. Around here he's considered a modern day Thor Heyerdahl, though. Everybody is looking forward to whatever it is he's going to spring on us in his keynote address on the last evening. His presentation is going to be filmed by the Kent Clarke people."

"Hence all those electrical cables in the lobby," I said.

"Yes. It's a bit of a mess, I know. But if you still want to attend, I'm sure you can. A couple of people canceled at the last minute. You probably got their room if you booked recently. We've already guaranteed the numbers for the meals and everything, so you could just take their places."

"Sure, we want to come," Moira said, starting to fill in

the registration form and gesturing to me to do the same. When we'd finished and handed over some cash, Brenda rose to go as a rather attractive man in khaki pants and shirt rose from his table across the room and passed near ours.

"Hello, Brenda," he said.

Brenda merely nodded in his direction and turned back to us rather more quickly than normal politeness would permit. "I'll be back in a minute with your name badges and tickets for the cocktail party, which is just getting underway," she said. "Your first pisco sour is on the house."

"What sour?" Moira said after Brenda has bustled off.

"Pisco. Distilled from grapes. Very popular South American cocktail."

"Hmm," she said. "Does it have a little umbrella in it?"

"I don't think so," I said.

"Well, that's something. One of the things on my 'never again' list is drinks with umbrellas in them. Do you think they'd make me a very dry, very cold martini instead?"

"What was that about savoring the experience?" I said.

"You have a point. Sour, I'm thinking, is not just the pisco, but also Brenda when it comes to that rather attractive man who just walked by."

"She was a little abrupt, wasn't she?"

"Maybe we will see him at the cocktail party, and we can make nice," she said. "He looked interesting."

"Not fascinating?" I said. She reached across the table and pinched my arm.

Dinner finished, we headed out to the patio and the welcome cocktail party for this little conference to which we seemed to have managed to attach ourselves. The pisco sours arrived quickly, milky white and frothy in tall slim champagne glasses. Moira sipped hers carefully. "Yum," she pronounced at last. "I may have to have more than one."

My first impression of the congress was that it was a little unusual. It may have been a matter of interpretation, but when I hear the word *congress*, with a capital *C*, attached to an event like this, I expect a rather large crowd, maybe hundreds of people, with several tracks of programming, and huge banquets and all. There couldn't have been more than forty or fifty people at the opening reception for the First Annual Moai Congress, including the mayor of Rapa Nui, who gave a very nice speech welcoming us all, and his modest entourage.

Even so, for a few minutes we stood like wallflowers on the fringe of the event, but soon Dave Maddox came over with a "Hey, girls," and we were drawn into the crowd. Jasper whatever his name was who swam with icebergs came over to shake hands and welcome us to the conference. He was attractive in a rather contrived way—perfect haircut, nicely pressed trousers, and I think he was wearing makeup, although maybe that was for filming. In any event, he didn't linger long. His target was quite obviously a woman in a saffron-colored sarong outfit that showed lots of skin. I swear she wasn't wearing a stitch under it. "That has to be Hottie Matu'a," I said to Moira.

We were introduced to a young man in his late twenties whose name was Brian Murphy, not Bob as Dave had insisted. At first I thought Brian was rather rude, peering as he did at the breasts of every woman in the place, but I soon figured out it was our name tags, hung on little strings around our necks, that he was interested in. Brian, it seems, was an archaeology graduate who'd been supporting himself as a computer programmer but was there to find himself a job in his chosen field. "I'm Birdman," he whispered conspiratorially.

"What?" I said.

"Sorry," he said. "Not one of the maniacs, I guess." I was tempted to say that if I stayed with this group for more than a day or two I most certainly would be.

I then made conversation with a Chilean by the name of

Enrique Gonzales who had brought an English grammar book to the party. Enrique's family, loyal to Salvador Allende, had fled Chile for Russia when General Augusto Pinochet brutally took power and established a military dictatorship that was to last almost twenty-five years. Enrique had left as a child and returned as an adult. "We will speak English, please," he said. "For practice. I came home to make study as tourist guide. I am fluent in Russian, and so I wait for Russian tourists. How many Russians do you think have come here in the last three years?"

"I have no idea?" I said.

"Guess, please," he said.

"A thousand," I said.

"There are no Russian tourists coming to Chile, maybe only three in two years," he said. "So now I learn English and make specialty of Rapa Nui for tourists. Most Chileans do not come to Easter Island. It is too far. So this will be for me a specialization."

"Good for you," I said. "Do you know all about Rapa Nui?"

"No. That is why I come here," he said. "To learn." I thought this was refreshing, someone who knew as little as I did, but this moment of camaraderie was not to last long. "I wanted very much to be Enrique-Mau," he said. "You know, like *ariki mau*, the rapanui term for king, and my name together. But someone else had it already. So I am Tongenrique. Is also good, no?"

"Fascinating," I said.

Seth, the history teacher from Albuquerque and expert in rongorongo, came over, and he and Moira were soon engaged in deep conversation. From it I decided that rongorongo was some kind of script that had recently been deciphered, at least in part, and that it was usually carved on wooden tablets. I may have been wrong. Tired of pretending to know what I didn't, I wandered off to admire the view beyond the patio. It was now dark, but I could still see a line of surf where the sea met the coast, and the shadow of steep hills beyond the lights of the hotel. Away from the lights, the southern sky was filled with stars.

"Lost?" a voice behind me said. I turned to see the attractive man who had been snubbed by Brenda. "I see they let you in. Dave Maddox has been lobbying hard on your behalf."

"My friend Moira's behalf really," I said.

"So you didn't get an invitation?"

"We didn't," I said. "And you?"

"I got an invitation, as did a number of my colleagues. Most of them declined, but I wouldn't miss this for anything." He laughed as he said it. "I'm Rory Carlyle. I'm currently teaching in Australia, but working here for a few months. I and some students of mine are doing an archaeological survey of Poike. I'm giving a talk about it tomorrow, relating local myths to actual archaeological data."

I introduced myself and told him how interesting I thought his work would be, not mentioning, of course, that I didn't know what a Poike was.

"Oh, it is," he said. "But I just had to tear myself away to hear the latest theories." There was a hint of something in his voice, I'm not sure what. Laughter at best, but more likely sarcasm. "So you have an interest in Rapa Nui?" he probed. "Some particular aspect of it?"

Many possible answers to that question flitted through my brain. I knew Moira would not be pleased, but I couldn't stop myself. "You know what?" I said. "I know nothing about this place you couldn't get from a documentary on television or in a guidebook except that I haven't read the guidebook because I didn't have the time to buy one, and Moira won't share hers yet. But I've wanted to see Rapa Nui and those wonderful stone carvings my whole life, and the opportunity presented itself. I have no idea what

I'm doing at an academic congress. I could be standing on this Poike thing you mentioned right this minute, and I wouldn't know it. Furthermore, I have only the haziest idea that I may have seen Jasper what's his name on television once. I think he was riding a camel somewhere. There, I've said it."

Rory threw back his head and roared with laughter. "You know something?" he said, wiping a tear from his eye. "I'd be willing to bet you know as much as at least half the people here."

"What's so funny?" Moira said, coming over to join us. "I'm Moira, by the way."

"This is Rory," I said. "He's doing an archaeological survey of Poike."

"Fascinating," she said.

"I take it your friend knows more about Rapa Nui than you do," Rory said.

"I've confessed my utter and complete ignorance about this place," I told Moira. "Just my own personal lack of knowledge," I added, just in case she doubted my loyalty.

"Do you have a specific area of interest, Moira?" Rory asked.

"You are such a brat, Lara," Moira said. "My specific area of interest at the moment is aromatherapy, Rory. It's very big in my world, right now. Ditto whatever she said, only more so. Lara owns an antique store, and she knows about old stuff. I have a spa."

"At least she's read the guidebook," I said.

"I am delighted to make both your acquaintances," Rory said. "And lest you feel embarrassed, let me tell you something." He paused for a moment and sipped some wine. "You must have seen the banner outside the hotel, the one that says welcome to the first annual Rapa Nui Moai Congress."

"Hard to miss it," I said.

"Indeed. Let's just say that maybe what it should have said is welcome to the lunatic fringe."

"Perfect," Moira laughed. "As Lara is probably too nice to tell you, I'm feeling just a little mentally unhinged myself."

"Perfect," he agreed.

We spent a pleasant half hour or so with Rory. He was funny, intelligent, and reasonably good looking. I could tell Moira thought so, too. He obviously loved Rapa Nui, the island, the people, the work he was doing. At the end of our conversation, I knew that Poike was a peninsula at one end of the island, the location of one of three volcanoes that had formed the island a very, very long time ago, and a place where legend had it that a great battle between the tribes of Rapa Nui had been fought. I also knew Rory was single.

The party was just breaking up when the most extraordinary thing happened. We'd spread out by this time, past the pool area and onto a grassy area between the hotel and the sea. Several delegates were out on the grass chatting.

There was a pile of earth near the edge of the cliff, by a wood post and wire gated fence whose role, presumably, was to keep people and animals from going over the side. One moment there was no one there. The next, an older man, dark of complexion and attire, stood staring intently at the dirt. Rory went over to talk to him, and we followed. The man said something to Rory in a language I did not recognize, and then as quickly as he had appeared, he walked away. Rory looked bemused.

"What was that about?" Moira said, watching the man's retreating back.

"That was Felipe Tepano," Rory said. "He's something of a legend in the archaeological community. He's been working on projects here for almost forty years. He helps me out sometimes with my excavation work. I stay at his wife's guest house on the other side of Hanga Roa when I'm here.

Felipe does some work on the hotel grounds from time to time as well, I believe."

"And?" Moira said.

"And," Rory said. "He just told me that someone will die here, right where we're standing. He says that someone will die here very soon."

2

RANO RARAKU—In retrospect, I'd come to view my first full day on Rapa Nui, during which an amorphous blob called the Moai Congress slowly became a group of mere names, then gradually, distinct individuals with all the foibles, passions, and temperaments that went with them, with my first glimpse of the quarry. From a distance, Rano Raraku looks like any other hillside on the island, a grassy, windswept surface dotted with large rocks, spewed in some ancient cataclysm from one of the volcanoes that formed the island hundreds of thousands of years ago. As one moves closer, however, the rocks begin to take form. Huge stone faces and torsos come into focus. Some stand erect, perhaps fifteen or twenty feet tall. Others, held in place by the dust of centuries, lean poised as if forever caught on the cusp of toppling.

Closer still, features begin to appear. The moai are similar, all with thin lips and sharp chins, large and upswept noses, elongated earlobes, and, where the torso can be seen, arms flexed, thin fingers pressed against stone bellies. All are sightless, staring vacantly across the landscape toward the sea. Still, they are not identical; each is individually carved, and with some study, the small differences that make them each unique become apparent. There are hundreds of them, a sight so amazing that Moira and I stood motionless for several minutes, transfixed by what we saw.

Then Moira, with a whoop of pleasure, ran down a dusty path and wrapped her arms around one of them. Praying to whatever gods looked after technopeasants like me, I raised the camera and snapped my first photo. The light was so bright I couldn't see the image on the screen and could only hope I had captured the moment. It was not that I thought I would forget Rano Raraku. That place, and the awe it inspired, would be with me forever. But I wanted to be able to share it with Rob, as he'd suggested, and to give Moira a keepsake of what was such a special moment for her.

The quarry will remain burned in my memory for another reason, an episode that, while mildly unpleasant at the time, was to have ramifications far beyond anything I could have imagined. For several minutes, though, Moira and I just wandered companionably among the moai, enjoying the hot sun and the fact that we were there. The first photo under my belt, I began snapping away with abandon.

"Shall we try to climb up to the rim of the volcano and see what's on the other side?" Moira asked.

"Sure," I said, and we took a rocky, dusty path that headed upward. It was an easy enough climb, although the sun by now was hot, tempered only by the wind.

Moira, who had taken the lead, stopped abruptly at the summit. "You will not believe this," she said, turning back to me, as I took the last couple of steps to the top. At first I didn't know what she was talking about, my attention caught by a startlingly blue lake, partially filled with reeds, that lay at the bottom of the crater below us and the inner slopes of the volcano peppered with even more moai, that I immediately began to photograph. I looked at Moira who pointed to our left, where a man stood, feet firmly planted on the summit, in front of a video camera.

"I'm standing on the slopes of the volcano, Rano Raraku, on the island some of us know as Easter Island, or Isla de Pascua, others as Rapa Nui, but one the native peoples used to call Te-Pito-te-Henua, or the navel of the world," Jasper Robinson said, gesturing toward the sea, as the camera panned across the landscape. "You can see why the inhabitants might think so because this is possibly the most isolated inhabited island on the planet. It is here, on the slopes of Rano Raraku, that the magnificent moai, the huge stone statues that have made Rapa Nui famous, were born," Robinson said, now staring straight at the camera, as he opened his arms wide in an encompassing gesture and the wind whipped his carefully coifed hair. A very young woman who had pierced rings almost every place you could think of putting them and a small lizard tattooed on her upper arm watched with a bored expression on her face.

"Call me crazy," Moira murmured. "But I was not expecting a film crew here."

"Doesn't do much for the ambiance, does it?" I said.

"This is a magnificent setting," the man went on, "still charged, I think, with the energy that those who carved the moai brought to the task. These monolithic stone sculptures are absolutely unique. You do not find anything quite like them anywhere else in the world. There are almost three hundred moai here in the quarry, each weighing several tons, and all at different stages of development. About a hundred and sixty of them are unfinished. Some, as you can see, were completed, and now stand upright, buried to their necks in the soil. Others lie partially carved, still attached to the volcanic rock from which they were created. Beyond that, about a hundred more of them line one of two ancient roads that lead from this quarry down toward the sea."

I heard footsteps crunching on stones behind me and turned to see Dave, who wore the same outfit as yesterday, with the exception of a green bandana, obviously a trademark of his, followed by six or seven delegates to the Moai Congress who had come on the bus with us that morning.

"Are these people going to follow us wherever we go?" Moira said.

"I guess so. They're filming a documentary on Jasper's work and theories," Dave said. "It's called *Rapa Nui: The Mystery Solved*."

"Which mystery would that be?" Moira said. She'd given up, as I had, pretending she knew anything. A tall blonde woman with large sunglasses and a straw hat glared in our general direction.

"The moai were carved using these," Robinson said, stooping to pick up what looked to be a lump of stone. "These are called *toki*, stone tools made of basalt. Thousands of them were found all over the site. Imagine carving these stone giants using only these toki. It is an amazing feat. The burning question is who carved these statues and not only carved them but moved them down the slopes—remember they each weigh several tons—and then raised them on ceremonial platforms called ahu," Robinson went on, taking a few paces toward the camera.

"I'll tell you what the Rapa Nui themselves say," he said, gesturing to a group of workmen who were leaning on shovels and laughing as they watched the action. The camera panned in their direction, and the men, embarrassed, dropped their tools and ran away, giggling as they went. The camera followed their retreating backs. "They say their ancestors carved them, but then the statues walked to the platforms all by themselves." He shrugged at the camera. "I guess we know that didn't happen." He laughed, gesturing once again toward the retreating workmen. The camera followed his hand.

"Do we believe them? Or do we believe that some other race, descendants of the builders of the great stone cities of South America, landed here and both built and transported these great monuments? That's the question we are going to explore over the next two hours."

"Horse manure!" a loud voice exclaimed, and we turned to see a giant of a man coming toward us. He had the bluest eyes I have ever seen, and his gray hair was parted in the middle and worn in long braids. He strode across the rocky terrain as if he owned the place. He was, it was clear, someone to be reckoned with, and he looked really peeved.

"Cut," a rather scruffy-looking man in horn-rimmed glasses and long hair that fell in his eyes yelled. "Could we have silence here, please?" he said, looking right at us as the giant among men joined our little group. "We are shooting a documentary."

"Stand clear!" Dave whispered. "Trouble coming."

"You call this a documentary?" the tall man said. "I call it science fiction, pure and simple."

"Do you mind?" the scruffy guy said.

"That's okay, Mike," Jasper Robinson said. "There are skeptics everywhere. We can take a break for a few minutes. I need to review my notes anyway. Were you able to stay with me through all that, Danny Boy?"

"Take a break," the director said, rather reluctantly. "Nice improvisation there, Jasper. And yes, Danny Boy kept up with you. Great footage." The cameraman, presumably Danny, waved. The bored young woman bestirred herself and applied a powder puff to Jasper Robinson's face before straightening the collar on his cream-colored golf shirt—which set his biceps off nicely—and brushing some dust from his khaki pants. She had not changed expression once that I noticed, not even when the blue-eyed giant had arrived on the scene.

"That was unconscionable," the tall man said, making his way over to where Robinson and the crew stood. "You panned the camera over those poor workmen to imply that they were incapable of much of anything. You took advantage of them to make your own point, and you are a bigot. You made them look like idiots."

"People can judge for themselves, Fairweather," Jasper said.

"That would be Doctor Fairweather," the other man said. "You know, it's several years of university study and after that years and years of field work before one begins to venture opinions on archaeology. I graduated with honors from USC. Where did you say you got your degree?"

"That is just the kind of *ad hominem* response I have come to expect from the academic establishment, of which you are surely one of the most reactionary representatives," Jasper said. "I believe my research speaks for itself. You'll have the chance to present your point of view at the conference, or at least you would have been able to do so if you hadn't declined to participate."

"What does ad hominem mean?" the woman we'd guessed might be Hottie Matu'a the previous evening and who had identified herself to us as Yvonne from Kansas asked.

"He means that Fairweather attacked the man rather than the argument," I said.

"He's made it personal, that's for sure," Yvonne replied, trying to kick some little stones out of her sandals, which were entirely inappropriate for the terrain, and tugging at her shorts, which were riding up on her in what looked to be a most uncomfortable way. She waved rather coyly at

Jasper, and he rewarded her with a big wink. The relationship, apparently, was progressing nicely.

"And will I be filmed here, too?" Fairweather asked, loudly. "No, I won't, because you will only have your own ridiculous ideas on film."

"I am going to present a paper the day after tomorrow that will show you just how wrong you are, Fairweather. About me and about Rapa Nui. I'll give you a second chance. Do come. You have my personal invitation. I hope you accept it, because I look forward to seeing the expression on your face when I reveal my little surprise," Jasper said.

By this time, the two men were almost nose to nose, both red-faced and obviously angry. "I vote we just leave them to it and continue to look around," I said to Moira.

"Right behind you," she said. As we turned back, I noticed the tall, slim woman in the sun hat who had grimaced at us exchanging a glance with the cameraman, who nodded. I was pretty sure I knew what that nonverbal communication was about. Danny Boy was telling her that yes, he had let the camera roll through the entire encounter between Robinson and Fairweather. I wasn't sure what I thought of the heated discussion, but I didn't think filming it was the sporting thing to do.

Determined not to let the incident spoil our visit, Moira and I wandered a little longer on the grassy slopes, stopping to look, to touch, to admire the distant sea. Way off in the distance, close to the water, we could see a long line of moai, their backs to the sea. "Ahu Tongariki," Dave said, joining us for a moment. "It's been restored, as have several others, so you get to see what they would have looked like at the height of the moai carving period. There are fifteen of them on that ahu. It's an incredible sight from here, but wait until you see them up close. We'll go down there later."

"Are they still fighting up there?" Moira asked.

"Fairweather's gone," Dave said. "He was pretty upset. At least he left before they came to blows."

"Who was the glamorous woman, the tall blonde in the big hat?" I asked.

"Kent Clarke, the film producer," Dave replied.

"But what is her name?" I said.

"Kent Clarke. That's her name."

"What do you bet her father wanted a boy?" Moira said.

"Either that or she made it up," I replied. "Show biz and all."

Dave laughed. "I'm afraid it's time to go back, girls. Sorry."

The van was abuzz, as could be expected, with talk of the little contretemps between Robinson and Fairweather.

"I don't know what to think," a woman by the name of Susie Scace said. "I came to hear Robinson. I'd be the first to admit it. He doesn't have the academic credentials, it's true. But you can't fault the work he's done in Chile, and he's done amazing things in Bolivia and Peru, too. I do believe there is such a thing as a talented amateur—somebody who just has a feel for the subject. Maybe he couldn't afford to go to university like Fairweather."

"He sure gets his hands on the big bucks," an impish little man with a white goatee and big ears interjected. He made me think of hobbits and was sitting near the back of the bus with a woman I assumed to be his wife. "I am deeply envious, having worn holes in the knees of my pants begging for money for my own work over the years. If it were not for my wife, Judith, here and her hugely successful medical practice, I would not have been able to come."

"You're a kept man are you, Lewis?" Dave said good-naturedly.

"I am," he said. "Retired last year."

"He's an expensive little muffin," his wife said.

"I'm Lewis Hood, also known as Poikeman," he said, waving in our general direction. Moira and I introduced ourselves.

"They're not maniacs," Dave said. "Poikeman won't mean anything."

"I have no idea what they're talking about either," Judith said, smiling at us.

"I wish I'd been there when Fairweather showed up," Brian Murphy, the young man from the University of Texas looking for a job, said. "Fairweather was trained by Bill Mulloy. Mulloy!"

"Who's Bill Mulloy?" Moira said.

"Wow, you don't know?" Brian said. "He's a legend. Mulloy came out with Thor Heyerdahl in the midfifties. Long after Heyerdahl left, Mulloy worked on. He was responsible for some of the best archaeological work done on the island. He and his team restored Ahu Akivi and the ceremonial village at Orongo. We'll be seeing them later. He's dead now."

"He's buried here," an older man offered. "That's how much the place meant to him. He worked here for years and years. I'm Albert Morris, by the way. To modify a phrase, please don't call me Al. I'm Albert, currently from Montana. I'm retired, too. I was a PR consultant in Washington until a couple of years ago, a spin doctor, to use the vernacular. I'm fascinated by archaeology, so I volunteer at dig sites all over the world. Anybody who'll have me."

"Do you notice how we're always giving ourselves away?" Moira murmured. "Laying bare our complete ignorance of people like Bill Mulloy for everyone to see?"

"All I'm saying is that people can teach themselves about a subject. Learning does not all happen in the formal education system," Susie said.

"I couldn't agree more, Sandy," Dave said. "Take me, for example. I'm a builder, a developer. But I have a theory as to

how the moai got from the quarry to the ahu. Just figured it
out one day. I hope you'll all come to my presentation. It's
the day after tomorrow, at eleven in the morning. You'll
have lots of time to get over your hangovers from the night
before, so you will have no excuse not to come."

"What I would like to know," said a woman who looked
to me as if she'd been blown off course on her way to an au-
dition for a remake of a 1940s' movie set in Budapest and
ended up on Rapa Nui by mistake. She was dressed in a
style I would describe as pseudo-gypsy, a brightly colored
dress with a gathered skirt, a scarf over her head, and far too
much in the way of both makeup and bracelets. "Was anyone here present when that man made his prediction about
an imminent death at our hotel?"

"Did that really happen?" Lewis Hood said. "Everybody
was talking about it at breakfast, but nobody actually heard
the guy say it."

"We did," Moira said. "The man's name is Tepano, and
he spoke in Rapanui, but Rory Carlyle understood and told
us what he said." There had only been a handful of people
present when Tepano had made his pronouncement, but
news obviously traveled fast in this pack.

"I think that's really spooky," Yvonne said. "I keep looking at that pile of dirt. I can't stop. You can see it from the
dining room. Sometimes I think it looks bigger than it did
the last time I looked at it, and I'm afraid someone is buried
there."

"Nonsense," Albert said.

"It is far from nonsense," the gypsy, who had introduced
herself that morning as Cassandra, said. "I believe the people here know things most of the rest of us don't, that they
are in touch with powers the rest of us have lost the ability
to contact. Here people are in touch with their *aku-aku*, the
spirits, who are very much with us. Rapa Nui may be all

that's left of the lost continent of Lemuria, and we know what that means."

"We do?" Yvonne said.

"You mean Atlantis, don't you?" Moira said.

"Atlantis is in the Atlantic Ocean," the woman said in a condescending tone. "Lemuria, or the Land of Mu, is the continent that once joined India and Australia."

"I'm thinking you are maybe not glad you asked this question," Enrique Gonzales said.

"There I go again," Moira said. "Looking like a complete ignoramus."

"And this has what to do with the dire prediction of last night?" Albert said.

"The people of Lemuria were very artistic and spiritual," the woman said. She had a compelling voice, deep and throaty, and I found myself hanging on every word, even if I thought everything she said was hogwash. "Unlike the people of Atlantis, I might add, who were much more scientific. It's possible that both Atlantis and Lemuria were destroyed by a scientific experiment on Atlantis gone wrong."

"Could this possibly be the lunatic fringe Rory was telling us about?" Moira whispered. "I don't feel so bad now."

"The people of Lemuria had extraordinary powers," the woman said. "Powers way beyond anything we know today. I believe, as many do, that they came from another planet."

I heard a quiet snort from Seth Connelly, the rongorongo expert, who had heretofore kept his mouth shut. "Somebody here is from another planet," he muttered.

"Rapa Nui people may have retained some of the powers of the Lemurians," the woman said. "The people here know about the spirit world. They know the aku-aku are very much with us. I believe their ability to sense the aku-aku comes from some vestigial power transferred to them by the Lemurians."

"Vestigial?" Yvonne said.

"My theory," Susie, practical woman that she obviously was, said, "is that intuition or dreams about the future are nothing more than our subconscious trying to tell us something. You know, you dream about the wheels falling off your car because there really is something wrong, some vibrations or something, that your subconscious detected even if you didn't consciously notice, and the dreams are trying to warn you. Am I making sense?"

"Spooky," Yvonne repeated. I resisted pointing out that even if one accepted the argument about dreams and the state of your car, which I probably did, it did not establish what it was about the pile of dirt that could have indicated to Tepano's subconscious that somebody was going to end up dead there. One thing I had in common with Yvonne, though, was that every time the pile of dirt was within eyesight, I couldn't keep my eyes off it.

"If anybody is going to die there," Lewis said. "It's going to be Jasper Robinson. And my money will be on that fellow Fairweather as the culprit. They should just pick him up immediately." We all laughed, all except the gypsy, that is.

"I think Jasper was unkind to those workmen," Susie said. "I'd agree with Robinson that the idea that the moai walked to the ahu is pretty preposterous, but still, he shouldn't have made fun of them like that."

"Who is to say they didn't walk?" the gypsy said. "Power is concentrated here."

"That walking moai story, however preposterous, does rather speak to the moai being moved in a vertical position," Albert said. He was having no truck with the gypsy.

"Just come to my presentation," Dave repeated.

"I'll come," Lewis said. "That final session will be quite something, though. I don't expect there'll be an empty seat in the place when Robinson speaks once this episode is reported to the rest of the group when we get back."

"There's lots going on between now and then," Dave said. "There are papers being presented from noon today on. I'll hope to see you all at mine." Moira rolled her eyes.

"Evil forces may be gathering," the gypsy said. "Remember what Cassandra de Santiago has told you."

"Look," Moira exclaimed, and we all turned in the direction she was pointing as the van slowed to a halt. We were down by the sea, and between us and the surf was the most extraordinary sight. Fifteen towering moai stood in a line on a long platform, backs to the sea, sightless eyes staring across the landscape toward the quarry.

"Ahu Tongariki," Dave said. "Impressive, isn't it? What did I tell ya?"

It was: the moai framed by the crashing sea behind and headlands beyond. I have traveled so much in my life that, sad to say, it takes a fair amount to truly impress me, but even for me, Ahu Tongariki was a jaw-dropping place. I could hardly believe my eyes.

"Tongenrique," Enrique said, tapping me on the shoulder to get my attention. "My name, like I told you."

"Right," I said. What was he going on about?

"I like this place," I said to Moira. "I believe it is actually going to live up to expectations."

"Me, too," she said. "Even with that Cassandra de Santiago person around. Do we think she made up that name?"

"Count on it," I said.

"An abnormally large proportion of people with made-up names at the congress," she said. "Poikeman, indeed!"

We spent the afternoon at the hotel, in a large building just off the main road, taking in the lectures—lectures, I might add, with titles such as *Lapita cultural complex and ancestral*

Polynesia or *The myth of Hotu Matu'a: The reliability of oral tradition in the study of the Rapa Nui prehistory.*

It did not take me very long to realize that for all the backslapping, shoulder-punching bonhomie, and the hey-great-to-see-yous, several of the people attending the Moai Congress didn't like each other very much. Indeed, if the congress could be said to have a personality, it was one of thinly veiled, but genteel, hostility. There was the very public spat between Robinson and Fairweather to be sure, but beyond that I began to notice that certain people went out of their way to avoid each other or looked for opportunities to argue over some esoteric point. These were academic disagreements, but it seemed to me the feelings went way beyond the professional and were charged, in some cases, with a level of animosity that surprised me.

That first afternoon alone, a delegate by the name of Edwina Rasmussen, a short, intense woman of rather unpleasant disposition, publicly called into question Brian Murphy's credentials and then talked loudly throughout his presentation; Brenda Butters walked out of Rory Carlyle's speech in a rather obvious fashion; and Jasper Robinson smirked and squirmed through any of the papers that did not support his theories.

There was clearly a very fundamental disagreement between those who believed that Rapa Nui had been settled by Polynesian mariners and the other group, which was convinced that Rapa Nui had been inhabited originally by people from South America, Peru, and Bolivia primarily, who had brought their great stonemaking skills to carve and erect the moai. Some went even further, postulating, as Moira's hero Thor Heyerdahl had, that the New World was civilized a very long time ago by people from as far away as Egypt and that these people in turn had discovered Rapa Nui.

It seemed to me that science was on the side of those who

supported the Polynesian theory, but science did not in and of itself stop the arguments from the other side.

Then there was the disagreement as to whether local legends and myths were just that or if they represented real events and people—history, in other words. For example, was there really a Hotu Matu'a, who in legend was the leader who brought the first people to Rapa Nui and became their first ariki mau, or king, or was this simply an interesting tale?

By the end of the afternoon, my "never again" life list had a new entry: I will never attend any event with the word *congress* in it again. I was convinced all this suppressed tension was giving me a headache. Moira must have felt it, too. "I don't think we actually need to attend the mixer this evening, do you?" she said. "I vote we get away from here. I think we should go into Hanga Roa for a look at the town—it's not on the archaeology tours—and stay for dinner and a drink or three. It's on me."

We went out to the main road and hailed a taxi, leaving Dave telling a group of delegates about the terrific time slot he had and how they must come to hear his presentation, and in a few minutes found ourselves on the main street of Hanga Roa, a sprawling town of low-rise buildings, never more than two stories, where apparently most of the 3,500 inhabitants of the island live.

We had no specific plans, which was very pleasant after what had been a rather structured day at the congress, so we just wandered along, looking at the various restaurants and souvenir shops, trying to get our bearings. I found an Internet cafe and picked up my email—three from Clive asking me where I'd put things. I'd left him a list of everything he needed for the antique show, but obviously it was easier to send an email asking for the answer than it was to open the file. I resolved not to mention this to Moira. There was also an email from Rob. My heart soared when I read the first sentence in which he told me my kitchen counter had finally arrived, but it sank at the second in which he broke the news that the hole for the sink was cut in the wrong place and we were back at square one.

Next, we found the town's church at the top of a slight incline, and the doors being open, we went in. While much like any other church on the outside, inside it was a surprise. The church enjoyed a rather unusual melding of Christianity with an ancient local religion, that syncretism most obviously expressed by wood statues, all carved by hand. There were saints, recognizably Christian, but carved wearing Rapa Nui attire. One saint had the face of a bird. I was enchanted, and Moira had trouble pulling me away.

Across the street from the church was a craft market—several rooms of little booths selling crafts and souvenirs. Almost everyone was selling wood carvings. There were thousands of carvings, many of the moai. I went immediately into my shopkeeper mode, looking for something special I could ship home to the shop. Then it struck me. I was on vacation. There was nothing I had to do, no purchase I had to make for the shop, no appointments with agents, no new suppliers to track down.

Still, I couldn't stop myself from looking. The carvings varied considerably in quality, and they were not inexpensive. Having said that, some were really lovely. Although my home will soon collapse under the weight of all the treasures I have brought back from my trips over the years, I couldn't resist buying one. Then, in keeping with my holiday mood, dampened only slightly by the news about the kitchen, I bought a flowered shirt for Rob. It was relatively subdued—lovely taupe and cream flowers on a black background—but still, as soon as I'd handed over the cash, I realized I couldn't see him wearing it. That's what happens to you when you go on vacation, I decided. Your reason, to say nothing of your innate good taste, deserts you. It's all that sun on your head. "I think you are going to have to keep me away from the stores and markets," I told Moira. "Let's go see some sights instead."

"We'll head for that little cove," she said. "The *caleta,* it's called, according to my map. Watch your step. No doubt you have noticed that there are many things that distinguish this street from the one on which you and I own businesses, the most obvious being horse poop. Did you notice how many people have horses in their backyard?"

"Hard to miss," I said. "Obviously these horses have the run of the town. I thought when that fellow Fairweather shouted 'horse manure' out at the quarry this morning, that it was just a rather quaint expression. Here it is entirely appropriate. The other feature that distinguishes this place from home is cell phones or rather the lack thereof."

"That, too," Moira agreed. "Horse poop and no cell phones. I'm sure they'll get cell phones soon enough, but I'm not sure what they're going to do about the horse poop. Look! What's this?" We had come upon a building where several people, obviously residents, crowded around an open door. "Come on. Let's see what's going on."

"I hope we aren't crashing a funeral," I said.

"You are such a drag, Lara," she sighed.

What was going on was some extraordinary singing, a group of young men and women who were singing in quite wonderful harmony and with great enthusiasm. The beat was infectious, and soon my toes were tapping. Nobody seemed to mind that we were there, and indeed several people made some room so we could see better.

A tall, attractive woman with beautiful tawny skin and dark hair and eyes smiled at us, and Moira asked what was going on. "Preparation for Tapati Rapa Nui," the woman said. "You would call it a folklore festival, I think. At the end of January, or early February, of every year, we celebrate our heritage. We recreate some of the rituals of our past—

for example, those associated with the cult of the bird man at Orongo. The island is packed with tourists for a couple of weeks. Young men have to swim out to a little islet called Motu Nui and wait for the first bird's egg. Have you been to the ceremonial center of Orongo yet?"

"Tomorrow morning," Moira said.

"That's where the cult of the bird man ceremonies took place for about two hundred years, until the missionaries arrived in the late eighteen hundreds, and the island was converted to Christianity. At the festival, we try to recreate those ceremonies. There is lots of dancing and singing, and there are all kinds of competitions. There is also a festival queen. Two young women are in the running this year, and their friends and families participate in the festival activities in an effort to help them. Everyone does what they can to help the candidate of their choice. One of the two girls, Gabriela, is a member of my family, so I will be supporting her.

"The stakes are very high," she said. "This year's winner gets a university education in Chile, completely paid for. Last year there was a very nice car as a prize. Stay as long as you like," she said. We did listen for a while longer, but I think we both felt like interlopers, so after a few minutes we moved on.

The caleta was very pleasant—a group of pretty buildings facing tiny boats in brilliant yellow, blue, and red bobbing in the wake. A moai stood there, back to the sea, gazing over the town. We continued along, the sea on our left, wandering farther afield. We seemed to be on the outskirts of the town when we came upon a small cemetery overlooking the Pacific. It was not large, and while the gate was shut, it was held only by a loosely twisted rope, so we went in and wandered among the simple graves, most with just a white wooden cross, the graves themselves planted with bright flowers. On the crosses were unfamiliar names like Pakarati, Tepano, Nahoe, Hotus, and Rapu, interspersed with many Spanish and even some English names.

It was getting late in the day, but Moira spotted another group of moai on their ahu on the headlands past the cemetery, so we walked on. A gate blocked the road, but it was easy enough, as it had been at the cemetery, to pry it open enough to get by. A few people watched us, but no one made any attempt to stop us.

As we stood gazing at five moai on an ahu positioned once again with their backs to the sea, we heard some shouts and turned back to the road to see several horses coming our way, accompanied by two men on horseback. The horses were lovely, a striking reddish color, with dark manes and pale faces, but somewhere not far away someone honked a car horn, and the horses bolted straight for us. There were at least fifteen of them, and their hooves on the rocky soil sounded like thunder. Moira and I clutched at each other and stood facing them, poised to run, although I, for one, had no idea which way to turn. When they were close enough that we could hear and almost feel their breath, and it seemed certain we were going to be trampled, the pack parted and swerved to either side of us, and in a moment or two they were gone. It took only a few seconds, but it was terrifying.

"That was exciting," Moira observed dryly when we'd found our voices again. "Let's go back to the harbor. I saw some restaurants there. It would be nice to have dinner by the sea. I like looking at it, even if the moai don't. I'm sure there is an explanation of why they all have their backs to the water, but I haven't heard it yet. Dave probably knows, but I'm afraid to ask him, lest he hold me hostage until I come to hear his paper."

We chose a charming little restaurant with windows on three sides wide open to the street and the harbor, decorated with cheerful blue linens and large and bright posters. The restaurant was deserted with the exception of us, the proprietor, and the chef. Moira ordered a bottle of Chilean sauvignon blanc on the proprietor's recommendation, and we were soon feeling relaxed and grateful to be alone.

A rain shower swept through, and soon we were listening to rain on metal rooftops and a pleasant trickle of water from the eaves. "Didn't you just love the quarry?" Moira said, taking a sip of wine. "I can't believe what we saw today. For some reason, I thought that every picture of a moai I saw over the thirty years since I read Heyerdahl was the same one over and over. At most I thought there might be twenty of them. I had no idea there were almost a thousand all over the island!"

"It is magic," I agreed. "I'm thinking, though, that maybe we should rent a four-wheel-drive vehicle and explore at least part of the island ourselves."

Moira smiled. "That sounds like a very good idea. Will you ever forgive me for making you sign up for this conference?"

I thought about that for a moment. "No," I said, and we both cracked up.

"It's a snake pit," Moira said. "All those arguments! Can you believe these people could have a heated discussion for a whole hour over a potato? What were they going on about? Do you have any idea?"

"It's key to the argument that the carvers of the moai came from South America. The sweet potato is indigenous to South America, but not to Polynesia, so if it's found on Rapa Nui, which it is, then it must have been brought here by people from South America. At least that's the theory. The side that argues for Polynesian carvers says that pollen analysis places the potato here long before anybody arrived, and it's therefore not relevant."

"I'm tempted to say, 'Who cares?'" Moira said. "The moai

are extraordinary no matter who carved them. I was enraptured by Heyerdahl in my school days and rather taken by his idea of a race of tall, red-headed stonemasons who had journeyed to Rapa Nui, but I'm just as happy to have the moai carved by Polynesians. It's very impressive that they could sail so far across the Pacific and navigate by star maps so long ago. If they could do that, why couldn't they carve moai? But obviously there are some here who do care."

"I'd say they care way too much. I have always believed, perhaps naively, that all who worked in the field were interested in sharing ideas, in advancing the world's knowledge through civilized discussion and study."

"Silly you," Moira said. "Weren't they just dreadful to that nice young man, Brian Murphy? I don't pretend to understand what he was talking about, but surely he didn't deserve the treatment he got at the hands of that awful Edwina Rasmussen, nor did Susie Scace, who seems to be a lovely person."

"You were right to suggest we go up and talk to Brian at the break," I said. "Everyone crowded around Jasper and just left the kid standing there."

"He was so pathetically grateful to us, wasn't he?" Moira said. "He must have known we were the last people on the planet to judge his work, but he sure was glad to talk to us. You know who Edwina reminds me of? Rosa Klebb, the villain with the killer shoes in the James Bond movie, *From Russia with Love*."

"Ouch," I said. "You're right, though."

"And Brenda Butters hates Rory because . . . ?"

"Because he doesn't support Jasper's theories and has no trouble saying so, loudly and often."

"I thought Jasper Robinson was particularly disagreeable," she said. "All those lengthy speeches when it came time for questions, intended to display his erudition and provide good footage for the camera, rather than actually asking a real question. If I had been moderating those sessions, I'd have cut Jasper off in about ten seconds. He is a very attractive man, though. Insecure, I'll bet you—one of those men who are always trying to prove themselves. Guess how many wives he's had."

"I have no idea. Three?"

"Four," she said. "Susie Scace told me. He appears to be after number five in Yvonne, who is absolutely starstruck. She hangs on his every utterance. He, of course, is just lapping up all that adoration. It's enough to make me gag. What did you think of the presentation on Lemuria, the lost continent, by that peculiar woman Cassandra de Santiago? Did she invent Lemuria all by herself?"

"Apparently not," I said. "I asked Susie Scace. There are people who think there was a very ancient civilization in the Pacific, one that disappeared just like Atlantis."

"I still think it's odd to have that kind of paper at an academic congress."

"It is that," I agreed. "Dave said the congress was by invitation. I wonder why these strange people got invited?"

"Beats me," Moira said.

"The schedule is a little odd, too," I said. "Most of the conferences I attend have the keynote speaker at the start, not the end."

"Big leadup to the big man," Moira said. "It has the advantage for Jasper of not giving anyone time to argue with him afterward, unless that fellow Fairweather shows up and starts yelling again."

"I think they filmed that disagreement at the quarry this morning," I said. "I can't be sure, but I think so."

"That's not very nice. I vote we go to Orongo with the group tomorrow then just skip the afternoon sessions. We can either rent a car, or book another tour, or something. We don't have to go to everything."

"We have to go to Dave's," I said, and we both laughed.

"That's not until the next day," she said. "I'm going to settle up the bill here, and we should return to the hotel. We haven't had a vicious gossip session like this in years. I'm so glad you came with me."

"You haven't finished your dinner, Moira," I said.

"I've had enough," she said. "I think I have to have another of those pisco sour things. If Rory's there, we'll ask him why the moai all have their backs to the sea."

We walked back to the main street in search of a cab. Now that we knew about the Tapati Rapa Nui, it was clear the whole town was involved. Many stores had posted photos of the two young women competing to be queen: Gabriela, the one we'd been told about, and another named Lidia. They were both very pretty, and one of them looked familiar. The street was fairly deserted now, except for teenagers on motorbikes and a few patrons on the patios of restaurants. Mike and the cameraman, Danny Boy, they'd called him, waved from one of them. I guess we'd been forgiven for talking during filming at the quarry.

By now it was getting a bit dark, so we hailed a cab and went back. Rory came over the minute he saw us, saying "Pisco sours all 'round?"

The young woman who came to take our orders was wearing a name badge that proclaimed her to be Gabriela. We told her we'd heard about her and about her nomination. She was a very sweet young woman and even prettier in person than in her photographs, with a gorgeous smile. We couldn't talk long, of course, given she was at work, but it was fun to meet her, and we wished her luck.

Moira asked Rory right away about the moai, and he told us they were images of clan ancestors and that they were placed to look over the village, as a guardian of sorts, rather than out to sea.

"What toppled all the moai?" I asked. "We saw so many along the shore that are facedown, and there are only a few ahu that were destroyed. Was it an earthquake or something?"

"And why did they stop carving them?" Moira asked.

"Clan wars," Rory said. "We think that during a time when society here was under a great deal of stress, wars broke out between the clans. There are stories about wars between the *Hanau eepe* and the *Hanau momoko*. Heyerdahl translated this as a battle between the long ears and the short ears, but that's not accurate. It is more like fat and thin, or upper class and lower class. The clans toppled each other's moai."

"Sort of like Jasper Robinson and Gordon Fairweather," Lewis Hood said, pulling up a chair. "Or the people who argue over sweet potatoes."

"Sweet potatoes?" Yvonne said, also joining in. "I missed that session."

"Don't ask," Seth Connelly said, also joining us. "The explanation will take hours."

At this point, several of the other people who had been with us at the quarry came over to chat, and so we left it at that. Dave, of course, reminded us of his presentation, the one at the perfect time. Yvonne made a joke about the pile of dirt: She said they'd named it Tepano's Tomb. Brian came over to chat up Rory in the hopes of getting a summer job.

The show stopper, however, was the arrival of Enrique with a glass of red wine, a can of cola, and a glass. As we watched, he poured the wine into the glass and then topped it off with cola.

"Did you see that?" Albert said. "What are you doing to that perfectly decent wine, young man?"

"This is how we drink wine in Chile," Enrique said, adding a bit more cola. "It's good. Very refreshing. You should try it."

"I may have to take something to calm my nerves," Albert said.

"I have diazepam if you want it," Moira said.

"Last call," the bartender said.

"I should think so, after that," Albert said.

"One more round of pisco sours?" Rory said. He and Moira were getting on like a house on fire, and I was beginning to feel as interesting as wallpaper, so I decided to leave them to it and go back to the room by myself.

There were two possible ways to get there, one of which involved going outside onto the terrace and thence across the grass to the annex where our room was located. The second was to cut through the lounge. Given all the talk about fate, Lemurians, aku-aku, and so on that day, I've often since thought about my choice.

I chose the outside route. If I had taken the other route or had left five minutes earlier or later, I would not have seen what I did. As it was, two perplexing and disturbing events occurred.

It was a pleasant evening. I walked along the terrace, and as I was about to turn the corner I heard a sound, a jangling, that I rather believed I'd recognize if I thought about it. The source of the noise became evident the minute I poked my head around the corner: Cassandra de Santiago's bracelets. She had a tight grip on Gabriela, the waitress, and was actually shaking her. I was about to protest, when Cassandra raised one arm and hit the young woman right across the face. I was thunderstruck, but before I could find my voice, Gabriela slipped out of the older woman's grasp and ran away.

I knew the woman had been too busy intimidating Gabriela, and the younger woman too terrified, to notice me, and so rather than confront Cassandra, I turned on my heel and went back along the terrace and thence into the lounge very upset by what I'd seen and not entirely sure what I should do about it. This time, it was the sound of loud snoring that signaled that I was not alone. I tiptoed carefully past a large armchair on which Dave Maddox dozed. I was almost safely past when the book he had been reading slid off his lap to the floor right at my feet. Maddox started slightly, but did not wake up.

The book, a hardcover, had fallen tent-like, spine up. The pages were rather badly crushed. I was going to walk right by, but I love books, and the sight of this one being squashed like that was too much for me. I carefully leaned over to pick it up, intending to simply straighten the pages and put it on the table at Dave's side, all without waking him.

The book was interesting for a number of reasons, not the least of which was that while its dust cover proclaimed it to be the latest John Grisham thriller, the book inside was actually written by Eric Hebborn. Hebborn may not exactly be a household name, but in some circles he is extremely well-known. Hebborn, you see, was a master forger. He claimed to have fallen into that particular line of work when he was ripped off by an art dealer and decided to take his revenge. He was good at it, if one can use that adjective under the circumstances. He fooled a lot of people for a considerable period of time. His final gesture, adding insult to injury, was to write a book called *The Art Forger's Handbook,* in which he documented all the techniques that he had used to deceive everyone. It was this book I now held in my hand, and it was a very rarefied edition, worth at least two or three hundred dollars.

As I stood contemplating this, Maddox gave a snort and woke up. He was obviously startled to see me, so close to his chair. "Sorry if I woke you," I said. "I didn't realize you were here. You dropped your book." I smiled and handed it back to him.

"I guess I must be tired if I can't stay awake reading Grisham," he said. I had the feeling he was watching my reaction closely.

"It's been a busy day," I replied. "I don't think I'm going

to attempt to read tonight, not even something as exciting as Grisham. See you tomorrow." I headed for the door.

"Good night, Lynda," he said. "Don't forget to come to my presentation."

"I'll be there," I said.

My brief but eventful trip to the room had left me with a number of questions, not the least of which was what was Cassandra de Santiago doing terrifying a hotel waitress, one who just happened to be one of two contenders for Queen of Tapati Rapa Nui. And what was a builder whose hobby was figuring out how the moai of Rapa Nui were transported to the ahu doing with a copy of *The Art Forger's Handbook* disguised as a Grisham thriller? Rapa Nui seemed to attract a rather strange group of people, indeed.

3

ORONGO—*This is none of my business,* I told myself. *I am on vacation. It has nothing to do with me.* Dave Maddox could read whatever he liked. After all, had I not read *The Art Forger's Handbook*? Yes, indeed, I had. It was actually very useful for someone in my line of work to understand how forgeries are made. I had trouble coming up with reasons it would be useful for a builder or even someone interested in how the moai of Rapa Nui were transported and raised, but there was no reason why he couldn't read it if he wanted to.

Mind you, when I read it, I sat there bold as brass with the cover hanging out for anyone to see. I didn't try to disguise it as the latest Grisham, nor the work of a Pulitzer Prize winner, either. The cover business was a bit peculiar, it had to be said, although I suppose now that I thought about it, a customer or two might have had second thoughts about buying something from an antique dealer who was reading a book about forgery. Perhaps Dave thought reading such a thing at an academic conference would be frowned upon. There would be nothing here he could forge, would there? Carve a twenty-five-foot moai and make it look to be six hundred years old? What would be the benefit of that, even if he could do it? Fake a petroglyph or two? Not much point in that either. Even if that were what he intended, though, it had nothing to do with me. *I am on vacation. This is none of my business.* That would be my mantra.

I was having more trouble with Cassandra. She was a flake, obviously, all that talk about alien beings populating a lost continent in the Pacific. I'm not saying there isn't a lost continent. But aliens? Still, she could think whatever she wanted. What she couldn't do was terrorize the wait staff at the hotel, in particular a pleasant young woman who just wanted to get a university education.

This has nothing to do with you, Lara, I told myself over and over again. Here I was at one of the most interesting places on Rapa Nui, the center of the bird man cult at Orongo, and I was watching my fellow delegates rather than enjoying the site. This was unfortunate, because the place is spectacular, perched high on a cliff above the sea, with a wonderful view of three tiny islets, one of which, Motu Nui, featured prominently in the rituals centered on the bird man, *tangata manu,* rituals that replaced the worship of ancestors as represented by the moai. The site, near the crater at Rano Kao, is embellished with hundreds of petroglyphs, many of them depicting birds or the bird man. Along with the petroglyphs are the remains of a sacred village, made up of distinctive boat-shaped houses called *hare paenga,* used during the ceremony.

Rory had chosen to accompany us that morning. What he said was that he wanted to make sure we were getting the right information about what we were seeing. I thought it had more to do with Moira. I tried to listen while he explained about the arrival of the birds and the competition between four powerful individuals and their representatives, called *hopi manu,* to find the first egg. The stakes were high, rather like the competition for Tapati queen: in the latter case, a university education, and in the former, the right to rule the island for the next year. But always, out of the corner of my eye, I was watching the others.

Cassandra, in an even more outrageous getup than the previous day, kept putting her hands on the petroglyphs, closing her eyes, and moaning slightly as if being visited by the spirit of the stone, or something. It was, in my opinion, unconvincing, if not just plain nauseating, but Yvonne seemed to be quite taken with it all.

"What are you sensing?" she kept saying.

"The forces are gathering," Cassandra said.

"Spooky," Yvonne said. I thought what was really spooky was that Yvonne hadn't broken her ankle yet, given she was wearing even more inappropriate shoes than the day before. The other person who seemed in imminent danger of breaking something was Enrique, who kept his nose in his guidebook rather than eyes on the rocky ground as we went along.

Edwina Rasmussen, the Rosa Klebb look-alike, was there, umbrella up for protection from the sun. She was unusually quiet, given that Rory's credentials were impeccable, and she therefore had no one to criticize.

Dave Maddox, too, was very subdued. He tended to wander off by himself rather than harangue the group, and he kept taking pieces of paper out of his pocket and reading them as he walked. Considering how high up we were and how rough the terrain, I thought this a very bad idea. I went over to talk to him.

"Did you finish the Grisham?" I asked and then wished I hadn't. I couldn't seem to hold to a resolution for more than two minutes.

"What?" he said, looking startled. "Oh, no I didn't.

Went straight to bed and slept like a baby. Probably get back to it tomorrow night, after my presentation is done. I can relax a bit then."

"Are you rehearsing?" I asked. "I notice you keep looking at some notes."

"I am. I seem to have a bad case of stage fright," Maddox said. "I'm kind of wondering why I got invited here."

"Why not?" I said.

"I don't know. All I did was post my theories on the Internet, and lo and behold I got the invitation. Jasper himself invited me. Well, not exactly Jasper, I suppose. Brenda Butters, the registrar. But she said Jasper had asked her to get in touch with me. I was pretty excited, as you can probably imagine."

"You'll be great," I said. I had no idea whether he would be or not, but he looked kind of pathetic. For all his bombast, he was just a regular guy. "There'd be something the matter with you if you weren't a bit nervous ahead of time."

"I suppose," he said. "But there are all these people with so much more experience than me. I've always been interested in these moai, and I was watching a documentary on television that showed a bunch of guys trying to raise one. I thought they were going about it all wrong. I suddenly had an idea about how it could have been done, using poles and rope, both of which would have been available at the time, and a system of wooden levers. It was a theoretical model only, you understand, untested. Since then, though, I have read about all the people who actually came here and tried to move them out of the quarry and then raise them on the ahu—people like Heyerdahl, Mulloy, Jo Anne Van Tilberg and Charles Love, and that Czech engineer, Pavel Pavel, I think his name is. These people are huge! I mean what am I, Dave Maddox, a small developer from Orlando, doing here?"

"Perhaps you're here because you have an idea that Jasper

thinks is different and will work," I said. "Jasper, after all, is hardly one to insist upon academic credentials, is he? Why don't you go and talk to him? I'll bet you'll feel a lot better after you do."

"Maybe," he said. "You will come tomorrow, won't you?"

"Of course I will," I said, patting his arm. "Moira will, too."

"You girls are terrific," he said, smiling rather wanly.

The team from Kent Clarke Films was there, too—Kent Clarke herself and Mike and Danny Boy. Kent ignored all of us, but the other two were definitely more accessible. When I inadvertently interrupted them, they told me not to worry. They were just scouting out the location.

"Speaking of interruptions," I said. "That was one big one yesterday at Rano Raraku."

"It was deadly," Danny Boy said.

"In case you can't understand the lingo," Mike said. "Deadly is good. Danny Boy has a touch of the Irish in him."

"I prefer Daniel," the younger man said. "I'm Daniel Striker, and my pal here is the director, Mike Sheppard. It is the great J. R. who started this Danny Boy business."

"I got the distinct impression that you filmed the interruption, Daniel," I said.

"That could be true," he said.

"Might add a little drama to an otherwise profoundly boring documentary," Mike said.

"Is it boring? The people attending the congress seem to think it's the most exciting event in decades."

"No accounting for tastes," Mike said. "Hard to make speeches look interesting. But we're waiting for the great man himself to make some pronouncement at the end."

"Did you come out just for this?" I asked.

"I did," Mike said. "I do work for Kent Clarke Films

from time to time. I flew in from Australia where I just fin-ished another gig. Danny, that is Daniel, lives here."

"Half the year. I came out originally to be the assistant to the assistant to the assistant camera guy when they filmed *Rapa Nui* here," Daniel said. "The one produced by Kevin Costner."

"You shouldn't be telling people that," Mike intervened. "That was one dog of a film."

Daniel laughed. "It was a job, which I needed given I'd dropped out of school and had been thrown out of my home, and it got me into the film business. It also brought me here, for which I'm grateful. Met my wife here. She's a Rapa. We're working on our third kid. Two girls already and maybe a boy on the way."

"He's hoping one of his girls will be Tapati queen in a few years," Mike said. "Take a little pressure off her dad with the prize."

Vying to be Tapati queen was not necessarily a wonderful experience, as we found out when we got back to the hotel. A tearful Gabriela was sitting with the woman who'd talked to us at the Tapati rehearsal, and when she saw us coming, she got up and ran away.

"*Iorana*," the woman said, rather wanly. I had decided that *iorana* was hello in rapanui.

"What's wrong?" Moira said.

"I'm not sure," the woman said. "Are you staying here?"

"We are," Moira said, introducing us both. "We talked at the rehearsal in town."

"Yes, I remember. I'm Victoria Pakarati," the woman said. "Are you at this Moai Congress by any chance?"

"We are, but only by chance," I said. "It was on when we got here, so we signed up."

"So you're not presenting or anything?"

"Hardly," Moira said. "Everything we know about Rapa

Nui we've learned since we got here. But what is wrong with Gabriela?"

"I don't know, but she has told her mother that she is withdrawing from the competition for queen of Tapati. The family is terribly disappointed and asked me to talk to her. They think it's just a case of jitters. I think it's worse than that, that something has happened, but I don't know what it is, and I can't deal with it if she won't tell me. She is such a lovely young person, a good student, a devoted daughter. She is one of ten children and a tremendous help with the younger ones. She works in her spare time at the hotel to make some money to help out the family. I just don't know what this can be about."

"I may have some idea," I said and related what I had overheard the previous evening.

"That awful woman hit her!" Moira exclaimed.

"I'm afraid so," I said.

"Who is this woman?" Victoria said. "Is she the one that goes on about the Lemurians?"

"Yes, indeed," Moira said.

"But who is she really?" Victoria asked. "Cassandra de Santiago can't be her real name, can it?"

"I have no idea. In fact, I have no idea who any of these people are," I said. "This is the oddest conference I've ever attended."

"Gordon says it's a complete sham, that it's all a big publicity stunt for Jasper Robinson, that none of the experts one would normally associate with the study of Rapa Nui, the people with established reputations in the field, are here, nor were they invited. Instead we have the Cassandra de Santiagos of the world. I know Gordon is biased, but he may have a point. What I don't understand is why anyone would bother setting this whole thing up, sham or otherwise. Just do the documentary and be done with it."

"Gordon?" Moira said.

"Sorry. Gordon is my husband, Gordon Fairweather."

"Dr. Fairweather," Moira said.

"Yes. Do you know him?"

"Not exactly," Moira said. "We saw him up at the quarry yesterday."

"Oh, dear," she said. "Gordon says he made a complete ass of himself up there."

"He expressed strong opinions," I said. "I had a fair amount of sympathy for him. Robinson did use the opportunity that presented itself to make fun of the Rapa Nui workmen."

"That's what Gordon said. His language was considerably stronger than that. Look, I know I'm biased, and Gordon does have a temper, but he is a lovely man."

"What are we going to do about Gabriela?" I said. "If it would help, I'll tell her I saw that odious woman attacking her and how inappropriate I thought it was. Maybe if she knows I was a witness, she will talk about it. Did I mention that before she hit her, Cassandra actually had Gabriela by the shoulders and was shaking her?"

"Good grief!" Moira said. "I vote we leave Gabriela out of it and just confront Cassandra, three to one. That's what you do to bullies. You bully them back."

Victoria smiled. "I knew you were good people the minute I saw you in town. Why don't we start with Gabriela and take it from there. I'd appreciate it, Lara, if you would tell her what you saw and how awful you think it was."

But Gabriela wasn't talking. When I related my tale, she just sat there sobbing, but she didn't open her mouth.

"That's it, then," Moira said. "You stay here with Gabriela, Victoria. Lara, you come with me." Gabriela shook her head vehemently, but Moira and I were not to be deterred.

Cassandra de Santiago was just taking her seat for the

start of the day's first presentation when Moira and I suggested she might like to join us outside. When we were out of earshot, I told Cassandra what I'd seen.

"I don't know what you are talking about," the woman said.

"I saw you," I said.

"When and where was this incident supposed to have occurred?" she said. She was very angry, but then so was I.

I told her—about ten the previous evening on the back lawn off the terrace.

"It just so happens I was with Kent Clarke last evening. Go ahead and ask her." As if on cue, the producer herself hove into view. "Tell these extremely unpleasant women where I was last night," she said.

"You were with me, of course," Clarke said. "Being interviewed for the documentary. Why?"

"I'm being accused of intimidating one of the staff here," she said. "I am going to see to it that that young woman is fired." *Ouch,* I thought.

"But why?" she said.

"Ask them," Cassandra said, as she flounced off. "I have no idea."

Clarke peered at us over the top of her snazzy sunglasses. "Ladies?"

"I guess there has been some mistake," Moira said. I was speechless. I knew what I had seen.

"If you have come to make trouble here, ladies, then I suggest you just leave. This conference was by invitation only, and I don't recall seeing your names on Jasper's list."

"How did one get an invitation to this thing?" I said. Clarke just walked away.

"You're sure, are you?" Moira asked when Kent was out of earshot. "No, don't answer that. What kind of friend am I? Of course, you're sure. The woman is a liar. And that makes Kent Clarke a liar, too."

"I'm thinking for the life list that 'I will never interfere in someone else's business again' would be good," I said. I dreaded going back to Victoria Pakarati to tell her what had transpired. I needn't have worried. When we got to the lounge, both she and Gabriela were gone. A waiter gave us a message to the effect that Gabriela wasn't feeling well and that Victoria had taken her home. Victoria would be in touch later, the waiter said.

"Now what?" Moira said.

"I think we should get away from here for a while," I said. "Rent a vehicle of some sort and just go exploring. Confronting Cassandra was a bad idea, and maybe we should disappear for a while."

"I think you're right," Moira said. "I hate to think of that awful women hitting Gabriela. I mean, that is just so tacky. But we did our best. Even if she lied through her teeth, it might give her pause to know you saw her, and maybe she won't do it again. So, yes, let's go exploring. That's what we came to do."

That's what we did. We rented a four-wheel-drive Suzuki and spent the whole afternoon exploring. I will not say it's impossible to get lost on Rapa Nui, as I was to find out soon enough, but there are not a lot of roads. The only paved one hugs the coast for a good part of the island, only cutting inland at Poike. We explored ahu after ahu, the huge moai all toppled, most of them facedown. It seemed inconceivable to me that people would go to such extraordinary lengths to both carve and transport these huge stone creatures and then topple them all. Even toppled, though, they dominated the landscape. Rapa Nui, the island, belonged to them.

"Sad, isn't it?" Moira said. "Rory said they continued to bury their dead in the ahu for a long time after. I wonder if there are bodies in these platforms?"

"Probably long since removed," I said, as we moved on.

We ended our island tour at Anakena Beach where Hotu Matu'a was supposed to have first landed and where Thor Heyerdahl had set up camp fifty years ago. There was an ahu there, too: Ahu Nau Nau with seven moai, four with red topknots, and another single moai on the slope of a hill, dedicated to Heyerdahl. It was a rather splendid sand beach, lined with the only palm trees of any size I'd seen on the island, and given we'd taken our bathing suits at Moira's suggestion, we went to swim in the surf.

"You're right, Moira," I said. "This is what we came to do, not to watch crazy people at a conference."

"Exactly," she said.

"Life list: I will take a vacation somewhere splendid every year," I said. "How's that for the positive statement?"

"For you, unprecedented," she said. "Finally, you are getting into the spirit of things. You do realize most people take a vacation of some sort every year?"

"I believe you and others have mentioned that before," I said.

"Remember it this time. I'm thinking we're not going back to the congress until late, either. We'll have dinner in town again."

We did, but somehow the tentacles of the Moai Congress reached out to find us, this time in the form of Gordon Fairweather and his family. We were sitting on the deck of a very pleasant restaurant when Fairweather, Victoria, and a sweet little girl of seven or eight, who they introduced as their daughter, Edith, came in, along with a young man Fairweather introduced as his right hand, Christian Hotus, and Victoria's mother, Isabella. The family took the table next to ours.

"These are the lovely people who are trying to help me with Gabriela," Victoria said. She was casually dressed, as pretty well everyone was on the island, in a sarong and short cotton top that showed off a little turtle tattoo around her navel.

"Have we met?" Fairweather said. "You look familiar."

"You're not going to like the answer to that question," Victoria said. "You saw them up at the quarry yesterday. Furthermore, I'm afraid they saw you."

Fairweather groaned and hid his face in his hands. "I will never apologize to Robinson, but I would like to apologize to you," Fairweather said. "You were just visiting the quarry, and I'm sure you found it all very uncomfortable."

"It's okay," we both said.

"I told you they were nice," Victoria said.

"You may not think so when I tell you what happened when we talked to Cassandra," I said. I related the whole sordid affair, and then I said, "I don't care what she thinks about me, but she said she'd have Gabriela fired. I am terribly afraid I've made matters worse."

"No worry on that score," Fairweather said. "I'm afraid Gabriela has quit her job."

"We've asked her to sleep on her decision to withdraw from Tapati Rapa Nui, and she's agreed, I think, to wait until tomorrow. But she is quite adamant about it, and she will not explain why, even to her mother," Victoria said. "If you had no success talking to that woman and Gabriela won't tell us anything, I just can't think what else we can do. Let's not talk about it anymore," she said with a shake of her head.

We chatted about the island and what we'd seen at Orongo that day. We both said we'd been blown away by the site, which we had, even if I'd spent a good part of the time bucking up Dave Maddox.

"Gordon thinks Orongo is a terribly sad place," Victoria said.

"And it is, if you know the history well," he said.

"But the Tapati," Moira said. "Doesn't it take place at Orongo, at least part of it? Isn't it a happy kind of festival?"

"Sure, it is. And someday our daughter is going to be Tapati queen," he said, giving Edith a little squeeze. "I love this island and the people. I think the women are particularly attractive." Victoria laughed. "I'm on sabbatical this year finishing a book I'm writing about it," he continued, "but usually we live here part of the year and part of the year in Australia where I now teach. As much as I like Rapa Nui, I can't ignore the fact that it has a very tragic history. You may not realize it, but thirty thousand years ago this was a lush tropical paradise. There was all kinds of vegetation, palm trees eighty feet high. Even fifteen hundred years ago, when man first arrived here, it was relatively fertile, if not as much so as other Pacific islands."

"What happened?" Moira said.

"The island became deforested over several centuries of man's habitation here. First of all, it is a very small island. The population grew. Wood was needed to build boats and houses, keep warm, and for several centuries a great deal of it, we believe, was needed to move the moai from the quarry down to the respective ahu. There were other problems as well—rats that fed on the palm nuts, for instance.

"So here were the finest mariners the ancient world produced, and they had no wood to build boats. They couldn't leave, even if they wanted to. The population grew to the point that the island could not sustain it. Starvation ensued. Warfare broke out between the tribes and individual clans, probably over resources. That is when the moai were toppled. There is some evidence of cannibalism, although I'm not one who is completely convinced on that subject. The world of the moai builders essentially came to an end."

"But it was replaced by the bird man cult, wasn't it?" Moira said. "Isn't that what I heard this morning?"

"It was, but think about it. These rituals were timed to

coincide with the arrival of the birds. It is true that birds and their eggs are good food sources. But more importantly, the birds arrive at the same time as the large tuna in the deep water way off the coast. Now a good catch of tuna would feed a lot of people. But no wood. No boats. No tuna. I have a feeling that those who participated in the bird man rituals must have heard the old stories about the arrival of the tuna. The people here have a very rich storytelling tradition. So here they are, stuck on an island with no resources, and they know that once upon a time, they could have got out to the tuna."

"That's terrible," Moira said.

"And it gets worse," Christian interjected. "Care to guess why?"

"I'm betting we showed up," I said.

"Exactly," Fairweather said. "The arrival of the Europeans. That essentially destroyed Rapa Nui culture virtually overnight. The first documented visit by a European was that of the Dutchman Josef Roggeveen. He arrived in 1722, at Easter, hence the name. At that time the moai were still standing on the ahu. The Spanish claimed the island in 1770, Cook visited after that, then the French. By the time a Russian arrived in 1804, there were only about twenty ahu still standing.

"After that it was a free-for-all. Various people took over the island for commercial reasons, and slavers were constantly raiding it. One particularly terrible event took place in 1862. All the able men of the island, including the priests and even the ariki mau, were kidnapped and taken to work the guano fields in Peru, where many died from the terrible conditions. While Christianity had not yet been brought to Rapa Nui—the priests didn't arrive until 1864 and didn't stay until 1866—the Bishop of Tahiti heard of their plight and insisted the islanders be sent home. Very few made it, but those who did brought smallpox with them. Within a very short time, the population of the island was down to exactly 110 people, where there had been thousands, some say as many as ten to fifteen thousand, before.

"It is a terrible story in many ways," Fairweather said. "The horrendous treatment and deaths of the people from smallpox, of course, but think also of all that was lost with them—the family stories, the folk tales, the myths they valued, and the secrets these families shared. Even their written language, rongorongo, was lost."

"How depressing," Moira said. "So are you going to accept Robinson's invitation to his presentation tomorrow night?"

"Haven't decided," he said. "A colleague of mine, Rory Carlyle, will be there. We drew lots and he lost, so he had to attend on behalf of a few of us who are working here."

"We met him," I said. "He refers to the congress as the lunatic fringe."

Fairweather laughed. "Trust Rory, he always has an interesting turn of phrase. He's filling in for me at the University of Melbourne while I'm on sabbatical."

"Isn't he working up on Poike, too?" Moira said.

"He is," Christian said. "We all are."

"Speaking of Rory, there was a man at the hotel the night before last by the name of Felipe Tepano," I said. "He predicted to Rory that someone was going to die on a particular spot."

Victoria Pakarati looked startled, then perturbed. "I don't like the sound of that," she said, looking over at Christian, who frowned. We'd been speaking English, which had left Victoria's mother out of the conversation, but now Victoria translated for her mother. The older woman shifted uneasily.

"Come now, all of you," Fairweather said. "It's nonsense."

"I'm not sure," Victoria said. "There have been other times."

"The motorcycle accident," Christian said.

"Yes." She turned to us. "I don't want to alarm you, but strange things happen here from time to time. Someone else made a similar prediction about a particular place on a road, and that very night, two young people on a motorcycle lost control, and died on the very spot."

"Coincidence," Fairweather said. "A good Catholic like you shouldn't be telling tales like that."

"I'm not a Catholic," she said.

"Then why is it you haven't missed the nine o'clock Mass on Sunday morning in the five years we've been together?" he said, smiling.

"I'm a Rapa Nui Catholic," she said. "That's different."

"We saw the church yesterday," I said. "I think I understand what you're saying."

"Come to Mass on Sunday," she said. "You'll understand even better. But I wouldn't discount what Felipe Tepano says."

"He's a very powerful man in his family—the patriarch, I think you'd call him," Christian said. "I'm related to the Tepanos on my mother's side, and I can tell you people think he does have some spiritual power."

"Gordon laughs about Rapa Nui Catholics," Victoria said. "Men like Felipe Tepano go to Mass every single day, but when they leave, they also do prayers to the spirits of the island and to their family aku-aku. We don't see anything contradictory in that, do we, Christian?"

"No, we don't," the young man said. "At least the older generation doesn't."

Edith was starting to get restless, so it was obviously time to go. Victoria had the last word. "If Gordon decides to go tomorrow, I'm counting on you to keep him in his seat and quiet," she said.

"Tough job," Christian said, laughing.

When we got back to the hotel, some of the congress delegates were sitting either in the dining room finishing their dinners, or out on the terrace or around the pool having a drink. Dave was deep in conversation with Kent Clarke, and he didn't seem any too happy about it. Jasper Robinson was nowhere to be seen, but then Yvonne wasn't either, a fact that was remarked upon by more than one person.

Daniel and Mike were holding up one end of the bar, a spot they seemed to have staked out for the duration of the congress, and we went to join them. "I hear you filmed an interview with Cassandra de Santiago last night," I said. "That must have been entertaining for you, Mike." Moira, who would have no trouble guessing what I was up to—which is to say, checking out an alibi—was no doubt doing some mental eye rolling, but she said nothing.

"Entertaining? That's a good word for it," Mike said.

"A bit of a nutter if you ask me," Daniel said.

"Why have a nutter on a documentary?" I asked.

"Like the film *Rapa Nui,* this one's a dog," Mike said.

"It is that," Daniel said. "I should know."

"Kind of eats into your drinking time, doesn't it, filming it in the evening?" I said. "Are you on call twenty-four hours?"

"Kent thought the nutter would be better at night, you know, kind of dark and creepy," Mike said, as Daniel rocked with laughter.

"Who's the bored-looking young woman who hangs around while you're filming and straightens Jasper's collar and stuff?" Moira said.

"Kent's daughter, don't you know. A bit of nepotism in the film business," Daniel said. "Or is it necrophilia? The girl can barely speak. Is she alive?"

"You're bad," Mike said. "But she just hangs about, that's for certain. Her name is Brittany."

"I'm surprised a woman named Kent Clarke wouldn't

call her daughter something more masculine, Sydney or something," Moira said.

"Lois," Daniel said. "As in Lois Lane. That's what I would have done. Anyway, I'm heading home. Thanks for the brew, Mike."

"I'm turning in, too," Mike said. "Long day tomorrow, and I've got to have a look at what we got today and get tomorrow organized."

"The logistics man," Daniel said. "He worries about the details. All I have to do is point the camera where he tells me."

"And make everything look nice," Mike said. He stumbled slightly as he stood up.

"Nice," Daniel agreed, reaching out a steadying hand.

I was thinking Moira and I would also turn in for the night, but Rory showed up at this point and came over the minute he saw us. We told him we'd met Fairweather and his family.

"Great guy," Rory said. "I heard about the set-to up at Rano Raraku. He does have a temper, but basically he's one of the good ones. Couldn't talk him into joining me here at the congress, though."

"He may come tomorrow evening," Moira said. "Robinson invited him."

"They may have to tie him down," Rory laughed.

"Actually his wife gave us the responsibility of keeping him still and quiet," I said.

"Not an assignment I'd relish," Rory said. He signaled the waiter. "The usual? Pisco sours?" he asked.

"I think I'm going to pass," I said. I'd been keeping an eagle eye out for Cassandra, given she was the last person I wanted to see that evening, and I had just caught a glimpse of her heading for the terrace.

Avoiding Cassandra, however, was more difficult than I

had thought. As I walked through the lounge, I saw to my dismay that she had changed direction and we were now on a collision course if I continued on my chosen route to the room. Furthermore, she stopped to talk to Mike on the walk between my current position and my goal. Fortunately, the lounge was empty except for Seth Connelly, who was reading in the armchair that had been occupied by Dave Maddox the night before. He greeted me in a most friendly fashion, so I didn't feel I could just turn around and walk out the way I had come.

"I've the better part of a bottle of wine, here," he said. "Come and have a glass with me." I chose a chair where I hoped Cassandra would not see me if she decided to go out to the terrace through this room.

Seth was very entertaining, as it turned out. He hadn't had much to say at the congress, but when I asked him about rongorongo, he was positively effusive. "It's a writing system," he said. "One of the most amazing ever. There is no precedent for it in ancient Polynesia. The old Polynesian cultures could neither read nor write. Rapa Nui was the same until the arrival of the Spanish in 1770. That year, the Spanish claimed the island. The Spanish insisted the *ariki,* the leaders, sign a document ceding the island to the Spanish crown. The Rapa Nui put little marks on the page, symbols of importance to them. What is amazing is that they obviously figured out that the Spanish symbols on the document represented spoken language, and after the Spanish left, the Rapa Nui came up with their own written language. Don't you think that's amazing? I don't think there has ever been anything like this in the entire history of literacy."

"Amazing," I agreed. "And is it still used?"

"I'm afraid not," he said. "Not everyone would have been able to read and write it in the first place. There would be wise men, called *maori rongorongo,* who specialized in it. Now nobody can. Progress has been made in deciphering it, but there isn't much to work with. While rongorongo was occasionally written on stone, it was usually carved on wood tablets, and a lot of these have just disintegrated in this climate. There are only fourteen tablets—twenty-eight if you count fragments—known worldwide. A rongorongo tablet is a very rare find."

"So this is your area of expertise?"

"I just work at it for my personal satisfaction. I teach history for a living. I came out here in the hope of seeing Gordon Fairweather again. Pity he's not at the conference."

"He may come tomorrow night," I said.

"Indeed! I hope so. Misery loves company."

"I take it you are not keen on Jasper Robinson?"

"I think Robinson has had some extraordinary discoveries."

"But?" I said.

"But I can't stand him," Seth said. "If the story about what happened at the quarry is true, if I'd been there instead of Fairweather, I'd have said a lot worse than 'horse manure.'" That sounded a lot like braggadocio to me. Seth was shy, almost painfully so.

We went on talking until I'd finished my glass of wine. Seth's enthusiasm was infectious, and I'd spent a very pleasant and enlightening half hour or so with him. I had completely forgotten about Cassandra, but she was nowhere to be seen, so I decided to make a run for it, leaving Seth to his book.

I wanted to go to sleep, but I couldn't, at least not right away. I had been of two minds about leaving Rory and Moira alone together. In fact, if I hadn't seen Cassandra heading my way, I'd almost certainly have stayed. I wasn't sure how I felt about the budding relationship between them. I did know I felt a pang as I watched the two of them, their heads bent close to each other, perhaps to be heard above the din, but more likely because they preferred it that way.

I know I criticize Clive a lot. He has a rather superficial glibness that lends itself to ridicule. But in my heart of hearts, I do not delude myself into thinking our marriage fell apart entirely because of his faults and foibles. I am not the easiest person in the world to get along with. I'm stubborn and judgmental and occasionally just plain cranky. I am also a workaholic. There, I've said it.

I thought Moira and Clive, no matter how painful it had been for me when they got together, had a really good relationship. They were both the better for it, and I found myself hoping that Moira would not stray. The question was, to which of them did I owe the most loyalty? I had been married to Clive. That aside, we were in business together. If he found out about any straying and discovered that I knew and didn't tell him, our shop might go down the drain. On the other hand, Moira and I also went back a long way, and we were very good friends. I was the one she asked to come to Rapa Nui with her, the number one spot on her life list.

I also lay there thinking about Cassandra. I went back over the nasty little scene of the previous evening again and again. The truth was I had not seen her face. I saw Gabriela's and the terror in it, and I had seen the back of Cassandra and heard her bracelets jangling away. Cassandra's choice of apparel was very distinctive, to be sure. I hadn't seen another gypsy on the island. She was a big woman, though, and wore loose clothing. It was possible, if not probable, that someone else had put on her clothes. It could even have been a man, given her stature.

That's ridiculous, I thought. Even if I didn't see her face, I heard her voice. But maybe that wasn't exactly the case, either. The person in the gypsy garb had not spoken clearly. Rather she had hissed at Gabriela, a hoarse whisper, in fact. Could I swear the voice I had heard was Cassandra's? I decided I could not, although I remained convinced that it was.

All of this was giving me a headache. I decided I didn't want to talk to Moira about any of it and that I would turn out the light, pretending to be asleep when she came in.

I didn't have to pretend, though, because despite all the drama, I was out like a light and came to only briefly when Moira came in. "Did you have fun?" I managed to say. I believe she said yes and something to the effect that Rory was a lovely guy and they'd gone for a walk together.

I awoke again in the middle of the night and lay there for what seemed to be an eternity, unable to sleep, listening to Moira's breathing. I couldn't see my watch, but there was a crack in the curtains on the sliding door that led out to a tiny patio outside our room, and through it I could see the moon, a slim crescent. The wind had picked up, and something was banging outside. It was one of those sounds, a creak and then a thunk at irregular intervals, that gets under your skin.

As quietly as I could, I pulled my jeans and a sweater on over my nightgown, then slid into my sandals. Moira murmured in her sleep, but didn't wake, as I carefully pried open the door wide enough to slip out.

It was absolutely beautiful outside, warm and windy. The dark sky was filled with more stars than I had ever seen in my life, testament to the remoteness of the island, and for a few minutes I stood, head back, looking at them. I could see the outline of the cliff behind the hotel. Somewhere I heard a horse neigh, and there was a shuffling sound nearby, an animal perhaps, rooting about.

The banging was coming from something a few yards away, near the dining room, so I walked quietly toward it. The lights of the hotel had been dimmed, but there was a slight glow from inside.

It didn't take long to find the source of the sound. It was the gate near the edge of the cliff and Felipe Tepano's pile of dirt. Perhaps the wind had loosened the catch. I can remember having only two coherent thoughts as I reached over to close it. One was that Felipe Tepano was right. The second was that Dave Maddox wasn't going to make it to his perfectly timed session later that day.

4

ANA KAI TANGATA—"Trampled by a horse?!" Moira said. Her tone was skeptical, something for which I could hardly blame her.

"That's what they're saying," I replied. "They" were the people charged with the responsibility of enforcing the law on Rapa Nui, the Carabineros de Chile, and it was in their headquarters on a dirt road out by the airport that I found myself.

"I don't believe it!" Moira said.

"I did hear a horse," I said. "And we might have been trampled ourselves, if you will recall, when we were out at the ahu near the cemetery. More to the point, however, the police say there are all kinds of hoof prints around where I found him."

"Horses are a big problem here," Rory said. He and Moira had come to lend their support, which was nice of them. I noticed they were holding hands. "There are way too many of them. They're everywhere. A lot of them are wild, or at least semi-wild. You could get rid of half the horses on the island and there would still be too many."

"They say he may have tried riding the horse. One of his shoes was found several yards away," I said.

"He decided to go riding in the middle of the night?"

"It wasn't exactly the middle of the night," I said. "It was dark, but it was close to six."

"Rapa Nui is on entirely artificial time," Rory said. "Because it belongs to Chile, even though it is 2,400 miles out from Santiago, the island tries to stay close to Chile time here. It's way darker than it should be in the morning and stays light well into the evening."

"He must have been drunk as a skunk," Moira said.

"He was well on his way when I last saw him," Rory said. "He purchased a bottle of pisco in the bar and was heading off to his room. Notice I said a bottle, not a glass."

"He said he was taking it home to the States with him," Moira said. "But I suppose that is what people who are trying to hide their drinking say. Perhaps he had a problem."

"I don't know, but would he drink so much that he'd go out and try to ride a horse in the dark?" I said. "His paper was supposed to be today, and he was so excited about it. He was nervous, yes, but despite that I am certain he had every intention of showing up. You think he'd stay sober long enough to deliver it."

"Maybe he just wasn't used to pisco," Rory said. "It's very pleasant to drink with a little whipped egg white and lime juice in a pisco sour, but it is distilled liquor and can be pretty lethal if you drink it straight."

"You are free to go now," a not unpleasant police officer by the name of Pablo Fuentes said. "We thank you, Señora, for helping us with the investigation. It all seems very straightforward. I will have someone drive you back to your hotel."

"I'll do that," Rory said. I was grateful for the ride. I was tired after a couple of hours conversing only in Spanish, which I hadn't used much for a year or two, and three rather wild- and ferocious-looking dogs evidently considered the road just outside the headquarters of the carabineros their personal turf.

When we got back to the hotel, Moira approached with a glass of water in one hand and a pill in the other. "Sleep," she said. "I got these after my operation. You will be out for about six hours, and you will feel better."

For some reason, I am uncomfortable with sleeping pills. I knew Moira took them. I'd seen her do so on more than one occasion since we'd set off together on this trip. I don't like the way I feel when I wake up, I don't like the dreams I have when I'm out, and I have a rather irrational fear of something bad happening while I sleep. Given a choice between that and spending six hours thinking about the pulp that was once the left side of Dave Maddox's face, however, I opted for the pill.

Soon I was dreaming away, unfortunately about horses. There were horses in my house, in the shop, in the backyard. They were everywhere. At some point, they galloped into a row, and I realized I was watching the Royal Canadian Mounted Police. Leading the group, to my surprise, was Rob. He was in dress uniform, red jacket and all, and he looked, I must say, rather fetching.

Now, it is true Rob is a Mountie. I suppose he must know how to ride a horse. I, however, in all the years I've known him, have never seen him do it.

In any event, Rob rode right up to where I stood, and towering over me from the vantage point of the saddle, said, "Remember what I told you about horses." He then rode off to join the others. The ranks divided as they came up to me, swung around on either side, and in a moment or two they were gone. It was then that I woke up.

"Good, you're awake," Moira said. "I've brought you something to eat. Then you're going to have a shower and get dressed. You have forty-five minutes until Jasper Robinson begins to speak."

Stickler for the social niceties that I am, I would have thought that the trampling death of a delegate to a conference as small as this would have brought the proceedings to a halt, at least for a day. But I had forgotten that this wasn't a real conference, at least not as far as Gordon Fairweather was concerned, and it was the documentary that was driving it. The show, as they say, must go on.

I knew I'd had some weird dreams, and I had a feeling there was something I was supposed to remember, but whatever it was, it was gone. I felt groggy and stupid, and I didn't want to go anywhere, but Moira was insistent. I knew she was right, but it all seemed way too difficult.

The meeting room was full when we got there, with standing room only at the back. For a minute I thought maybe I could crawl back into bed, but Rory had saved us seats. Moira sat beside Rory, and I was seated between Gordon Fairweather, who had evidently decided to attend, and Seth Connelly, the rongorongo expert. Albert Morris, Lewis and Judith Hood, Edwina, Enrique, and Yvonne sat immediately behind us. I hoped Gordon wouldn't start yelling during Robinson's talk, because I'd had more than enough drama for one day and my head was starting to hurt. There was a spot just over my left eye that was throbbing, and as the camera with its accompanying spotlight swept the crowd, I had to cover my eyes. I was also feeling slightly claustrophobic in the middle of the row. There was a larger meeting room in another building, and I couldn't for the life of me figure out why they wouldn't have used it. Silly me. Clearly I would never have a career in publicity and public relations, because when I mentioned it to Moira she pointed out that they wanted the room to look really crowded for the cameras.

About fifteen minutes past the appointed starting time, the lights in the room dimmed, which came as a relief, if only a temporary one, and Jasper Robinson jogged out from behind a curtain accompanied by music that sounded somewhat anthem-like. I idly wondered if I had wandered into a religious revival meeting by mistake. Robinson bounded up the steps and thence to the microphone, smiling and waving like an evangelist—or was it a candidate for president he most resembled? I couldn't decide. Moira started to giggle, Gordon Fairweather looked heavenward for support, and Rory, staring at his shoes, shook his head in amazement. I wanted to throw up.

The room may have been small, but the screen to one side of it was large, as was Jasper Robinson's head on it. Rock concert, I decided. Not a campaign stump, not a religious meeting. A rock concert. I was right, too, because just then a group of dancers dressed in traditional Rapa Nui attire came out to perform, accompanied by a group of musicians and two women who sang. Jasper swayed and clapped in time to the music. I looked around the room. Everyone, with the exception of Rory, Fairweather, and I, seemed to be lapping it up. Even Moira was smiling, but she may have just been laughing at the absurdity of it all.

Then as quickly as it had started, the warm-up act was finished, and the dancers, who had actually done an excellent job even if the context was a little odd, dispersed. I can remember thinking that when I felt better, I might like to see them perform again. On the large screen a photograph of a moai appeared, and across it the words *Rapa Nui: The Mystery Solved* appeared. "Good evening, ladies and gentlemen, colleagues, and all those who love knowledge," Robinson said. There was applause. I guess nobody in the room was prepared to admit they hated knowledge. "I am here to-night to present for your consideration my latest work on the mystery of the moai of Rapa Nui." He paused and there was a smattering of applause again. "I'd like to begin, if I may, with a personal note."

A photo of an older man in a blue shirt and sun hat, smil-ing, appeared on the screen. "It was my privilege to spend some time with the late Thor Heyerdahl," Jasper said. "Heyerdahl has been an inspiration throughout my life. He was not an archaeologist, as some of you in this room like to point out, but he was driven by a fierce commitment to his work, and his death is a tremendous loss. Easter Island, I know, was very dear to his heart. He believed, as most of you know, that the moai of Easter Island were carved by people from the South American mainland, people with highly evolved skills at stonework and from a sophisticated culture that was responsible for the great cities of Peru and Bolivia.

"For fifty years, the experts, some of whom are in this room," Robinson said, with a touch of sarcasm in his tone when he said the word *experts,* "have been trying to prove that settlement of Rapa Nui from the east, from the main-land, is not possible. My question for all of us this evening is what if the experts are wrong?"

"Not again," Rory sighed.

A new slide appeared: *There is extensive archaeological evi-dence for the early settlement of Rapa Nui by Polynesians. If South Americans settled on Rapa Nui, where is the evidence?—Rory Carlyle.* Rory and Gordon exchanged glances, Rory's rather pained.

"Heyerdahl knew perfectly well that Polynesians had set-tled Rapa Nui, Dr. Carlyle," Robinson said. "But he be-lieved very strongly that there had been two waves of settlement of the island, one from South America that brought the great stonemasons to Rapa Nui, the second from central Polynesia. What evidence did he produce that would support that? First this." A slide showing Felipe Tepano sitting on a rock surrounded by a number of children, all apparently listening intently, came up on the screen. Behind them were a couple of horses, and for a few seconds I was drawn back into my dream. In this particular fragment of memory, there was a horse in the showroom at McClintoch and Swain. In the dream I had thought this was highly unusual and not a good idea, but it didn't seem to bother Clive at all. Pity he wasn't so reasonable in real life. I had this overwhelming sense that there was something I had to do, or remember, and whatever it was, it hovered somewhere near my conscious mind, but it wouldn't reveal itself. I turned my attention back to Jasper Robinson.

"Rapa Nui oral tradition tells of two waves of settlement of the island. One, of course, is the story of Hotu Matu'a, the first king, or *Ariki Mau*. But there is a story of seven others who came ahead of Hotu Matu'a, and there are stories of pale, redheaded men on the island. It is even possible that Hotu Matu'a was pale-skinned. We know how valued pale skin has been over the centuries here; witness the practice of placing people in caves to whiten their skin. Those who do not accept Heyerdahl's theories are happy enough to believe the folk tales about the arrival of Hotu Matu'a, but ignore the stories that suggest the arrival of a different people. This is hardly good science.

"But is oral tradition, suspect at the best of times, the only discussion point this evening? It is not." A photo of a potato appeared on the screen.

"Not that potato business again," I heard Lewis Hood say in the row behind.

"Get to the point, man," Albert Morris said.

"*Ipomoea batatas*," Robinson said. "A type of sweet potato. This has been the spanner in the works, as we would say in England, the monkey wrench, where discussions of the original inhabitants of Rapa Nui are concerned. It sticks in the craw of our so-called experts, believe me."

"Since when was he English?" Fairweather muttered. He must have seen the look I sent his way because he leaned over and said, "Don't worry. I'll behave."

"*Ipomoea batatas* is, I'm certain we will all agree, indigenous to the Americas, not to Polynesia. Yet it has been on Easter Island for a very long time and may indeed predate the arrival of the ancestors of the people who now live here. It is easily transported by people, that we know. Recent work shows us that it was in Polynesia by about A.D. 700. How did it get there? At this time, we simply do not know."

"Is that true?" Moira asked Rory.

"Sort of," he replied.

"I still don't get it," Yvonne said. "Even though Jasper already explained it to me."

"Shush," Edwina said. "Why are you here if you won't pay attention?"

"Heyerdahl believed it came direct to Easter Island from the source in South America," Jasper said. "Given that we don't know how it got here, is this any more improbable than saying Polynesians got to South America and took it back with them? I do not believe so. Those who support transfer from Polynesia point to the fact that they can find no evidence for the sweet potato on Rapa Nui before A.D. 1600, but surely this is not entirely fair, given that *ipomoea batatas* does not preserve well in sediment. This one fact alone should force us to at least revisit the possibility that people like Thor Heyerdahl were right and that the first settlers on Rapa Nui were from South America. But no. The orthodox view now is that Heyerdahl was completely incorrect, and the search for the moai builders has moved on."

Up on the screen there appeared what looked like a reed of some kind—bulrushes, we'd call them at home. "The tortora reed," Robinson said. "Also indigenous to South America." The slide disappeared quickly to be replaced with another, this one showing two men astride a boat, paddling out to sea. "This slide shows us small boats made of this same tortora reed," Robinson continued. "The photograph was taken just off the coast of northern Peru, where boats of this type are common. The tortora reed is found in the crater lakes of Rapa Nui, and we have drawings of Rapa Nui people on craft like this. What would the self-proclaimed experts have to say about this?"

"What does he mean self-proclaimed?" Seth Connelly muttered. "If anybody is a self-proclaimed expert, it's Robinson."

Another slide appeared: *The transfer of plants cannot be used as proof of the transfer of culture.—Gordon Fairweather.*

"Your turn," Rory said to Fairweather.

"That is most excellent statement," Enrique said. "I will use it for my tourists."

"Quite right, Fairweather," Robinson said. Gordon looked wary. "But these are arguments we've been having for decades. What would it take to prove to you that a transfer of culture had taken place between South America and Rapa Nui, a transfer originating on the mainland, I might add? What if there were new evidence of a cultural transfer from South America to Rapa Nui?"

Another slide appeared. I held my hand over my left eye to see it better, but it didn't help much. I had no idea what I was looking at. It was a series of figures carved into something, most likely a piece of wood. "This is a photograph of the large Santiago tablet, now in the Museo Nacional de Historia Naturel. On it, of course, is carved the writing system we call rongorongo."

As Jasper spoke, another slide appeared: *Rongorongo, while an extraordinary achievement for which there are no known antecedents anywhere in Polynesia, was essentially a short-lived phe-*

nomenon, beginning shortly after the acquisition of the island for Spain and ending in 1864 when the men called maori rongorongo were either captured in slave raids or felled by smallpox. With them the knowledge of how to read rongorongo was lost.—Gordon Fairweather.

"Is he going to try to tell us something different?" Connelly said.

"Both Gordon Fairweather and Rory Carlyle, whose views I have tried to make sure you understand in the interests of a full airing of opinion, are with us tonight," Robinson said. Something akin to the sound of a small animal being strangled emanated from the general direction of Gordon's throat. "Fairweather," Robinson repeated, "makes three points here. The first is that there is no precedent for rongorongo in Polynesia. He is quite right, and I will ask you to remember that fact."

"Why do I think your words are about to be twisted into something unrecognizable?" Rory said.

"His second point I will return to, but his third, that the ability to read rongorongo disappeared with the capture and deaths of the Maori rongorongo is also correct. Certainly there was no one in the early part of the twentieth century who could read it. But to continue with Dr. Connelly's interesting point of view—"

"Interesting?" Fairweather said. "Is that what you call it?"

"Gordon," Moira said, in a warning tone.

"It is Fairweather's second point that I am most interested in tonight and that is that rongorongo dates to the annexation of this island and its subsequent renaming as San Carlos by the Spanish in 1770. I realize I am repeating what a lot of you already know, but I want to make sure everyone understands this because it is key to what I am going to show you later. According to that theory, the inhabitants of Rapa Nui watched the Spanish in all their imperial finery

claim the island and were consequently asked to sign a document that sealed the acquisition. The Rapa Nui elders put
some marks on the document, drawings of what they
knew—a bird for example—and the Spanish left never to
return. That document has survived.

"Then, so the story goes, the people of Rapa Nui, realizing that what the Spanish wrote represented in some way
the spoken word, came up with their own writing system,
the one we now know as rongorongo. If true, this is an
extraordinary achievement—to design a writing system on
the spot as it were, as opposed to the way most writing sys-
tems evolve, over centuries."

"What does he mean, if true?" Connelly said.

"I have a feeling we are about to find out," Rory said.

"My question to you all, and specifically to Dr. Fairweather, is what if rongorongo is much, much older than
that, and what if its origins can be found elsewhere? We already know it doesn't come from Polynesia. Would a more
ancient form of rongorongo qualify as evidence of cultural
transfer, Dr. Fairweather?"

Robinson paused dramatically. I looked over at Rory and
Gordon, then back to Seth. All three, as if attached together
with string, slowly leaned forward in their seats.

After a few seconds in which you could hear the prover-
bial pin drop, a slide appeared on the screen. The slide was
relatively dark, which was a merciful relief for me as my
head was really throbbing now, and strange lights kept
jumping about in front of my eyes. There was no way,
though, that I was going to leave until I knew what Robinson had to say. The photograph on the slide was definitely
not taken on Rapa Nui, but I had no idea where it had
been. It was a desolate place, an earthly lunar landscape in a
way, without so much as a blade of grass to be seen, just
sand and rock. Nonetheless it was very beautiful. The picture must have been taken at either dawn or dusk, because

mountains in the background had a pink tinge, as did the sand.

"Some of you will know that I have been working with some success in northern Chile," Robinson said, with a self-satisfied little laugh. "And it is in northern Chile that I found something that will interest you all. This is the Valle de la Muerte, Death Valley, in other words, in the Atacama Desert of northern Chile, near the border with Bolivia. The valley, not far from San Pedro de Atacama, was discovered by a priest by the name of padre Gustavo Le Paige. It is now a popular tourist attraction. This part of the world is best known perhaps for salt flats, flamingo habitats, the highest geysers in the world at a startling fourteen thousand feet plus."

"Flamingos? Is he ever going to get to the point?" Albert asked. "I have discovered a rather delectable wine from the Maipo region and it is waiting for me in my room." Brenda Butters, in the row in front of us, turned around and glared. I sympathized with Albert. I was sure Moira had a bottle of painkillers in the room, and I wanted to have at it as well.

"You supply the wine. I'll bring the cola," Lewis chortled, ignoring Brenda's stare.

"It is interesting for another reason, which is that it may well be the driest place on the planet. That means, of course, that we are able to find ancient objects that in another climate would have long since decayed. So it is here that we find extraordinarily well-preserved mummies, for example, and an ancient mud brick pueblo, Aldea de Tulor, that dates to about 800 B.C. In other words, the region is home to a very ancient culture.

"Just a mile or two from Death Valley there is a side slip off a similar canyon, and it is here that I discovered something that is going to rewrite the history of Rapa Nui." He paused dramatically. There was a hush. No one moved. It was as if the whole room was holding its breath. Several seconds ticked by.

A new slide appeared on the screen. It looked like a burlap bag filled out into a round ball with a rather small and dessicated head that stuck out of the top of it.

"Eeeww," Yvonne said. "What is that?!"

"Some of you will recognize this as a mummy bundle," Jasper said. "It was found in a tomb that I excavated in the canyon. Notice, please, an object with the bundle. I will show you a closer view of that object now."

Another slide appeared. To me it just looked like a holiday snapshot, the kind I was taking with my fancy new camera, only I hoped mine would be better. Two people were standing in the same kind of desert landscape we'd seen a minute earlier.

"You will perhaps recognize the two people in the photograph. On the right is Edwina Rasmussen, my esteemed colleague, and I am, of course, on the left." Both were smiling, and Jasper was holding something in his hand.

"You are all probably wondering what I'm holding," he said.

"Tell us," several in the audience called out. Jasper paused for more effect. He had everyone in the room's attention.

"Next slide, please," he said, and a close-up of his hands holding what looked to be a piece of wood with something carved on it appeared. I had to cover my left eye again to make it out at all. I still didn't know what it was, but it resembled the Santiago tablet Robinson had just shown. In other words, this carving had to be rongorongo.

"In case you're wondering," Robinson said. "This was found near San Pedro de Atacama in northern Chile as I have just said, in a grave that has been dated to 200 C.E., almost fifteen hundred years before rongorongo is supposed to have been invented on Rapa Nui. It has survived because of the exceptionally dry climate."

He paused dramatically. "The inescapable conclusion is that rongorongo originated on the mainland and was carried to Rapa Nui. Not the other way around." The room burst into applause.

The lights came up, and shooting pains stabbed my eyes. Two members of the warmup act rolled a glass case on a trolley out on to the stage. Flashbulbs started popping immediately, and soon the audience was on its feet, clapping rhythmically. At that moment I would have preferred to hear howling hounds of hell over that noise. Rongorongo was going to have to wait. I stood up, crawled over everyone between me and the aisle, and then bolted out the door. I made it as far as a hibiscus bush before I threw up. I staggered back to the room, crawled into bed, and pulled the blanket over my head to make the lights stop strobing.

"Migraine," the Chilean doctor said, in English for Moira's benefit, an hour or so later. I suppose that was something of a relief. I was sure I was having a stroke and would die, which didn't seem such a bad idea. "Have you had one before?"

"No," I mumbled.

"I'm told they are very unpleasant," he said. I could have told him that, too. I'd never had a headache even remotely like it. I wanted them to turn out the light and go away so I could die in peace.

"Unfortunately, once you have one, the likelihood of more is rather high," he said. If I could have managed to sit up without vomiting, I would have scratched his eyes out. Alas, I couldn't move.

"Perhaps that is a detail she doesn't need right at this moment," Moira, bless her heart, said.

"I'm going to give her something for the pain," the doctor said, as if I weren't there.

I've tried taking something for the pain, you idiot. I can't keep it down.

"I understand she had an unpleasant experience earlier today, and that may well have set this off," he said.

No kidding! The guy was a genius. I decided that before I joined Dave Maddox in the netherworld I had to ask Moira what Seth, Rory, and Gordon had said about Jasper's rongorongo revelation, if that's what it was, and to request that she tell Rob that I loved him, or something equally touching. Instead, a few seconds later I'd been jabbed in the posterior and was out cold again, dreaming of horses. This time it was I who was lying on the pile of dirt known as Tepano's tomb. Felipe Tepano was there, on the patio, telling anyone who would listen that someone else was going to die on the same spot. I knew I was that someone because I was certain I'd had been kicked in the head by a horse. I tried to cry out for help, but couldn't make a sound. The only person who noticed me was Cassandra, who not only came over, but pulled me up and started shaking me. "I have put a curse on you," she said. "You insulted me. I have put a curse on you just as I did on Dave. I have the power. My aku-aku is very strong."

But then, suddenly there were Rob and the Mounties to the rescue. *I've had this dream before,* I thought.

"It's just a migraine. You'll be fine," Rob said. "Remember what I told you about horses." I promised him that this time I would, no matter what. As he wheeled his horse to the left to leave, he said, over his shoulder, "There's something else you've missed, by the way."

When I came to, the room was dark, and Moira was snoring slightly. I glanced around. A tiny fringe of light showed under the curtain, but I could look at it without flinching. Furthermore, the pain in the head had stopped, and I could sit up—I tried this very gingerly—without throwing up. Apparently the worst was over. I lay there quietly grateful, feeling much more kindly toward the doctor, and thinking about my dream. This time I could recall it all very well. The trouble was, I couldn't remember what Rob had told me about horses. Then it came to me. Rob said that horses will always go around you. Even if you were lying unconscious on the ground, he said, they would not trample you. If Rob was right, and I had no reason to think he wasn't, then what exactly had happened to Dave Maddox? And what was it I'd missed?

So there I was once again, creeping out of the room in an effort not to wake Moira. This time I took my new camera. The sky was soft gray tinged with pink this time, and there were angry dark clouds off in the distance. It was possible this was going to be a stormy day, which made what I was going to do all the more urgent.

I went directly to Tepano's tomb, which had a pathetic piece of yellow plastic fluttering away in its general location. No one had made any effort to cover up the scene of death, to protect it from the wind and what looked to be an approaching downpour. There were lots of footprints in the dirt, but also hoof prints as well. I could see why the carabineros had reached the conclusion they had. I took a picture of the spot, and also the gate, the one I'd found unhinged. Then I walked the full length of the fence until it reached the sea in one direction and a rock face in the other.

When I had completed the circuit, I was startled to see the Chilean policeman Pablo Fuentes watching me from the vantage point of the terrace. "Sometimes it is not a good idea to revisit the site of an unpleasant experience, Señora," he said, walking down to me.

"And sometimes it is," I said.

"How so?" he said.

"He wasn't killed by a horse," I said.

"Why would you say that, Señora?"

"My spouse is a member of the Royal Canadian Mounted Police," I said.

"A Mountie," he exclaimed. "Most excellent."

"He told me that horses would go around you even if you were lying on the ground unconscious."

"I am not a Mountie and know nothing about horses, but if he says so, then it must be true." I couldn't tell whether he was being facetious or not. "Other than what the Mountie has told you, can you find any support for your point of view?" he asked. Now I knew he was humoring me.

"Do you see any horse poop on this side of the fence?" I said.

Fuentes looked amused, but at least he looked around for a minute before he pronounced, "No."

"There's lots of horse poop on this island, at Rano Raraku, on the road to Orongo, and even on the main street of Hanga Roa. And there is lots of horse poop out there," I said, pointing to the area beyond the fence. "But never in the three days I've been here have I ever seen horse poop on the hotel grounds."

"But there are horses just outside the fence, Señora," he said. He looked as if he was having great difficulty not laughing.

"There certainly are," I agreed. "So how did the horse get into the hotel grounds?"

"It jumped the fence, I suppose," he said.

"Okay," I said. "Show me where. Show me one hoof print anywhere near the fence on either side of it." He was sufficiently interested in what I had to say to walk the length of the fence as I had.

"Where did you find Maddox's shoe?" I asked. "This side or the other side?"

"This side," he said.

"So what happened here? Maddox lost a shoe climbing the fence to get to a horse on the other side, went out to the road, along it, down the hotel lane, through the lounge, and across the terrace?"

Fuentes was beginning to look annoyed. "What happened here was a bad accident," he said.

"I don't think so," I said. I went through the gate now, being careful not to step on any hoof print as I did so, and walked up to the edge of the cliff, peering over the side very cautiously. I do not like heights. "There's a dead horse down there," I said after a moment or two.

"There is?" Fuentes said, stepping as carefully as I had through the gate and joining me at the edge. The horse lay on its side on the rocks below. From time to time a wave washed over it. The poor horse was very definitely dead.

"I suppose that must be the horse," he said. "You may have inadvertently disproved your own hypothesis."

"I don't think so," I said. "How did the horse get down there and Maddox end up here? Please don't tell me the horse felt so bad after trampling Maddox that it threw itself off the cliff."

"Señora," he said, in a pained tone. "It is too bad about the horse. I suppose I will have to send someone down there to have a look. I think you are hinting that Señor Maddox may have been murdered. I do not agree with you. Murder is almost unheard of on Rapa Nui. I think the only one in living memory occurred when a man killed his wife some time back."

"I'm glad to hear murderers do not run rampant on the island, but the people we are talking about are not from Rapa Nui," I said.

"As far as I know, tourists do not regularly murder each other here, either," he said. "However, lest you think I am being derelict in my duty, I will tell you that I have asked that a pathologist be sent out from Santiago. The doctors who examined the victim and pronounced on his death are somewhat divided in their opinion, shall we say, and so I have asked for an expert to settle this. Unfortunately the pathologist is not going to make today's flight. He will come in tomorrow."

"What do you mean divided in their opinion?" I said. "Could one of their opinions coincide with mine?"

"No, Señora," he said. "One of them thinks Señor Maddox may have hit his head on a stone."

"Which stone?" I said.

"The one his head was resting on. You have perhaps not noticed that there is a lot of rock on Rapa Nui?" he said. He was getting a bit testy. "There was alcohol and barbiturates in his blood. That much we have been able to ascertain here," he said.

"Enough to kill him?" I asked.

"Perhaps not," he conceded. "But maybe enough to make him sufficiently loco to go out and try to ride a horse."

"Everyone is leaving today or tomorrow," I said. "Before the pathologist gets here."

"Not today, Señora. There is an inbound flight from Santiago, but no return. The flight goes on to Tahiti today. It will not be back until tomorrow."

"So nobody from the congress is going to Tahiti?"

Fuentes pulled a small notebook out of his pocket. "Two of you: Señora Susan Scace, Señor Seth Connelly. I am here early in order to take their statements before they leave."

"Maybe you should take their passports until the pathologist gets here."

"I am having some difficulty thinking how I would explain to my superiors in Valparaiso why I impounded the passports of two foreign nationals on the basis of horse poop."

He had a point, I suppose. "What else is down there?" I asked. "There seems to be a path leading down to the water across the way, on the other side of the cove."

"*Ana Kai Tangata,*" he said. "Ana means cave in Rapanui.

That is Eat Man Cave. There are two possible interpretations of the name. One is that this is where Rapa males came for picnics. The other is—"

"I know what the other one is," I said. "Maybe they were starving. Their children were starving. Perhaps in desperate circumstances people do the unthinkable."

"Perhaps," he said. "You should go and see the cave. I do not go sightseeing myself, but I understand there are paintings of birds on the walls."

Fuentes waved goodbye and started back toward the hotel. I was tempted to follow. I realized I was hungry, which, given the state of my insides the previous evening, was a very good sign. I could hear the clink of dishes in the dining room, and while it was still a bit early, I wondered if I might persuade them to make me a large breakfast.

Instead, I followed the path along the edge of the cliff until I came to a rocky path heading down toward the sea. The path wasn't exactly an easy one, nor was it particularly difficult as long as you watched where you put your feet. Soon I was down at the water level, with the waves crashing against stone just a few yards away. In a few strides I was up in the cave. A section of the upper wall of the cave was, as Fuentes had said, painted. You could make out birds in blue and red and white. The paintings were sufficiently high on the wall that some sort of scaffolding would have been required—wood supports, I supposed, if wood were then available, a pile of stones if it wasn't. Fuentes was right about one thing: One commodity this island would never run out of is rock.

I sat there for a while thinking about both the cave and my conversation with Fuentes. If Ana Kai Tangata was haunted by evil spirits emanating from either the victims or the perpetrators of the cannibalism implied in the cave's name, I couldn't feel them. The danger seemed much more imminent than that. I felt trapped in some kind of web with whatever evil was out there, on an island where there are only a few flights a week, some of which went some- where I didn't intend to go. What was it like, I wondered, to live on an island so far from everything else? Everything you need, or just want, from a lot of your food to the small- est part for your car engine to a grand piano, had to come from somewhere else, by and large, and travel great dis- tances to get to you.

All I could see through the cave entrance was water, the gray of the sky and the gray of the water meeting at a hori- zon that seemed very far off. I knew once I stepped out of the cave, the horizon would seem limitless. Pablo Fuentes didn't believe me. I wasn't even sure Moira would. Te-Pito- Te-Henua, they called it—the navel of the world. As stun- ning as this island might be, when it came right down to it, at this moment at least, there was not a lot to be said for be- ing alone at the center of the world.

With those morbid thoughts, I picked my way carefully across the rocks to the dead horse. I wondered if Fuentes would feel differently about the passports of foreign nation- als when he saw the poor horse had been killed by a bullet through its brain.

5

•

AHU AKIVI—As it turned out, the flight to Tahiti was not
an issue. The plane got in from Santiago all right, but tech-
nical difficulties delayed its onward journey by five hours,
by which time Pablo Fuentes had had to rethink his attitude
toward any number of things.

But that was to come later. After my visit to the cave and
the excursion along the shoreline, I came up the path to find
Moira standing on the cliff edge in a complete flap. "Where
have you been?" she demanded. "I've been looking for you
everywhere. Susie Scace said she'd seen you walking along
the cliff and I was afraid something awful had happened."

"Moira!" I exclaimed. "I just went for a walk."

"You can't just go off like that without telling me," she
said.

"You were asleep, Moira," I said.

"You're right," she said in a second or two. "This place
must be getting to me. I'll be glad when all these people

have left, and we can get on with our holiday. How's your head?"

"It's fine. Life list: I will never have a migraine again," I said. She managed to smile. "Let's go get breakfast. I'm starving, and I have to hear what happened after I left Jasper's talk."

"Not that much, really," she said, as I tucked into a rather large plate of eggs. "Two of those dancers came out pushing a glass case to center stage, followed by the rest of them, who did what I can only describe as a victory dance around that thing, whatever it was. Then Jasper invited Rory and Gordon to be the first to see the tablet, which I gather he has named the San Pedro tablet. I guess Rory's curiosity overcame his humiliation because he actually went up and looked at it. Gordon wouldn't go."

"And?"

"They behaved like perfect gentlemen, even if Gordon refused to go on stage. You have to give them credit. Rory even shook Jasper's hand and said if the tablet stood up to further study, he was to be congratulated for a significant find. Something like that, anyway. It must have pained him greatly to say it. After that, everyone was allowed to go up on the stage to have a look. I went up there, but I had no idea what I was looking at. Everyone else was pointing out some of the little figures and saying it looked just like the Santiago staff. What do I know? But we may have inadvertently stumbled into something really special at this congress. We may get to eat out on this for years. Jasper said *National Geographic* was interested in an article, as was *Archaeology* magazine. We'll be able to say we were there when Jasper made his big announcement. Not that anybody else but you will have a clue what rongorongo is."

"Has anyone seen Jasper?" Kent Clarke said in a loud voice at the dining room door. Everyone said no. "We're supposed to be filming," she said in an exasperated tone.

"Tell him I'm looking for him if he comes in here, please." She vanished just as quickly as she'd come.

"She's obviously used to being in charge," Moira said. "I hope I don't speak to my staff that way. Life list: Speak civilly to staff at all times."

"I suppose she's under some pressure," I said. "According to Mike and Daniel, this is one dog of a documentary she's making."

"I thought I was going to be seeing him. I thought we had a date," Yvonne said from the next table. "Story of my life. They all dump me for some reason. I suppose I wasn't smart enough for Jasper. I'm not dumb, you know. I just didn't get much of an education. I'm trying to learn stuff. That's why I signed up for that Internet group and came here." She rose from her chair and ran from the room sobbing.

"I'm thinking this is opportunity for me," Enrique said as he rushed past our table in her path.

"Was she talking to us or the tablecloth?" Moira said.

"I have no idea," I said. "But it seems the Jasper thing is off. So what's the drill for today? Are we going to Ahu Akivi with the rest of them? What are your plans?"

"I'm afraid to tell you," she said.

"You have a date with Jasper?" I said.

"No," she said. "It's worse."

She's going off to spend the afternoon with Rory doing the unthinkable, I thought. Will I or won't I tell Clive? I waited.

"Promise you won't scream, or anything?" she said.

I promised. It was a promise I hoped I'd be able to keep.

"I'm going to get a tattoo," she said.

"What?" I shrieked.

"You promised not to scream," she said.

"Sorry," I whispered. "A tattoo?" It wasn't the idea of the tattoo itself that surprised me; it was the idea that Moira, spa owner and seeker of skin perfection, would even consider one. This was the new Moira indeed. I looked at her carefully. I rarely saw Moira without makeup or with a single hair out of place. It had happened gradually, over the space of a few days here, but Moira had essentially transformed herself. She'd toned the makeup down to pale lipstick and some eyeliner, and her hairstyle was considerably more relaxed than usual. I decided this was a good thing.

"Haven't you noticed that almost everyone here, the people who live here, I mean, have tattoos?" she said. "Rory told me that when the Europeans first came, they found people with their entire bodies covered in tattoos. He said there are names for each of the different tattoos—you know, one name for the face, another for the tattoos on the buttocks. You get the idea."

"You're having your buttocks tattooed?" I said.

"No," she said. "Did you see that lovely little turtle Victoria Pakarati had tattooed around her navel?" I nodded. "I'm thinking of having something like that done."

"Okay," I said.

"Rory's going to take me to a parlor he knows about, a place with clean needles, et cetera. When I get there, I will, of course, cast my Meller Spa eye over the place to make sure it meets my standards of cleanliness. If it does, I'm going for it. Rory claims he has a tattoo himself, too, one I haven't seen, so I can only imagine where it is. Do you want to come with me? Get a little butterfly or something at the base of your spine?"

"Nooo," I said.

"You are such a poop, Lara," she said. "What are you going to do, then, while I'm breaking free of all the constraints that have held me captive for many years?"

"One little tattoo will do that?" I said. "Maybe I should reconsider." She laughed. "I guess I'll go to Ahu Akivi with the gang," I said. "We missed it on our island tour. Then I may go into Hanga Roa to shop for souvenirs. What I'd really like to do, if it is in any way possible, is see that tablet of Jasper's," I added. "I spent some time talking to Seth Connelly about rongorongo, and he made it all seem very exciting. It's a better story if the people of Rapa Nui invented the language virtually overnight and all by themselves, but either way, I'd like to see it. I'm sorry I missed the opportunity. I wonder where it is. I assume Jasper wouldn't just have it lying around his hotel room, would he? It's got to be priceless."

"That's a good question," she said. "Maybe the museum in town has it in safekeeping, or something."

"Another question, now that I think about it, is how did he get it here without anyone knowing about it? I sure wouldn't want to put it in my checked luggage, given the number of times airlines have lost my bags," I said. "He must have had a lot of help from somebody. When I see Jasper, though, I might ask if I could have a quick peek at it," I said. "If I suck up to him the way you did to . . ." I stopped. "That was tasteless of me. I was going to say Dave Maddox, of course. He seems to have just disappeared, don't you think? Even I, who found him dead, was going to joke about the way you had him wrapped around your little finger that first night."

"It seems like a very long time ago, doesn't it?" Moira said. "I think poor old Dave probably has gotten lost in the frenzy to discuss Jasper Robinson's startling discovery. Now that you mention it, I didn't hear his name much at all yesterday and certainly not at all so far today. He was kind of sad, wasn't he, the way he was so overly jolly all the time. All that stuff about coming to his session. He must have said that to me ten thousand times in the two days I knew him. I think it just put people off. I made fun of him a lot, though, and I regret it now. If it would make you feel any better, when the time came for his session, Susie, Yvonne, and Brian went for a drink and toasted his memory. You were under the influence of the sleeping pill I gave you at the time."

"I suppose that's something," I said. In fact, though, not everyone had been able to delete Dave from their memory file. Brenda Butters came up to our table only minutes later. "I have a favor to ask," she said in a voice so low I could hardly hear her. "I'm wondering, er, the hotel wants us to clear out Dave Maddox's room. He was due out today anyway. He was going to Tahiti for a week's vacation. The flight from Santiago will be in later this afternoon, and the hotel is full. They need the room. Given I'm the registrar for this event and the person who has been dealing with the hotel on all the arrangements, they've come to me."

"You'd like our help clearing his stuff out," Moira said. "I'm not sure Lara is feeling up to this. She had a terrible migraine last night. I actually had to get a doctor in to see her." She gave me a look that indicated she was trying to find us a way out of this.

"Is it okay with the carabineros?" I said.

"Yes," she replied. "The hotel called them, and that man who investigated the accident, Fuentes I think he said his name was, came over to say it was okay. I'm just not terribly comfortable doing this by myself, not because he's dead or anything, but because of valuables. I would just like a witness or two while I'm doing this."

"All right, then," I said. "I'll help. How long can it take? It's not as if it's his house or an office he's used for years. He's only been here a few days. Let's just get it done fast."

Moira looked surprised and none too pleased. I, of course, was curious to see what other surprises Dave had in store, even dead. It did not take us long to find out. Essentially, Dave had barely unpacked, just kept everything in his suitcase, which was a mess. I just put his suitcase on the bed and in the guise of repacking had a quick look through his stuff. There

was nothing out of the ordinary. Moira packed up the bathroom toiletries and put them in the bag. Brenda went
through the drawers.

The book with the Grisham dust cover was on the bed-
side table, but when I checked the contents quickly, it was
indeed a book by Grisham. That meant that *The Art Forger's
Handbook* had to be somewhere else, but I couldn't see it.
The other item that was distinguished by its absence was
the paper Dave was due to give the day he died. It was possible the paper had been folded up in the pocket of the
clothes he'd been wearing when I found him. Needless to
say, it was not something I'd thought to look for at the time.
The book, however, was too big for that.

Moira caught my attention. She was holding an empty
bottle of pisco. "Found it on the floor under the desk," she
said, with a knowing look.

When we were done, I said I was going to do one last
check and pulled open all the drawers, checked the cupboard and the bathroom, and even looked under the bed.
Moira looked at me with some amusement. "Shoes and
socks," I said.

Neither the paper, nor *The Art Forger's Handbook* were
anywhere to be found. I had one last thought and checked
the back of the closet. "The safe," I said. "It's locked, so
there must be something in it."

"Oh dear," Brenda said. "There's a fifty dollar deposit on
the keys for those things. We'd better go through his pockets to find it or the congress will be stuck with paying for
it."

We unpacked the suitcase. The key was not there. The
only key, in fact, was one for the suitcase itself. "I suppose it
might have fallen out when, you know, he tried riding that
horse," Moira said.

"I guess I'll just have to 'fess up about the key and eat the

fifty dollars," Brenda said. "I'll phone and get the hotel's."
But the phone in the room didn't work, so she went off to
Reception to get it. I continued to look around the room.

"I don't think it's here," Moira said.

"What?" I said.

"The key. That's what you're looking for, isn't it? Or is
it?"

I told her I didn't think Dave's death was an accident. I
told her about my dreams about horses.

"I hate to say it, but I think that migraine has damaged
some brain cells," she said. "I'm sure it's only temporary.
Why would anyone kill Dave? You think that someone got
ticked off because he got their name wrong for the hun-
dredth time, lost it completely, bashed in his head, and then
rode a horse over him?"

"It's true that if I killed everyone who called me Laura,
the streets of most urban centers would be piled high with
corpses," I said. "But something else was going on." I told
her about the book.

"I wouldn't want anyone at this conference knowing I
was reading a forger's textbook," she said. "Isn't it as simple
as that?"

"Let's just see what's in the safe," I said, as Brenda returned, key in hand. But there was nothing. The safe was
absolutely empty.

"I wonder why he bothered locking it," Brenda said.
"This is very irritating about the key. And the hotel is going
to charge us storage for his stuff, until his family makes
some arrangements."

"He has family?" Moira said.

"A brother, apparently," Brenda said. "Who didn't sound
too cut up when I called him to give him the news. I don't
think they were close. He's suggesting Dave just be buried
here. He said he'd send money."

"Poor Dave," Moira said. "He did seem to be something of a klutz. Maybe he locked it accidentally. The key could be on the floor of the cupboard."

But it wasn't. "Maybe the cleaning staff swept it up by accident," Brenda said.

I thought it was much more likely that someone had been in Dave's room just before or after he died, had found the key, emptied the safe, and left, locking it to slow people like me down. I went over to the sliding door and with one pull opened it. "This door is unlocked," I said.

"The police, maybe?" Moira said. *Maybe,* I thought.

"The rooms on this side of the hotel aren't air conditioned," Brenda said. "They're a bit cheaper. It gets pretty hot, I'm told, so he probably left the door open for some air."

"I'm sure you're right," Moira said, as I, growing more suspicious by the minute, went to take a second look at the phone that wouldn't work. It was easy to see why: The cord had been cut. I held it up for the other two to see.

"What would cause that, I wonder?" Brenda said.

I was tempted to say a knife, or scissors, but I held my tongue. Nobody was going to believe me on this one, including Moira. Even though I'd predicted she wouldn't, and even though I knew in my heart of hearts hers was the rational reaction, I was still a little hurt by it and feeling rather put upon. Then I had the most wonderful idea, one I went to implement the minute Moira headed off to get her tattoo.

"Brian!" I said to the nice young man who had unfortunately not yet snagged himself a job. "You are obviously the most technologically advanced person at this congress. I am really hoping you can help me."

"You flatter me," he said. "What seems to be the problem?"

"My partner, Rob, gave me this camera to bring on this

trip," I said. "I thought that was really nice of him, particularly given the fact he couldn't come with me."

He looked at it. "I'll say. This is a really good camera," he said. "Five megapixels. Great resolution."

"Yes," I said. I had no idea what he was talking about. "Rob couldn't get away from his job, you know. I thought it would be nice to send him some photos I took with the camera he gave me. I read the manual, and I think it should be possible, but I don't know how to do it."

"You just have to transfer them to your computer and then attach them to an email. Did you bring your laptop?"

"I didn't," I said.

"Okay," he said. "We'll use mine. I have software on my laptop that should work. But I'd have to hook your camera up to my laptop. I don't suppose you brought a connector for the camera for a USB port."

"Would this be it?" I said, handing him a cable. I'd been so intimidated by the manual, I'd brought everything that had come in the box with the camera. This was the first time I'd needed any of it.

"That's it!" he exclaimed. "We're in business. Now, I'll get my laptop and transfer your photos to it, and you can send them through my email. I can log on in Santiago."

"I'll pay the charges," I said.

"Don't worry," he said. "One of the advantages of living in the middle of frigging nowhere is that Chile takes good care of you. Valparaiso, on the mainland, even though it's 2,500 miles away, is a local call."

"But Santiago?" I said.

"Look," he said. "You and Moira were so nice to me when no one else in the whole world would talk to me. If I can repay you in even this small way, I am grateful."

"I really thought your paper was terrific and that those other people were horrid," I said.

"I rest my case," he said. "Okay, here we go," he said

when he returned with his laptop. "Now, you put in your partner's email address, say it's a message from you in the subject line, just so he doesn't think it's spam, and tell me what photos you want me to attach." I told him.

"Well, these are different," he said, looking at them. "All this dirt."

"Actually, Rob is a soil engineer," I said. "I agree with you, as would almost everyone else on the planet, but he'll be over the moon with these photos." *You are a pig, Lara*, I thought. *Life list: I will never lie to a nice young man again.*

"I think you'll have to send two or three separate emails, with all these attachments," he said. "Now here's the space for you to write your own message."

I wrote my own message all right. Over the course of three emails, I told Rob my feelings about Dave Maddox and about how nobody believed me. I said I hoped he'd take a look at the photos I'd taken and send a reply, not by replying to Brian Murphy, of course, but to me.

"Is that a dead horse?" Brian said, as he attached the last photo.

"It is," I replied. "Sad, isn't it? But so artistic, don't you think? Rob is also a farmer on the weekends. And a painter. He uses scenes like this as his subject matter. I know he'll find this interesting." *I am damned,* I thought. *My aku-aku will torment me forever for this.*

As soon as the emails were on their way, I hurried into Hanga Roa to the Internet cafe and logged on. I'd sent the emails to both Rob's home address and work, hoping he was at his desk one place or the other with the email beeping to tell him there was a message from me.

He must have been nearby, because there was already a message from him asking me what I was up to and about how I should just come home. I sent him another in which in a rather testy tone I pointed out that he'd offered to come and help me on these trips, and even though he wasn't there, I still wanted his help.

This time he was at his desk, because by the time I'd managed to reply to another inane request from Clive, Rob had replied again. This time the message said: *The dead horse on the rocks did not make the prints on the dirt where the body was found. The dead horse was wild, i.e., unshod. The prints on that Tomb thing, whatever it is you keep calling it, are horseshoes.*

Ha, I thought. *I knew it.* Then I realized I wasn't much further ahead. I had merely eliminated one horse among what had to be thousands on the island. Fuentes would just say another horse killed Dave.

Do you think Maddox was trampled by a horse? I typed.

Could be, but only if the horse considered itself, or its foal, for example, to be threatened by him, the return email read. *Horseshoes are unique, made for a specific horse. You could look for distinguishing marks in the prints. I can't tell from your email. Be careful* were the last two words.

So real had been my dream about Rob on horseback, that I almost emailed him to ask what else it was I'd forgotten about Dave Maddox's death. That one would have stumped him, I'm sure. I sincerely hoped I would remember whatever it was I was supposed to soon, because this feeling of unease was starting to get to me. I didn't want to think about Dave Maddox's body at all, that crushed face still very fresh in my mind.

As an afterthought I asked Rob how my kitchen was coming along. The reply was that progress was being made at a rate that was essentially imperceptible. I wanted to cry.

Back at the hotel everyone was getting ready to go to Ahu Akivi on the last field trip of the conference. The flight to Tahiti was not until late in the day, so everyone was there. I put Susie Scace's bags in our room for safekeeping until it was time for her to go to the airport.

While we waited for the others to assemble, I went over to talk to Mike and Daniel, who were sitting surrounded by their gear, in the shade. Kent Clarke was standing beside a Jeep in the hotel drive, tapping her fingernails on the hood of the vehicle and looking about with a particularly vexed expression on her face. Brittany was sitting in the passenger seat looking, well, bored. She had acquired, I noticed, another tattoo, this one of a jelly fish, that sort of climbed up her neck, somehow.

"She's going to wear her fingers out," Daniel said, nodding in Kent's direction. "And then how will she be able to count out the vast sums of money she owes us, Mike?"

"Star gone walkabout?" I said.

"He probably drank himself into a stupor somewhere last night, savoring his triumph," Mike said. "I can see him now, sprawled on the floor behind the bar of some dive, arms still wrapped around that rongorongo thing."

"You're such a cynic, Mike," Daniel said. "You have no appreciation for greatness." He couldn't keep a straight face, however, and soon we were all laughing. I rather hoped Rory and Gordon would happen along so they could join in the fun, but perhaps their sense of humor had deserted them the previous evening, or they were off by themselves licking their wounds. Rory, now that I thought about it, wouldn't be here, because he was taking Moira to a tattoo parlor in Hanga Roa, of all things.

"Speaking of that rongorongo thing," I said. "Where is it? In safekeeping I presume?"

"No effing idea," Daniel said. "I just wish it looked at bit more impressive on film."

"I was kind of hoping to see it. I had a migraine and had to leave just as it was being wheeled on to the stage."

"We'll ask on your behalf when we finally see Jasper," Mike said.

"Given you're one of the few people at this congress who will actually talk to us plebs," Daniel said.

"You're kidding," I said. "I'd have thought everyone would be interested in hearing about the documentary."

"Nope," Mike said. "You and that dead guy, Maddox, were the only ones who'd have a conversation of any duration with the likes of us. He's gone, so that leaves you. So it will be our pleasure talking to the great one on your behalf."

"Thanks! I really want to see that thing. Dave was interested in the documentary?" I asked, I hoped casually.

"Yes, indeedy," Daniel said. "Bit of a bore, though. All that 'great to see you' stuff. I suppose I shouldn't speak ill of the dead. He was helping Kent with the research. Kent asked him and paid his way to the congress apparently. That's all I know really. I have no idea what he did for the airfare. Funny choice, I'd say, but there you are."

That seemed about all he was going to say. "So did last night make for better television?" I asked.

"The dancing girls in those feathered skirts and tiny bikini tops were good," Mike said.

"Too many white girls," Daniel said. "The spots in the dance company are all being taken by Chileans. It's a shame because it's Rapa culture they're representing, and furthermore, Rapa girls are really lovely."

"You would hardly be biased or anything, would you?" Mike said. "But to take your question seriously, Lara, no, slides and a talking head at a podium do not good television make. That's why we plan to take Jasper out, should he deign to show us his lovely face before the sun goes down, to shoot some footage at a cave where rongorongo tablets could, theoretically at least, be found. When that was done, we were going to have him give you all a little talk at Ahu Akivi and film that as well."

"You don't like him, do you?" I said.

"I do not have strong feelings on the subject," Mike said. "About him, or about his big discovery, if that is what it is. He's a job, one job in a not-so-illustrious career."

"By not having strong feelings he means he hates the guy," Daniel said. When Mike started to protest, Daniel put up his hand. "Don't try to deny it. J. R. is a turd. We all know that." Mike shrugged and then laughed. "Still, Mike and I keep begging Kent to let us work on every one of J. R.'s adventures."

"Our masochistic tendencies," Mike said. "I think this will be the last time for me, though. There is only so much of J. R. I can stomach."

"My wife, Eroria, certainly feels strongly," Daniel said. "She was much miffed last night when I told her what Jasper had to say about South American stonemasons. He has earned the undying enmity of Eroria and every other Rapa Nui on the island, I should think. In the interests of family harmony, I agreed with her. I have no effing clue, of course, whether he's right or not."

I noticed for the first time that Daniel had a tattoo, a lizard, on his left bicep. "Does everybody here really have a tattoo?" I asked.

"A lot do," he said. "Long tradition of it, I believe. Eroria treated me to this one when we got engaged."

There was something about this tattoo business that was bothering me, and I didn't know what it was. I had no problem with Moira getting one, and I thought I'd even consider something very discreet myself, except I couldn't bring myself to do it. I wondered what that was about. I'm sure it hurt a bit, but so did having your ears pierced, which I'd done maybe twenty-five years earlier and certainly never regretted. For some reason, though, right now I was filled with revulsion at the idea of a tattoo, something I'd never noticed in myself, not that I'd thought about it much, if ever, before.

By now the buses were ready to go, and our group headed out in two of them, followed by the Kent Clarke team in their van. Kent had decided that rather than waste more time, they'd film some footage of the group at the site to use as background at some point in the documentary.

I loved Ahu Akivi the moment I saw it, and the mere sight of it put troubling thoughts about tattoos out of my mind. Unlike other ahu that invariably hugged the coast, this one was inland, an ahu with seven moai gazing across the landscape toward the sea. I don't know why I liked it better, other than to say it had a certain grace that the larger Ahu Tongariki lacked, something Brian Murphy attributed to the sensitive restoration work of his hero, Bill Mulloy.

Christian Hotus, the young man Gordon had described as his right hand, was the guide for this excursion, the only one, given Jasper had still failed to show. Edwina Rasmussen could have done it, but she would much rather stand under her umbrella, which she used constantly outdoors in the sun, and criticize someone else, which is what she did all the while Christian talked. I, however, thought he did a better than credible job as guide, and the fact that he was Rapa Nui born and bred added a great deal.

According to him, there were two stories about the ahu, one that the seven moai represented seven sailors sent out by Hotu Matu'a to find the island he had seen in his dreams. The other, perhaps more realistic, was that these moai represented seven ancestors of the clan whose village the moai guarded. There was space for one more, perhaps to honor the man who had built the moai and had the seven carved, but the clan wars and the toppling of the moai made the raising of the eighth impossible.

We stood, a group of about twenty, in front of the ahu, while Christian pointed out various features, telling us that long after the moai had been toppled, the ahu had been a burial place. "Now," he said. "Follow me around the back, and I'll show you something interesting."

It was interesting, all right. What followed was a scene right out of the Keystone Kops. Christian rounded the end of the ahu, and I was right behind him, snapping photographs. Oblivious to everything beyond what I could see through the camera lens, I walked straight into Christian, who had come to an abrupt stop. When I saw what had happened to him, I stopped dead in my tracks, too. Then Enrique, who had his guidebook up to his nose, bumped into me, and then Brian, who was rhapsodizing about the work of Bill Mulloy, ran into Enrique. We then had the pedestrian equivalent of a pileup on the freeway. One after another, those coming around the side of the ahu, all gawking at something other than where they were going, bumped into the person just ahead. Susie was almost knocked down. Over to the side, Daniel, who, like me, was oblivious to anything that could not be seen through the camera lens, kept right on filming, panning across the back of the ahu, not noticing the absolute chaos just to his left.

The cause of this uproar was the great Jasper Robinson himself. He was sitting on the ground, leaning against the stones of the ahu, legs stretched out in front of him, looking for all the world as if he'd been waiting for us forever.

"What is he doing there?" Edwina carped the minute she saw him. "We could have been hurt."

"If you didn't want to see me, you could have just said so, Jasper," Yvonne said loudly.

"For heaven's sake, Jasper," Kent Clarke said, striding purposefully up to the seated Jasper. "Do you not realize how expensive it is to have a crew on standby for hours on end?" And then she fainted dead away.

6

"WHAT DO YOU THINK?" Moira said, pointing to what I suppose would be a little hummingbird when the red welts calmed down, on her upper arm right at her shoulder.

"Very cute," I said.

"I think this may be the bravest thing I've ever done," she said.

"Probably," I said.

"I kind of lost my nerve on the belly button idea," she said. "For one thing, I felt a little squeamish, and also I wasn't sure how Clive would feel about a hummingbird around my navel."

"Good idea," I said. "This looks nice, and it's discreet."

"Exactly. You, too, could have one," she said. "This is on my shoulder and is therefore called a . . . just a minute, I'll remember, *he pare*. If it were on my thigh, it would *he kona*. Just so you know. Remind me I have to put antibacterial cream on it from time to time. Guess where I got it? You'll never guess. Daniel Striker's wife, Eroria, did it. You know, the cameraman. His wife is a real artist, and she does tattoos both here and in Australia where they live part of the year." She stopped for a moment and looked at me. "You're looking a bit green about the gills, Lara. Are you getting another migraine? Is there a problem?"

So I told her. "Jasper is dead!?" she gasped. "Murdered?"

"I'm afraid so," I replied.

"And Dave? Are they saying the same thing about Dave?"

"Not yet, but I think they might once the pathologist gets here."

"When is that supposed to be?"

"Tomorrow," I said. "He's flying out from Santiago tomorrow."

"I didn't believe you, you know, about Dave. I am a jerk. That must have been something, finding Jasper like that," she said.

It was. Finding a dead guy leaning against an ahu may have made for much better television, but it also made Pablo Fuentes's life a living hell. Jasper, when we'd found him, was stone-cold dead and had been for several hours. No matter how much Fuentes wanted to rule this another accident, two corpses with their heads bashed in made at least one too many. But we'd got the horse business out of the way, or so I thought at the time. There were no hoof prints to be seen. No horse poop in the immediate vicinity, either.

Still, Fuentes wanted to make it an accident, even if it was pretty obvious that you couldn't just accidentally hit your head like that, all by yourself, unless you threw yourself off the third floor of a building, maybe, which he hadn't done, partly because I had yet to see a three-story building on Rapa Nui, and because even if there was one, it wasn't anywhere near Ahu Akivi.

The good news was that finding Jasper had cleared up my mental discomfort with tattoos, and that came as something of a relief, although given the circumstances it was hard to see why. Jasper's chest, as Dave Maddox's had been, was red and puffy from the effects of a very recently acquired tattoo. I'd just focused on Dave's face when I'd found him, I suppose, and blotted the rest of it out. No wonder the thought of tattoos made me nauseous.

The bad news was that Fuentes seemed to hold me personally responsible for the rather abrupt change in his job responsibilities which heretofore, as far as I could tell, consisted of riding around the island with three of his compadres in one of the distinctive cream and green Carabineros de Chile vehicles. I say this because the whole time I was on Rapa Nui—and it was days longer than I intended to be there—I never saw one of these vehicles with fewer than three or four men in it. I also heard very little evidence of crime, and, as Fuentes himself had told me, people didn't go around murdering others much on Rapa Nui. Perhaps being Chilean, assigned for a few months to an island at the end of the world, with people they could not entirely understand even if they spoke Spanish as a common language, the carabineros sought safety in numbers.

Called upon to act, Fuentes did two things. First he confiscated all the footage Kent Clarke Films had taken since their arrival several days earlier. His second act was to do what I'd told him to in the first place, that is to say, make all of us stay on the island whether we wanted to or not. He rather peremptorily summoned me to come with him to see the congress delegates, now all assembled in the meeting room.

"You will come with me," he said in a tone that brooked no disobedience.

"Where are we going?" was the best I could manage in reply, even though I wanted to tell him to stuff it, given he had been so patronizing when I'd told him Dave Maddox had been murdered.

"I am not comfortable speaking English to a crowd," Fuentes replied. "You will translate."

I felt I had no choice but to do so, thus earning myself the distinction of being the one person at the conference that they could all agree on. In other words, every single one of them hated me.

"You will stay here until the investigation into the murder of Jasper Robinson is completed," I said, at Fuentes's bidding. A groan surged from the audience in my general direction.

"While Corporal Fuentes has not yet taken the step of confiscating your passports, he wants you to know that your names have been given to the authorities at the airport, and also to customs and immigration officials in Santiago. There are no flights to Tahiti today, given that last night's flight has finally taken off. In other words," I said, ad-libbing for a moment, "he's telling us there is nowhere to go."

Another groan, louder than the first. "I'm a U.S. citizen," Edwina Rasmussen said. "I demand to meet with a consular official."

"That would be in Santiago, Madame," I said, after listening to his reply. "You may do so when you get there." Actually, I toned down what he said a little. I didn't want Edwina to hit me with her umbrella.

"When will we be allowed to leave?" Susie Scace asked.

"When I say so," I translated. "By which I mean Corporal Fuentes."

"Do we have to stay in the hotel?" Brian asked.

"No," Fuentes replied. Everybody thought that was a bonus, but maybe they hadn't really thought it through.

"I believe I may be of assistance," Cassandra de Santiago said. "I am in touch with the spirit world."

"No, thank you," I said. That was not even close to what

Fuentes said, but I'd have been embarrassed to translate what he did say out loud.

"So where is the San Pedro rongorongo tablet?" I asked Fuentes when everybody had filed angrily out of the room, most of them glaring at me as they did so.

"What are you talking about?" Fuentes asked me after a second or two. I told him that Jasper Robinson had unveiled a tablet covered in rongorongo script that he had found in the Atacama Desert.

"What is rongorongo?" he asked irritably, when I'd finished my reasonably lengthy description. This amazed me at first, but then I reminded myself that he was Chilean, nor Rapa Nui. It seemed a dumb idea, particularly right now, during the investigation into two suspicious deaths, to have a police presence that knew nothing about the culture in which they found themselves. I was sure my opinion would not be appreciated by Fuentes, however, so I told him about rongorongo, and how, given he'd taken all the Kent Clarke footage, he could see for himself what the tablet looked like. He stomped out of the room.

It didn't take a rocket scientist to figure out what Fuentes would do when he'd looked at Daniel's tapes. Once the policeman got around to acknowledging that murder was a distinct possibility, Gordon Fairweather was going to be number one suspect the moment the Rano Raraku footage appeared before his eyes.

I wanted to run to Hanga Roa to try to find Gordon or Victoria and warn them, but when it came right down to it, what difference would it make? Gordon could run, and he could probably hide for a day or two, but this was one small island to try and evade authorities on, and frankly there was nowhere else he could go. After a couple of hours of persuading myself to think this way, I gave up and went into town. I had no trouble finding out where Victoria Pakarati lived. Half the town was called Pakarati as near as I could tell, and a very tall white archaeologist with braids wasn't that hard to locate either.

Victoria answered the door. She had been crying. "Have they taken Gordon already?" I said.

She looked perplexed. "Has who taken Gordon where?" she asked.

I had rather just put my foot in it. "You've been crying. Is there anything I can do?" I said, changing tactics.

"It's Gabriela," she said. "She's in a coma. We don't know what happened. I'm looking after the little ones so that her mother can be with her," she said.

"How bad is it?" I said.

"Bad," she said, and then she started crying again. Two little boys who were watching from a doorway began to wail when they saw her.

"Where's Gordon?" I said.

"Up on Poike," she said, pulling herself together. "I've sent a message for him to come home."

Bad idea, I thought, but within seconds I heard footsteps behind me, and Gordon strode into the room. Little Edith ran in and grabbed him, "Papa, Papa, Gabriela," she kept saying over and over.

He was a man who took charge easily, and within minutes I was playing games with the little ones, while Gordon took his wife aside and calmed her down. Victoria went outside and came back with bananas and papayas she'd picked from her own garden, and soon we all had large glasses of freshly made juice in our hands. The little ones stopped crying. It looked like a perfectly normal day at home.

"I need to talk to you, Gordon," I said.

"Gordon, I've promised my sister I'd go to the hospital as soon as you got here," Victoria said. "You can go later. Will you stay with the children?"

"Of course," he said. "Maybe Lara would help me convince the boys to have a nap."

"Gordon," I said. "We need to talk."

"She's tried to kill herself," Victoria said. She was trying very hard not to cry.

"Gordon!" I said.

"Can't it wait?" he said.

"No, it cannot," I said, rather more loudly and firmly than would usually be necessary. "It's about Jasper Robinson. Have you heard the news?"

"What news? That he faked the San Pedro tablet? Now that would be news I'd like to hear."

"He's dead," I said. "We found him up at Ahu Akivi. It is possible he was murdered."

"Murdered!" both Gordon and Victoria exclaimed. "Have you heard this?" he said, turning to his wife.

"I've been looking after the children all day," she said. "Ever since Gabriela was found."

"I didn't like Robinson, as you know, but I wouldn't wish that on anyone," Gordon said.

"The police have confiscated all the film that was taken during the Moai Congress," I said. They both looked at me with a "so what?" expression on their faces. "I think they continued filming when you arrived at the rim of Rano Raraku."

Silence greeted that statement. "Oh, my God, Gordon," Victoria gasped, looking from one to the other of us as my words sank in at last. "That's what you meant when you got here, asking whether they'd taken Gordon already, isn't it? You were trying to warn us," she said. "Gordon, they have you threatening Robinson on tape!"

It was at this moment that the Carabineros de Chile pulled into the drive.

And so it was that I found myself negotiating mushy gears in a battered old truck with a fugitive in back.

I'm sure my life list, had I thought to consult it in the few seconds I took to make my decision, would have had an entry rather near the top that said I will never harbor a fugitive in a foreign country, especially one that is an island in the middle of nowhere. I'm not sure what had propelled me out the back door and into the truck. Perhaps it was the expression of anguish on Victoria's face, or the baffled expression on Edith's.

I had barreled along a poor road that ran parallel to the airport runway, before cutting inland on a road that was even worse, taking muffled directions from the back. "Where are we going?" I asked, trying not to move my lips as I did so, just in case someone was looking, which they probably weren't. Given the circumstances, however, I wasn't taking any chances, other than the big one I seemed to have taken on, in a moment of insanity.

"Cave," the muffled reply came back.

"What? Where?"

Gordon evidently took the blanket off his nose for a second. "The family cave," he said. "Victoria's family has a cave."

"Okay," I said. "Am I on the right track?" It was a good expression, because a track was pretty much what the road had become. I'd long since switched to four-wheel-drive. Every now and then, on my say so, Gordon would peek out the side window, get his bearings, and give me instructions. He was a big man, and I knew it was extremely uncomfortable for him curled up in the back. More than once a groan had escaped his lips as I'd taken a bump just a little too fast. Speed, however, did seem to be of the essence.

I finally reached the end of the trail and could see no way to go further. There was a wall of rock in front of me, and beyond that, maybe a hundred feet away, the sea. At Gordon's instruction, I got out, climbed the rock and looked around. There was no one to be seen in any direction, a bit surprising on an island that is twenty-five miles when measured at its very longest point, but people seemed to pretty much stick to to the area around Hanga Roa.

When I said to, Gordon unfolded himself from the back seat, and stood up.

"Nice job," he said to me. "Thank you."

"I know I'm stating the obvious here," I said, as we crouched over and maneuvered into the cave. "But there's nowhere for you to go, and you can't spend the rest of your life in a cave. Furthermore, won't the carabineros know that Victoria's family has a cave?"

"They're Chilean," he said. "The police are Chilean, the doctors are Chilean, even the teachers are often Chilean. No wonder the islanders worry about losing their identity here. The carabineros don't even patrol the island at night. The only crime here is excessive drinking. You know who keeps this island under control? A bunch of strapping Rapa youth who have no compunction about using night sticks when called upon and a bunch of grannies who haul their wayward sons-in-law out of the bar by the ear when need be. Do you really think the carabineros are going to find the family cave?"

"Someone could tell them," I said. I declined to mention that there were two crimes now on Rapa Nui, excessive drinking and murder.

"They won't find me, believe me," he said. I looked around. The mouth of the cave was easily seen, even from some distance. There were stone platforms covered in dried grasses, mattresses of a sort, inside, and outside was a place to cook. Still, I figured even Pablo Fuentes could find this place.

"My point is that, even if they can't find you, you can't stay in a cave for the rest of your life!"

"No," he said. "But I can stay in a cave until Victoria has a lawyer lined up and until she can get in touch with the

U.S. Embassy in Santiago and maybe even persuade them to send somebody out here. Chile was a military dictatorship until very recently. I'm not turning myself in until I have everything in place."

"Okay," I said. He had a point. Maybe having a lawyer present canceled out the obvious disadvantage of having made a run for it. "What do you want me to do now?"

"Will you take the truck up to Poike for me? Tell Christian or Rory what's up, and ask them to bring me some supplies, some food and water, and maybe some flashlight batteries. Victoria will have told the carabineros that I'm up on Poike but will be returning shortly. With any luck they won't go up there, but will wait for me in town. There's no road. You'll be using four-wheel-drive again. I'm hoping Rory or Christian can come up with some reason the car is there and I'm not. I'm really just buying time, I know."

"Okay," I said again. I rummaged around in my bag and handed him the emergency bag of trail mix I never travel without and the small bottle of water I had been carrying with me. Neither would last him for long. "Rory will be along soon," I said.

"I'm counting on it," he said. "Tell him just to come into the cave and speak loudly. He won't see me, but I will hear him and recognize his voice."

"I can pretty well see everything here," I said, dubiously. The cave was high enough to stand up in and went back fairly far. But there were no other entrances that I could see.

"Long and honorable tradition," Fairweather said, enigmatically. "Rory will understand."

I started to clamber out of the cave. "Lara," he said. "I don't know why you are helping a stranger, but thank you."

"That's okay," I said.

"You haven't asked me if I killed Jasper Robinson," he said.

"No," I replied. "It never occurred to me." He gave me a halfhearted smile and a wave, and I was on my way again.

"Rory will be here soon," I repeated. But it didn't quite turn out that way.

I had a tough time finding the place where Rory and Christian were working, but I finally did. They were a little surprised to see who got out of the truck and positively flabbergasted when I told them about Jasper.

"Murdered!" Rory said. "The guy was positively begging for it, but still!"

"Where are your students?" I said. I wanted as few witnesses to my presence there as possible.

"They've taken the van back to town," Rory said. "We're pretty much finished here for the day."

Then I told them about Gordon, the carabineros at his home, and our flight out the back door to the cave. "Gordon needs some time," I said. "When he doesn't show up at home, the carabineros will be here."

Christian had the hood up within seconds, rummaged around, and then tossed something into the grass. "Too bad the truck has broken down," he said, leaving the hood up. "Gordon went into town to get a part."

Rory smiled slightly. "Parts usually have to come in on the next plane," he said. "I guess it will be a while before Gordon is able to get his vehicle repaired."

"Right," I said. "But how did he get to town?" Nothing like having your story straight before the carabineros arrive.

"I took him," Christian said.

"What about the students? Would they have seen Gordon leave?"

"No," Rory said. "It was getting too hot, so we sent them home early. It was just the three of us up here."

"We should be okay," I said. "I am kind of hoping for a lift to town myself."

"No problem," Christian said, wheeling a motorbike out from behind a rock. "Hop on."

"You rode that thing on these trails?" I said. The idea

struck terror into my heart. I was more afraid of going back to Hanga Roa on the back of this thing than I was of Pablo Fuentes.

"Make sure the carabineros don't see Lara with you," Rory said. "It's the least we can do for her."

"Gordon thinks the carabineros won't find him in the cave, but I'm not convinced," I said.

"They won't," Christian said.

"Not a chance," Rory said.

"You all seem so sure," I said.

"Do you know about the *kio?*" Christian said. I shook my head. "That's the rapanui name for the people who hid out in caves called *kionga* during the clan wars and also when the slave ships showed up on the horizon. Whole extended families had places to hide until someone came and told them it was safe to come out. Believe me, they will not find Gordon until he wants to be found."

"I think you better get going," Rory said. "There's a fair amount of dust over there. I'd take the long way back if I were you."

Christian had the motorcycle revved up and I was behind him holding on for dear life in seconds, and we headed off in the opposite direction in our own cloud of dust.

"You'll be okay?" was the last thing Christian said to Rory as we pulled away.

"Liar is my middle name," Rory said grimly. "Get out of here."

We were halfway back to Hanga Roa when I realized there was something we'd forgotten. I pressed my mouth to Christian's ear. "Who came up to Poike to tell Gordon to go home?" I said.

Christian slowed down slightly. "I'll take care of it," he said.

But it was too late, and a series of disasters began to unfold. The young man Victoria had sent to get Gordon was Gabriela's brother, Santiago. When questioned by the carabineros, Santiago was very forthcoming, assuming, quite naturally, that this had something to do with whatever had befallen his sister. He told them he'd ridden his motorbike up to Poike to get his uncle and that Gordon had put the bike in the back of the truck and driven him home. Santiago, perhaps thinking he was providing his uncle Gordon with an alibi, was very specific about the time all this had happened and said that both Rory and Christian could also attest to these facts.

Rory, who'd undoubtedly lied through his teeth as he'd promised, was caught out in the lie, as was Christian. Both were brought in for questioning and then placed under house arrest. By evening, there was also an armed guard front and back at Victoria's home, she too having been caught in the same lie.

The only person whose role in all of this the carabineros did not seem to know about was a certain shopkeeper from Toronto. Fuentes, who was not stupid, was bound to wonder who had taken Gordon's truck—now that everyone knew it had at one point been in Hanga Roa—back to the dig site in Poike. I was almost certain neither Rory nor Christian would reveal my part in it, but I was a little concerned they might both claim to have been the person who drove it back, thereby giving Fuentes cause to wonder if someone else was involved. But no one came calling that first day, so I decided I was safe for the time being.

It took me an hour or two to realize that meant it was up to me to get food and water to Gordon. It was a burden that weighed heavily on me. Just looking around would tell you there was no foraging for berries on this island. If you couldn't eat grass or rocks you'd pretty much be out of luck. As for fresh water, the only source of it I'd seen were the lakes in the craters, and I had trouble imagining climbing down to one of those in the dark. I wasn't too worried about the food. Gordon was not fat by any means, but he was a big man, and he wasn't going to starve overnight. Water was more of a problem. I'd given him my liter bottle, but I'd already had some of it. I couldn't exactly remember how much. That meant I'd have to get up there soon.

No problem, I thought. I'll rent a vehicle, buy some food and water, and be on my way when no one is looking. I knew I wouldn't stand a chance of finding the cave in the dark, and it made more sense for me to be out during daylight hours anyway.

What I hadn't counted on was the San Pedro rongorongo tablet, or more specifically, its absence. The tablet was not immediately listed as stolen, just missing, given that its owner was permanently unable to tell anyone where he'd put it. The dancers who'd wheeled it on to the stage had not wheeled it off. That was left to Jasper, who had then had his fifteen minutes of glee after the dancers left the stage, when he asked Fairweather and Rory up to see it, and then stood by while everyone else oohed and aahed over it. What happened after that was a little vague. The glass case it had been housed in and the trolley it had rested upon both belonged to the hotel, and hotel staff had found both, empty, in the meeting room after everyone else had gone. They assumed that someone had taken care of the tablet. Undoubtedly someone had. The question was, who would that someone have been?

The carabineros, once advised of the evening's proceedings, had taken a good look through Jasper's room and declared definitively it wasn't there. The hotel manager said no arrangements had been made with the hotel for its safekeeping, and the night it had been unveiled was the first he ever heard of it.

Inquiries at the Sebastian Englert Museum in Hanga

Roa as to whether or not the tablet had been deposited with them met a similar response, with the additional comment that they had never heard of the San Pedro tablet at all.

Kent Clarke and the rest of the team at Kent Clarke Films all said that both Jasper and the tablet were still in the meeting room when they packed up their gear and left, Daniel to his home in Hanga Roa, Kent and Brittany to their room, and Mike to his end of the bar. Several members of the delegation remembered seeing him there, and none of them had seen the rongorongo tablet in his possession.

Kent told the police, or so she said, that she had asked Gordon Fairweather and Rory Carlyle to have a closer look at the tablet. She said she was not prepared to take Jasper's word that it was authentic and was hoping for a second opinion. She said that both men had agreed to take a look at it the next day. She said she was reasonably sure the tablet was still in the room when they left. There was a slight element of doubt in her statement, however, just enough to make both Gordon's and Rory's situation even worse than it already was.

The next morning, the carabineros swept into the hotel, asked all of us to stand by, and quite methodically searched our rooms while we watched. It took all day, and we were not allowed to leave the hotel.

By this time I was getting really worried and completely paranoid. I was convinced I was being watched every moment and worried that they'd managed to slip a bug into our hotel room while they searched, even though they'd made us watch while they went through our stuff. I hadn't said a word to anyone, not even Moira, who had not taken the news of Rory's incarceration well, and was now off in a little world of her own, usually by the pool.

I tried a couple of test runs into Hanga Roa by taxi, and on both occasions, within a few minutes, the carabineros had pulled in behind me, and when I got out, they cruised up and down the street watching me. Twenty-four hours a day, there was a police vehicle at the hotel entrance. So much for renting a car and making a dash for it. By now the better part of two days had gone by.

The only bright spot in all of this was that I figured out a way to keep tabs on Gabriela's condition. It occurred to me, in a rare moment of lucidity in those couple of days, that, given Gabriela had worked there, she might have a friend. That friend, it turned out, worked at reception. I mentioned that I hadn't seen Gabriela in the bar or dining room for a couple of days. Was she on a break? I asked.

"She's very sick," said the young woman, whose name, according to her badge, was Celia.

"That's too bad," I said. "I hope she'll get better soon. I'm rooting for her for Tapati queen."

Celia burst into tears. "They think she's tried to kill herself," she said. "She's in a coma!"

I feigned surprise and expressed genuine dismay. "What happened?" I exclaimed.

"Nobody knows. They think she may have taken it herself, but they can't find any poison around. Pills, perhaps, but nobody knows how she would have got them. They've sent some blood to Santiago for tests, and we're just waiting. I'm afraid she may die before they figure it out," the girl wailed.

"I knew she was unhappy about something," I said, rather tentatively.

"She was," Celia said. "She wouldn't tell me what it was. But to do something like this!" She stopped and looked at me for a minute. "When she came to the hotel to pick up her belongings, she told me two nice ladies from the hotel had tried to help her, but that no one could. Was that you and Ms. Meller?"

"We did try, without success," I said. "But I had no idea it was this bad."

"Nobody did," Celia said, but she gave me a little smile.

I hoped I had found an ally if I needed one. I even contemplated asking her to take a message for me to Victoria Pakarati; indeed I wrote a note and sealed it in a hotel envelope, but later when I went to reception to ask her, she was deep in conversation with Pablo Fuentes. They stopped talking the minute I walked in. Given I couldn't be sure of the tenor of that conversation, I just asked the first question that came into my head, something about the weather, and left with the letter still in my bag.

I finally poured out my heart to Moira. I asked her to go for a stroll on the hotel grounds with me and told her everything, then held my breath waiting for the reaction. "I'm glad you told me," she said. "I knew there was something bothering you. I was afraid you were annoyed with me about not believing you, and, I guess, about other things. Yes, I will help. We are intelligent women, to say nothing of devious when called for, and we will figure this out. If I can sum up what I think you've told me, Victoria can't go to her husband, nor can Rory and Christian, given they are both under house arrest. You can't go to Victoria because then they will be watching you. If any of her close relatives try to get to him, they'll be seen. So it's up to us. First we need food and water. Then we need a diversion."

"If we buy a lot of food and water, the guy who is following us around will begin to wonder," I said.

"Who said anything about buying?" she said.

It was another day before we could get everything organized. I was worried sick about Gordon by then. Every meal, we'd emptied the bread basket into our bags, and at breakfast we took lots of extra cheese and fruit, keeping it in the minibar in our room. The water was easy. We just ordered extra for our table every meal, and we did, in fact, go shopping, but only once. It was not the food that was slowing us down. It was devising a way for me to get it to him. We knew what we needed to do. We just had to find the right place to make it happen. We did the tourist routine, looking at the menus at every restaurant, buying T-shirts, walking up and down the streets of Hanga Roa stopping to look at everything.

Finally we were ready. We went into town, followed closely by one of Fuentes's men. We went into a car rental agency and came out with a white Suzuki four-wheel-drive, drove along the main street, parking in front of a restaurant carefully chosen, which we entered. I, as the one viewed with most suspicion, sat in the window with my menu and pretended to talk to Moira whose chair, had she been in it, was hidden from view. I smiled, I laughed, I didn't have a care in the world. In a few minutes she was back in her place, eating the cheese enchiladas I'd ordered for her. After lunch, we did a test drive to Anakena Beach, leaving the carabineros who'd been following us to sit in a hot van while we swam and sunbathed for the rest of the afternoon. We knew we were ready to roll.

But then Seth Connelly did something really, really stupid.

URE E REKA

THEY SHOULD NEVER have come back, Ure e Reka thought. *As much as they had dreamed of the return to their home, as harsh as the life had been, they should have stayed where they were.*

He could still feel his face burn at the humiliation of it, the way the men from the big ship had thrown their gifts onto the sand of the shore, forcing all of them to crawl on their hands and knees to retrieve them. And then, while they scrambled, those same bad men had grabbed them from behind, tied their hands, and carried them to the waiting boats. So many of them! Even the ariki mau and the other wise men of the clan Miru! Even his father, maori rongorongo.

They had been frightened then, on the long voyage to the terrible place, but it was nothing compared to what awaited them: the guano fields of the Chincha Islands, where they had worked in the stench and the heat, forced to the hard labor by the men who took them. He and the others could only dream of returning home.

But then, the word came, from some important ariki far away. They were to be returned to the island. Their fortune had been almost too happy to be believed.

Marama was the first man among them to fall ill. As the ship sank into the troughs, then rose again, he began to scream, tearing off his clothes as the fever took him. And then one by one the others had succumbed to the fever, and one by one they had died. His father had been among the last to be taken.

There were only a handful of them left, perhaps fifteen in all, of the thousand who were taken and the hundred who set sail for home, dumped on the beach they had been taken from so many months before.

His mother had been there, throwing herself into his arms. She too had later sickened and died, as the hideous fever swept on. Delirious, she told him to find his sister. She could not tell him where she was.

Already he knew he was ill. The sores had begun to appear on his flesh as it had with the others. If he found his sister, she too would die. No, she would have to fend for herself. What he needed to do before the fever had him in its grip was to hide the tablet, as his dying father had told him to do—the tablet, the kopeka, and the votives. His father had entrusted him with the location of the cave, and he would take it there. His father's aku-aku was very powerful. It would guard over the cave and its contents until someone came.

They should never have come back. Death had come with them.

1

TWO DAYS AFTER we'd found Jasper propped up against the back of Ahu Akivi and the day Moira and I were to put our meticulously planned strategy into action, all hell broke loose. It started, though, like just another day trapped in paradise. Most of us had found ways of coping under the circumstances. Some found new places to visit in town or elsewhere on the island, others simply enjoyed the pool and the ocean view. Most got together in the bar from time to time to whine to each other about our situation. The Kent Clarke crew was in some disarray, given the demise of their star. Kent took her daughter sightseeing, and Mike, as usual, held up his end of the bar, joined as often as not by Daniel, and now by Brian, who was having trouble convincing someone to give him a job, now that most of the people he wanted to see were either under house arrest or nowhere to be found.

Some had more unusual pursuits: Cassandra set herself

up to read tarot cards in the lounge for a fee. Yvonne and
Enrique had taken to writing each other poetry and reading
it aloud, something we all agreed was sweet even if the poetry itself was intolerably bad. Albert, with the help of
Lewis, was gradually working his way through the hotel's
wine cellar, keeping notes on every bottle he sampled.

Seth, though, pretty much kept to himself. Most of us,
and I include myself in this, I regret to say, simply forgot
about him. He'd not been the most sociable person to begin
with, but the evening we'd sat drinking his wine in the
lounge talking about rongorongo, I'd found him to be a
very pleasant companion and certainly rather voluble once
you got him on a subject that interested him, in that case,
rongorongo.

I'd tried once or twice to elicit a comment from him on
the San Pedro rongorongo tablet, but he wasn't doing much
talking after Dave died, not just to me, but to anyone. Now,
with the discovery of Jasper's body, Seth darted into the dining room the moment it opened, so he could get the same
table every meal, a table for two only, although he never
asked anyone to join him, and one that not only didn't have
a view, but was in a dark corner. I realize now he was keeping his back to the wall. Meal finished, he'd dash out again,
returning directly to his room. While I never saw it, I
wouldn't be surprised if he moved furniture in front of the
door. His room was in the same row as ours, and the curtains
were pulled day and night. Once or twice, when I took the
back route to the room, I saw the curtains move, so I guess
he was at his post as watch guard. He was alone and acting
like a caged animal, and I suppose he did what a caged animal would. Twenty-twenty hindsight is a wonderful thing,
of course, but in looking back on it, I think I could have,
perhaps should have, predicted what would happen.

Seth's plan wasn't bad, certainly no worse than the one
Moira and I had been plotting. It was in the execution that

it failed. He put it into action at almost the same moment we did. Moira and I had been sitting with some of the others looking out to sea, watching as the day's only flight came in. It was the occasion, almost every day, for some gnashing of teeth, with almost everyone saying how much they'd like to be on it when it left. Seth, however, was the only one of us who did anything.

Moira and I announced we were going into town and asked if anybody needed anything. The guard posted near the dining room barely noticed as we walked toward our Suzuki, parked not far from our room. As we sauntered in as nonchalant a manner as we could muster past one of the buildings, a door opened behind us, and Seth came out. We waved at him, but he didn't acknowledge our presence.

He was carrying one of the hotel laundry bags, and walking purposefully toward the reception area as if to drop it off. Before he got there, however, he abruptly turned and headed for a red Suzuki with rental stickers parked not far away. Upon reaching it, he tried to unlock the door. Unfortunately, he dropped the keys. Twice. By this time the guard posted at reception had noticed his nervous demeanor and started to walk toward him.

Instead of brazening it out, which would have been my inclination, Seth dropped the bag, which split open to reveal not laundry exactly, but a jacket, toiletries, and what looked suspiciously like a wallet, passport, and an airline ticket. The guard shouted at him to stop, but Seth wheeled around and started to run. By this time the other guard, roused by the shouting, had come around the corner, and immediately drew his gun. I was standing by the driver's side of our car, keys in hand, watching in a mixture of amazement and horror as Seth came straight at me.

"Don't shoot," Moira yelled.

"Don't do this, Seth," I said, but it was too late. As Seth slammed into me I could smell his fear, heard a desperate little gasp as he grabbed at the keys, which flew out of my hand and skidded across the pavement.

Seth made a dive for them at about the same time the guard did. Within seconds, Seth, nose bleeding, was pinned with his arms behind his back, as the other guard held a gun to his head.

The others by now had gathered round. "He could have been killed," Susie said, visibly pale. "How awful!"

"Are you all right?" Moira said, gesturing to my arm, which was already starting to bruise.

"I think so," I said.

"But what was he doing?" Yvonne asked.

"Making a run for the airport, I expect," Albert replied.

"I'm thinking it is not so intelligent to be doing this," Enrique said.

"You could say that," Lewis agreed.

"Or you could just call him an idiot," Brian added.

"Does this mean he's the murderer?" Yvonne said.

"Rather looks that way, I'm afraid," Albert said.

"What a pathetic excuse for a human being," Edwina said as Seth, now sobbing, was dragged away.

"Come on, let's have another drink," Mike said.

Thirty minutes later I had the unpleasant duty of translating Fuentes's words once again, notifying the group that we would all have to forfeit our passports and the keys to any rental cars we might have and were forthwith confined to the hotel. Hotel staff had been told they were not to arrange rental cars for any of us and to report to him if anyone attempted to leave.

"But if Seth is the murderer," Judith, the muffin's wife, and not one to be intimidated, said, "why can't we go home? I have a medical practice to attend to."

I translated. "He says we don't know that Seth is the murderer, and until Fuentes is satisfied of that, we're to stay."

"Come to think of it," Lewis said. "He doesn't strike me as a murderer, but then nobody does."

"We'll be told when we can go home," I concluded.

"There goes Plan A," Moira whispered, as dejected, we left the room.

"Is there a Plan B?" I asked.

"Does there need to be? I mean if Seth is the murderer . . . ?"

"I'm not sure, but let's assume we do need one," I said. It was just as well we did, because Saturday evening poor Seth was brought back to the hotel, but now confined to a room in the old part of the hotel, with no air-conditioning and no sliding doors at the back, with a guard on his room day and night. Meals were to be delivered to him at Fuentes's discretion and delivered under police escort. It seemed rather churlish to be sorry he wasn't arrested and charged, but I'm sure I was not the only person who would have been relieved if he had been.

The next day was Sunday. Moira and I were up really early and in the dining room stocking up on meat and cheese. At 8:15, we went out to Reception and asked them to call us a taxi. Fuentes appeared instantly. There must have been a little bell at the desk, or he had very good ears.

"You cannot leave the hotel, ladies," he said.

"We are going to church," Moira said. "We never miss Mass on Sundays. You cannot prevent us, surely, from participating in our worship." Have I mentioned Moira is Jewish?

Fuentes looked us over. We had each packed one dress for the trip, thinking we might have a fancy dinner out in Santiago, and we were wearing them, along with our sun hats. We also had our good sandals on. My dress, which fortunately was of the loose variety, covered a pair of shorts and a T-shirt. My running shoes were in my bag. The food was in Moira's.

"My officers would be happy to take you to the church,"

Fuentes said at last. "They will wait for you and bring you back."

"Thank you," we said.

The church was already filling up when we got there. The police dropped us right at the door and watched us walk in. I stood in the doorway long enough to see that they had shut off the engine very close to the door. They'd already put the seats back and were settling in. Within a few minutes, the church was packed with both worshipers and tourists. The front door was blocked by a group of people who had congregated there just to listen. It was standing room only.

As the singing began, Moira slipped the bag of groceries over to me, looked over her shoulder, and said, "Go!"

In a couple of seconds, I was out the side door. Plan A, and now Plan B, hinged on one thing: not one but two identical white Suzukis that we'd rented the previous day, initially intending to do a switch kind of operation, a plan scuppered by Seth's dash for freedom. One car was now at the hotel, under the watchful eye of the carabineros. The second was on a side street in town. While I'd been sitting in the window of the restaurant we'd entered shortly after we left the rental agency, pretending to talk to her, Moira had slipped out the back, picked up the second car, and parked it on the side street where I now headed. It was possible, of course, that the carabineros, who'd watched us go into the rental agency, would go in and find out we'd actually rented two. I didn't think they would. We'd gone into a rental agency and come out with a car. In five minutes, I was in the second car and on my way.

The rental agency was going to be none too thrilled with the state of the suspension on one of their vehicles, but I didn't care. I blasted up the road by the airport, turned inland at a trail, and bounced along for several minutes. I knew I had less than an hour to get to Gordon and get back to the church. The trouble was, I wasn't sure if I was on the right trail. Several cut off in different directions. I took one I was sure was it, but it just ended, not at the rock face I expected, but at a small copse of trees. After half an hour of this, I knew I was defeated. I was afraid I wouldn't even be able to find the main road again. Moira would be caught in the church without me, and we'd both be locked in our room. It wasn't in any of our interests to let that happen. I headed downward, hoping to pick up the main road, which I figured I had to come to eventually, looking left and right as often as I could without getting completely bogged down, to see if I could see the rock outcrop that contained the family cave. At last, when I was about to despair completely, I found the paved road, and headed back to town. It was the best I could do.

The last stragglers were leaving the church as I slipped in the side door and then walked out the front with Moira. "Wasn't the singing just marvelous?" Moira said as we climbed into our police escort's van.

"Lovely," I said. Someday I'd like to hear it. "I enjoyed it so much, I might like to go to Mass again tomorrow morning."

Moira paused for a moment. "Good idea," she said. "I'll speak to Corporal Fuentes about it."

"Tell me you found him and he's all right," she said, as we sauntered across the lawn to our room once the police dropped us off.

"I couldn't find the place," I said. "All the trails looked the same." There was a catch in my voice, and she put her arm through mine.

"Let's get into our bathing suits, go out to our favorite spot, and devise Plan C," she said.

"I've got to find a way to contact Victoria," I said, as we were back in our customary spots near the edge of the cliff. "Get her to draw a map to the cave. I know I started off right, but when I was with Gordon, he was giving me directions and I was just concentrating on not hitting a pothole so hard that I destroyed the truck. I didn't realize how many side trails there are. Some of them were pretty well traveled, so I figured it couldn't be one of those, but maybe it could. Maybe the carabineros have already been up to the cave, and it was their tracks I saw."

"But they would have found him if they'd gone up there," she said.

"Not according to Rory and Christian," I said. "And Gordon for that matter. They all claim he wouldn't be found."

"Victoria was not at Mass," she said. "I looked for her as planned, and I had the note ready to try to slip to her some way if I could catch her eye, but if she was there I couldn't find her."

"Did you manage the service all right?" I said.

"Sure," she said. "I did what you told me. I watched what everybody else did. I stood when they stood, I kneeled when they kneeled, and when they sang I just hummed along. It was gorgeous music by the way. They had a band even, with drums and guitars, and the hymns were in Rapanui. I loved it. Is it too late for me to convert?"

I smiled dutifully. I knew she was trying to cheer me up. "I guess the carabineros won't even let Victoria go to Mass. Do you remember that Gordon said she hadn't missed Sunday Mass in the five years he'd known her? I screwed up, Moira."

"Don't think that way," she said. "We'll come up with something."

After dinner, we went back to our room and at a reasonable hour turned out the light. By one a.m., I was out the sliding door at the back, over the fence, and out on the road. Plan C was underway. I got past the guard without any trouble and then jogged into town. I found Gordon's house and slipped into the neighbor's yard. I knew there was a clothesline out back—indeed the clothes on it had lent Gordon and me some cover when we made our hasty exit. It was, as I'd hoped, the kind on a pulley. As quickly and quietly as possible, I pinned a note, in a plastic bag, to the line, and reeled it up to the house before slipping away. By 1:45 I was back in my bed.

The storm hit the next morning. Lightning streaked across the sky, and the rain came down in torrents. The airport was closed. The lawn where Moira and I had held our planning sessions was a sea of mud. We took to writing each other notes in our room while we talked about something else. I was sure Gordon was dead, that the day before had been my last chance to save him, even when Moira passed a note across to me that said all Gordon had to do to get water was to stand outside, look up, and open his mouth. The trouble was there was no reason for there to be clothes on a clothesline in this weather. We agreed, however, that I would head out again that night.

I was soaking wet by the time I got there, having had to slide past the carabineros to get to our second rental car once again. The clothesline was absolutely bare. I was debating whether to try to get into the house when I heard a creak, and the line started to move. A note in a plastic bag slid silently over to me. I looked at the window close to where the line attached to the house and thought I saw something move, but I didn't hang around. It was still dark when I got to the car, but dawn would be coming soon enough. The terrible weather, I hoped, would give me some cover. I headed out of town on to the main road, and when the coast seemed to be clear, I switched on Moira's penlight and had a look at the map. I tried to do the route without headlights, but eventually had to switch them on.

Despite the map, once again I could not find the cave. The tracks were almost obliterated in the mud as water poured downhill. I found myself back at the copse of trees again, borderline hysterical by this point. To my relief, Victoria had marked the copse on the map, and I was able to get my bearings at last. I almost screamed with joy when the rocky outcrop appeared.

I crawled into the cave and swept the interior with the flashlight, which didn't do much good, given it was only a penlight. There was no one there, but I remembered Gordon's instructions for Rory. "Gordon," I said. "It's Lara. I'm alone." Nothing happened. My heart was in my throat. He was dead. I hadn't gotten there on time. "Gordon," I said again, this time a little louder. "It's Lara." I waited, holding my breath. Seconds ticked by. No one came.

In a panic I started scrabbling away at a pile of rocks to one side of the cave. Lo and behold, an opening appeared. I shone the pathetic light into it, and saw it was a shaft of some kind. It had been used by humans because there was a length of rope that hung down into it by a couple of feet, held there by another rock on the floor of the cave and covered with smaller stones so that it couldn't be seen. The shaft looked longer than I was tall, and even with a couple feet of rope, I didn't think I could go down there. But then I heard what I was reasonably sure was a groan. "I'm coming," I called.

The shaft was too narrow for me to even crawl on all fours, and I knew I'd have to wriggle my way in. Headfirst was not an option, because if I got stuck, I'd be there forever. Even with the penlight, I could see that the tunnel curved in such a way that if I went down on my back, I wouldn't be able to make the turn. So I lay flat on my stomach, stuck my feet into the downward tunnel, grabbed the rope over my head, and started to slide, using my elbows to brake the descent.

My feet hit rock on the turn when I was only a few feet down. I had no way of telling what lay beyond, and had a minor panic attack. For some reason, this position was very frightening for me. I know I'm uncomfortable with heights, but I've never known myself to be claustrophobic, never, that is, until then. The rock surface was only about four inches from my nose, and the lower I went the narrower the shaft seemed to be, although it was possible my imagination was in overdrive. I felt as if I was going to choke, and I was terrified that I wouldn't be able to pull myself back up lying on my back with my arms over my head.

I just couldn't go any farther. I did manage to pull myself up to the floor of the cave again and just sat there, breathing heavily. Then I heard the sound again. "Gordon?" I shouted into the shaft, and I was almost certain I heard a reply. If he was down there, then this had to be doable. I took a deep breath and went back into the shaft. This time, when my feet touched bottom, I swung them out into the space. I didn't know if it was another shaft like this one or the entrance to the abyss. Frightened, I decided I just could not do this, no matter what, and began to push myself back up.

But it was too late. I started to slide around the turn in the shaft, and then I fell a foot or two. I landed in a shower of stones on rock. I was in another shaft, mercifully horizontal this time and larger, enough for me to simply crouch over and make my way along. The flashlight was broken, but it didn't matter, because I could actually see light ahead of me. I thought at first that Gordon must have turned his flashlight on for my benefit, but when I stepped into a larger chamber, one in which I could actually stand upright, I realized that dawn was breaking, and there was a window at the far end of the cave. Just enough light was coming in that I could see Gordon sitting, his back to the cave wall. The first thought I had was that he was dead, sitting as he was, just like Jasper Robinson, but then he groaned. I'd brought one bottle of water with me, and I was over to him in a flash, pouring some into his open mouth. He opened his eyes immediately, grabbed the bottle, and drank.

"Breakfast," I said. "Sorry I'm late." It was a poor attempt at a joke, but if I hadn't said something like that, I'd have cried. He made an effort to smile.

"I brought mail, too," I said, handing him an envelope from Victoria. "The flashlight has quit, so you will have to go over to the light, while I go back up and get the rest of the supplies." He nodded, but he didn't move.

I had to take that awful shaft back up, but buoyed by my success, I made it quickly enough. I didn't think I'd have the strength to haul myself out too many more times, but I did manage to do it often enough to get the water and the food down there. Gordon was still sitting where I'd left him. It was then that I noticed his arm.

"What happened?" I said.

"It's my shoulder," he said. "I stumbled somehow. I guess I was getting a little impatient and careless, and I've either dislocated it or badly bruised it. The point is, I can't pull myself up that shaft."

"Maybe I could," I said, but I knew I couldn't. I could barely manage hauling myself up, and there was no way I could pull him up, even if I were Charles Atlas, because there wasn't enough room for both of us. This was really not good. I carefully pulled his shirt off his shoulder. I wouldn't know a dislocated shoulder if I fell over it, but there was no question he had one of the worst bruises I'd ever seen.

I made my way over to the opening in the rock and looked out. The storm continued to rage outside, but there was some shelter from the wet in the rock opening. Carefully I leaned out slightly and looked down. Vertigo kicked in immediately, and I staggered back from the edge. Very far below was the sea, churning against jagged rocks. I edged forward again and this time carefully looked up. The top of the cliff was maybe twenty feet up with no path, no toe- or finger-holds that I could see.

"I can certainly see why this was a good hiding place," I remarked, in what I hoped was a casual tone. "Nice and roomy, large picture window, outdoor facilities, though, I suppose."

"You just have to remember not to pee into the wind," he said. "Will you read me the note?" I did. In it, Victoria told him she loved him, that she had called the U.S. Embassy in Santiago, they had recommended a lawyer, and that same lawyer was supposed to have been on that day's flight, which had been canceled because of the storm. She would send the lawyer with one of the family members to get him as soon as he arrived. She said Edith was fine, but missed her papa. She said that they were keeping Gabriela comfortable while they tried to figure out what was wrong.

Gordon closed his eyes for a moment when I finished the letter. He seemed quite overcome. Then he asked about Rory and Christian and I had to tell him why they hadn't been able to bring the supplies. I considered telling him about the San Pedro rongorongo tablet, but I didn't. I didn't think he'd kill anyone, but I wasn't so sure he wouldn't make off with the tablet.

"This is one fine mess, isn't it, Lara?" he sighed. "And it is all of my making. If I hadn't lost my temper up there at Rano Raraku, I wouldn't be here and neither would you. I hope you will forgive me someday."

"Forget that," I said. "Let's just figure out how we're going to get you out of here, and soon." I gave him the little bottle of painkillers I had taken to carrying in my cosmetic bag ever since the migraine and piled the food and water up where he could reach them. He told me he could move about a little, but the shaft was out of the question.

"If the police want me, they'll have to get me out," he

said. I hated to leave him, but there was nothing else I could do. I had to get back before I was missed.

"I'll be back," I said.

He grabbed my hand with his good one. "Thank you," he said.

When I got back to town, it was light. I parked the vehicle closer to the hotel and on the side where I did not have to cross in front of the guard to get to the sliding glass door at the back of the room. It was open, of course, but the room was empty. I was chilled to the bone and got into the shower forthwith, then climbed under the covers and fell asleep.

I couldn't have slept more than a few minutes when the door opened, and Moira, with a policeman behind her peering over her shoulder, stepped into the room. "Are you feeling better?" she said. "I went to the gift shop and got you some pills for your tummy. I also brought you some breakfast and coffee," she said, "for when you're feeling up to it." The policeman looked at me, grunted, and left.

"You're good, Moira," I said.

"I know," she replied. She wrote me a note in which she told me she'd realized that the police were going to go door to door if people didn't show up for meals, so she'd gone and just told everybody I wasn't feeling well. The policeman had followed her back to the room, so she'd played her role to the hilt. While I was reading her note, she even took two pills out of the package and flushed them down the toilet in case someone checked to see if I'd taken anything for this tummy of mine.

"Details count," she said, as I devoured the breakfast she'd brought. I wrote her a very long note about Gordon, and she looked dismayed as she read it. At the end of it, I told her I'd be going out again that night.

"I sure hope this rain stops soon," she said. "For everyone's sake."

Victoria had written me a note as well. In it she said she

was planning to have a fit of hysterics that evening and that she was going to insist the police accompany her to the hospital to see Gabriela. I was to be there about midnight if I could.

Moira was rolling up a blanket and placing it in my bed as I slipped out the back door again in the dark. "In case they do a bed check," she scribbled. Fortunately, given where I'd left the vehicle, I didn't have to jog into town this time, nor did I have to cross the hotel entrance without being seen. I parked a block or two from the hospital. It was a good thing Victoria had included a map of its location in her note, because I would never have guessed this low-rise building that looked like a school maybe, or a retirement home, was the hospital. The only clue was an ambulance parked out front. After locating the policemen that I knew would have escorted Victoria to the hospital—they were in their vehicle on the street—I crept behind the ambulance and slipped in.

Victoria was watching for me and quickly pulled me behind the curtain that surrounded Gabriela's bed. I told Victoria that Gordon was all right, that I'd managed to get him food and water, and would do it again if necessary. She flung her arms around me and held on tight. Then I told her about his injury, and she teared up a bit.

"I've got to go," I said. "I don't want to stay any longer than is absolutely necessary. How is she?" I asked, gesturing toward Gabriela. It was a stupid question. I'm not sure I would even have recognized Gabriela under different circumstances. Her face was so white as to be almost unreal, there were tubes everywhere, and somewhere just outside the curtain some machine was thumping along. I think it was doing her breathing for her.

"Not good," she said. "We're still waiting for tests. They had to send the blood samples to Santiago! The doctors say there was alcohol and sleeping pills in her blood, but not enough to do this. She doesn't drink, you know. I'm not saying she doesn't go out with friends and maybe have the odd drink. Maybe she does. She likes to dance, so she goes to the clubs sometimes. But no one has ever seen her drunk, and we have no idea where she would get sleeping pills. I cannot understand this. Anyway, it doesn't matter if she did this to herself or not, I just want her to get better. She did wake up from time to time the first day or two, but she hasn't in a while. The nurses tell us to speak to her, that she may know who is here. I hope she does."

Gabriela looked so terrible that I could hardly stand to look at her, but I reached over and took her hand for a minute. "She didn't do this to herself," I said. "There is something else going on. I don't know how I know this. I just do."

"I keep thinking it must be something else, too," Victoria said. "If there isn't enough alcohol and drugs to put her into a coma, what did?"

"Hold Edith safe," I said.

"I will," she said. "Thank you for helping us."

I let go of Gabriela's hand and saw something that gave me pause. "What's that on her arm?" I said.

"It's a tattoo," Victoria said. "Or at least the start of one. I guess she must have had it done just before this happened. The doctors thought at first it might be the cause—septicemia, you know, from a dirty needle—but it isn't that. It's just a tattoo. You can see the lines where the tattoo artist drew them to help with the design. It's a tattoo of a little bird."

That's strange, I thought, but it would take me a while to figure out why.

I slipped back into our room, waking Moira as I did so. "How did it go?" she asked.

"Mission accomplished," I whispered.

"Brava!" she said.

"You know something, Moira?" I said, completely forgetting, in my general relief, that I wasn't supposed to talk in the room. "Now that I've managed to get food and water to Gordon, I want to go home. Once the storm abates and the airport opens, he'll have a lawyer and the support of his embassy. I don't for a minute think he killed Jasper Robinson, or especially, for that matter, Dave. But there is nothing more we can do for him. He's someone else's problem now. It is a fabulous place, this Rapa Nui. The antiquities are unparalleled, the people lovely, the scenery rather breathtaking, once you come to appreciate its relative barrenness and begin to see the subtleties in the landscape. But I've seen it. Now it's time to go home."

"What do you think it will take to get us off the island?" she said.

"Maybe having Gordon turn himself in," I said. "I hate to see him charged with a murder just so I can go home, but it's beginning to reach that point."

"I'm beginning to feel the same way," she said. "I'd like to see Rory before we go, though. I suppose if Gordon is charged, they'll at least let the others leave for home."

"It's still raining," I said. "I hope they get that airport open soon."

"Go to sleep," she said. I did. I was deep in the dream in which Rob was telling me I'd overlooked something very obvious, when the still of the night was rent by a bloodcurdling scream.

8

THAT SCREAM WAS one of the worst sounds I have ever heard in my life. It was barely human. Given the way the hotel was configured and the less than optimal sound insulation in it, I think just about everybody in the place heard it, too.

The first scream was followed by a second, and soon doors started slamming, and most of us found ourselves out on a wet lawn. The rain, at least, had stopped.

"Has somebody else been murdered?" Brenda Butters said, almost shaking with fear.

"Maybe it was an animal," Albert, clad in rather dapper red-and-white striped pajamas, proposed, unconvincingly.

"There were two screams," Lewis said.

"The second one was me," Yvonne said. "I was so startled by that awful sound that I screamed, too. Sorry." Enrique put his arm around Yvonne in a protective way.

"Who's not here?" Susie said. "That should tell us who screamed."

"Cassandra isn't," Yvonne said.

"Maybe Cassandra's aku-aku is strangling her," Lewis said.

The original scream, however, had emanated from the mouth of Seth Connelly. As soon as his door was opened by the police guard, though, Seth very calmly walked out. His eyes were open, but he wasn't very responsive. "He's sleep-walking," Judith Hood, the doctor, said. "Don't touch him."

We all tried to stay out of his way, the police guard holding a flashlight up as Seth wandered about. If there was somewhere particular he planned to go, it was not evident to me. Finally he walked right up to the group of us, eyes wide open, and said, in a very strange voice, "We're all going to die."

Yvonne screamed again. "Shush," Judith said. "Seth," she said, in a carefully modulated and practiced tone. "I want you to go back to your room, get into bed, and go back to sleep."

"Dave is dead. Jasper is dead. Soon I'll be dead," he said, but he did what he was told. Judith waited until he had settled down, then told us all to go back to bed.

"That is a very disturbed man," Judith said to the police guard. "I want to talk to your superior in the morning. He must be allowed out of that room."

"He's faking," Fuentes said, after the guard on the door summoned him the next morning at Judith's request. Moira and I had gone with her to provide moral support.

"I'm a doctor," Judith said. "I am giving you my professional opinion. I think this man is seriously delusional. We need to get him out of that room."

"Trust me," Fuentes said. "I've seen it all before." But in

the end, he gave in. Seth would be allowed to leave his room as long as a guard was with him.

But Seth didn't want out of the room. I did realize that if I felt rather claustrophobic on this island, poor Seth Connelly must be really suffering confined to his room. It was his own fault, certainly, and had caused me some difficulty to be sure. Still, he couldn't be having a fun time of it. Every time I walked by his room, I could see him in there sitting on the edge of the bed. The door was usually open so that he could see something other than four walls, and I guess he sat where he could see grass. When Judith talked to Fuentes the next day and got permission for him to leave the room to come to the dining room for his meals, however, Seth wouldn't budge.

"Does anyone know if he has family?" Judith asked us. "I think someone he trusts is going to have to come and take him home, and then get him some serious psychiatric help." Nobody knew anything about him. Judith then organized a rotation of people to visit him.

The first couple of visits went reasonably well, apparently. Everyone said he seemed to be fine. Mine, however, did not.

"Hi, Seth," I said rather tentatively. He did not look good. He hadn't shaved in days. He didn't smell good either. A little soap and water was definitely called for.

He scrambled to the other side of the bed. "Are you Anakena?" he said. "Have you come for me?"

"Seth," I said. "I'm Lara McClintoch, an antique dealer from Toronto. Unlike several of the people here, that is the only name I have. We had a lovely chat the other evening about rongorongo," I said. "Don't you remember?"

He looked at me closely. "You aren't Anakena?" he said.

"No," I replied. "I'm Lara. Anakena is a beach."

"We should never have come back," he said.

"Why not?" I said.

"Anakena knows," he said.

"Right," I said going into the bathroom and turning on the shower. "Now, you are going to have a shave and shower. Do you have any clean clothes?"

He looked around. "I guess some are cleaner than others," he said.

"Then get them, and go and clean yourself up," I said. I was treating him like a child, I knew that, but it seemed to be what it took, because he did what he was told. While he was in the shower, I did a quick sweep of the room. The only item of note was the copy of *The Art Forger's Handbook*, this time with its own cover. A few minutes later, Seth came out of the bathroom a relatively changed man.

"Okay, now," I said in my best schoolmarm voice. "Gather up your dirty clothes and fill out this form. I'm going to call for the housekeeper to do your laundry." I picked up the phone. "This phone doesn't work," I said.

"No," he said. I pulled the cord up and looked at it. I was about to say it looked just like the cord in Dave's room, but bit my tongue. If Seth thought he was going to end up like Dave on Tepano's Tomb, telling him that was going to send him right around the bend, given his fragile state. I took the laundry bag to reception and asked them to look after it.

When I got back to the room, Seth allowed as how he felt better now that he'd cleaned himself up. "I'm sorry I was so out of it when you first came," he said. "I don't know what's the matter with me. I've always been a little claustrophobic, you know. I can't go into caves," he added, stuttering over the word *caves*. "The idea of a submarine terrifies me. Maybe being on this little island . . ." His voice trailed off.

"It is difficult being here and knowing you can't leave," I agreed, and then I suggested he come to lunch with me. He got that haunted look again and refused. I realized that he seriously believed there was someone out there who wanted to kill him, and I suppose a hotel room with only one entrance and window, both guarded by a member of the Carabineros de Chile, looked like a pretty good arrangement to him, even if he was slightly claustrophobic. How he thought he was going to get home, however, was another matter.

"Okay," I sighed. This was tough going, but I'd promised Judith I'd take my turn, and take my turn I would.

"What did you think of the San Pedro rongorongo tablet?" I said.

His hands started to tremble. "It's genuine," he said. "We didn't want it to be, but it is."

"Why wouldn't you want it to be?" I asked. "Is it because you don't believe Rapa Nui was first settled from South America? Is that it?"

"It's not from South America," he said.

"What do you mean, it's not from South America? You're saying it's real, but not from the place Jasper claims it is," I said.

"Yes," he said.

"Gordon Fairweather and Rory Carlyle seemed to think it was a possibility that it did—come from South America, that is."

"That's because they didn't have a chance to take a good look at it the way I did," he said.

"Good for you," I said. "How did you manage that?" One part of my brain was telling me to have a look around the room to see where he'd hidden the tablet; another part was sure he was sliding into lunacy again right before my eyes.

"Dave let me see it," he said. "He had a good look at it as well. He said he thought the wood was wrong for Chile, but he'd have to check when he got home, or maybe on the Internet. Dave knows his wood, being a builder. Dave knew his wood," he corrected himself.

"How did Dave come to have the tablet?" I said. Dave

had been long gone when Jasper showed the tablet to the world. I was getting confused.

"He brought it with him," Seth said.

"The tablet was Dave's?"

"Of course not," Seth said. "Jasper asked Dave to bring it with him. A diversion, I suppose, or maybe he didn't want to risk being caught with it. Jasper just flits into a location, gets himself filmed doing something spectacular, and then flies out again. He's always been like that, even when he was young. Dave met Jasper in Miami, and Dave made a little stand for the tablet, so it would be upright on the stage, and then brought it with him. I think Dave just put it in his carry-on luggage and brought it out. Dave didn't think it was much of a risk, because they're looking for rongorongo being smuggled out of here, not coming in."

"So why did Jasper ask Dave to do it?"

"They go back a long way. We all do," he said. "Dave was coming out here early to see that everything got set up right and then to be official greeter. Brenda Butters is a good organizer, which is why Jasper asked her to help with the registrations and everything, but she isn't very good at the social stuff."

"You and Jasper and Dave all go back a long way?" I asked.

He didn't answer.

"So Dave thought the wood was wrong, did he? What did you think?"

"I know the tablet didn't come from Chile. Dave wanted to believe it did, but I knew he was wrong. When he started to think the wood was wrong, then he wanted it to be a forgery. We borrowed a book about forgeries, and Dave studied it. It's here somewhere."

"Is that it?" I said, pointing to the Hebborn.

"Yes," he said, picking it up and handing it to me.

"Dave was reading it to see how the forgery might be done."

"When was this?"

"We talked about it the night he died," Seth said. "He came to my room to get the tablet late that night after they closed the bar and everyone had turned in for the night. We had to give it to Jasper and that Kent Clarke woman so they could get it ready for the presentation. He took it with him."

"So where is the San Pedro tablet now?" I asked.

"I have no idea," he said. "It doesn't matter where it is."

It does if it has something to do with Dave and Jasper's deaths, I thought, but once again I kept that thought to myself. "But it's missing. Someone must have thought it worth stealing."

"Or Jasper made it disappear because he didn't really want anyone who knew anything about it to have a close look," he said. "It is not from Chile. It was Jasper's vanity, his determination to find something that supported his theories, that blinded him to the obvious."

"I'm not getting this," I said. "Are you saying that Jasper just pretended to discover the tablet in Chile? That he just walked out of the desert into some town and said, 'Look what I found'?"

"No, I'm saying someone put it there for Jasper to find," Seth said. "It was a message, even if Jasper didn't realize it at first."

"Wouldn't that be a lot of trouble? That canyon looked pretty deserted and far from, well, everywhere."

"Not for Anakena," Seth said. "And not for Jasper."

"Anakena is a beach," I repeated.

Seth was obviously in bad shape. "You didn't like Jasper, I know," I added. "You said you'd known him a long time. Why did you stay in touch?"

"Who said anything about staying in touch? I hadn't

seen him in thirty years when I got here. I'm getting a little tired," he said.

"Dave kept something locked in his safety deposit box," I said, thinking if anybody knew it would be Seth. "It wasn't his money or his passport. Do you know what it was?"

"I expect it was the photograph," he said. "I shouldn't have brought it. We shouldn't have come at all."

"Photograph of what?"

"Anakena knows."

"Where would this photograph be now?" I said, ignoring his reference to Anakena.

"I imagine it has been destroyed. That's what I would have done."

"Was Dave drunk when he came to see you the night he died?" I asked. Perhaps this was a question Seth would be capable of answering.

"No," he said. "He showed me a bottle of pisco he'd bought to take home with him. But he hadn't drunk any. Everybody thinks it was an accident, that he tried to ride a horse in the middle of the night."

"I don't," I said. "I think he was murdered." There, I'd said it.

"Yes," Seth said. He seemed remarkably calm all of a sudden.

"Who do you think did it?" I asked.

"Anakena," he said. "Whoever that is." Then he climbed into bed, curled up into the fetal position, and closed his eyes. I took that as my signal to leave.

I wanted to say something to comfort him. He was obviously in very bad shape, with all that talk of Anakena and messages. The only helpful thing I could think of was that the sun was out, Gordon's lawyer was on the way, and if he turned himself in, then maybe we'd all be able to go home. But there was only so much of that I could tell without betraying Gordon and possibly making trouble for myself. That the sun was out would be about as far as I could go, and somehow I didn't think that would help, given Seth wouldn't go out of his room to stand in it. "I'll bring you some dinner later," was all I said.

I went to get my own lunch. The dining room had closed already, but they took pity on me and made me a sandwich. Susie Scace was sitting alone at a table on the terrace, so I asked if I could join her.

"Do you mind if I ask if you're one of the people with a funny nickname of some kind?" I said.

"Nana o Keke," she said. "At your service."

"What is that all about, or is it some big secret?"

"No secret, really. Not now anyway. A number of us are here because we participate in a group on the Internet called the Moaimaniacs. We all use an alias, so part of the fun of coming here was to meet people and try to put them together with their alias. Some were easy. Cassandra was on it, I know, because of all that stuff about Lemuria. On the Internet, she calls herself Mu—Mu being the earth mother and the goddess after whom they're supposed to have named Lemuria. She always speaks of herself in the third person, as in 'Mu believes Rapa Nui to be the tip of her continent,' or 'Mu would be interested in learning more about whatever,' that sort of thing. I had no trouble identifying her right away. I hope you'll forgive me for saying so, but I found her tiresome on the Internet and even more tiresome in person."

"You won't get any argument from me there," I said. "I think she's awful."

"Dave Maddox, poor man, was MoaiMan, Seth is RongoReader, and Brian is Birdman. Everyone tried to choose something that related both to Rapa Nui, of course, but also their particular area of interest. Brian is interested in doing some research at Orongo, which is the site of the bird man cult. Dave, well, you know all about his moving Moai theories. And Seth is really into rongorongo. Have you taken your turn visiting him by the way? He seemed relatively okay when I was there, but I think maybe he's on the edge of a complete breakdown, perhaps because of Jasper and Dave. What did you think?"

I agreed Seth was in pretty bad shape. "What about your alias? Nana o Keke, did you say?"

"I'm embarrassed to tell you," she said. "Because it isn't very good, not nearly as clever as some of the others. My grandchildren call me Nana, and Ana o Keke is the cave of the white virgins. Therefore, Nana o Keke. Seeing as how I'm a grandmother, the virgin part didn't make a lot of sense, but I liked the rhythm of it.

"Let's see, who else?" she said, counting off on her fingers. "There were supposed to be eleven of us here. Albert Morris is Ariki-mo, a clever play on the title for king, ariki mau, and his last name, and Brenda Butters is Avareipu. That would be Hotu Matu'a's sister, or wife, depending on which version of the myth of the first settler you care for. Enrique, that dear boy with his nose in a guidebook all the time, is Tongenrique, also clever.

"Edwina Rasmussen is Vinapu, because she supports Jasper's theories of settlement from South America. Vinapu is an ahu where the stonework is believed to resemble that of Cusco, Peru, and one that people point to as evidence of South Amerindian settlement. Edwina didn't participate much in the Internet dialogue, just corrected us from time to time, which is what she has continued to do here, I'm afraid. My favorite, though, is Poikeman. That would be Lewis. I think it suits him to a T, don't you? He sort of looks like the toy, doesn't he? What is it his wife calls him? A little muffin?"

"I'm missing somebody, though. Yvonne! How could I forget? She's Hottie Matu'a. I suppose some of the locals would think that sacrilege or something, taking the name of their first king in vain, but you've got to admit it suits her." She laughed.

"Where did the idea for the congress start? Was it on the Internet?"

"I don't know really. There was an announcement posted to our list that the event was happening and when. There was an email giving us all the information about hotels and so on, and the registration form came from Avareipu, that is to say Brenda Butters, although I didn't know that was her name at the time. All the Moaimaniacs were invited. I think there are fifteen of us, but only eleven were able to get here. I've managed to identify all but one."

"Which one would that be?" I said.

"I'm missing Anakena," she said. "I'm surprised, because Anakena was the one who urged us all to come. I suppose he or she could have suggested it and then not been able to come themselves, which would have been a shame. Either that or they're here and just prefer not to have us know who they are. I can't imagine why, because it's been fun meeting everyone."

So that was what Seth meant. "Could Anakena have been Jasper?" I asked.

"I suppose it could, but I don't think so. Jasper provided the Internet site, and he may have followed the conversation, but if so, he was a lurker—you know, someone who reads but never identifies themselves. He had a number of chat groups on his Web site for places he'd done work and had one of his spectacular adventures. Ours is Moaimaniacs@jasperrobinsongroups.com. A bit of a mouthful. His schedule was posted on the group from time to time, along with press releases and so on. My recollection is that they were posted by Jasper@JasperRobinson.com. He didn't strike me as the kind of guy to use an alias. He pretty much wanted everybody to know who he was."

"Has the conference lived up to your expectations? Other than . . ."

"The guest of honor, plus one of the maniacs, ending up dead?" she said. "Yes and no. Jasper's presentation was a knockout, of course. Who would have guessed he'd turn up a rongorongo tablet in Chile! The field trips were also great, although I'd have appreciated a bit more explanation about what we were seeing. It was great when Rory Carlyle came and told us about trying to link Rapa Nui myth with real archaeological data. My one complaint was that I thought there were going to be a lot more expert speakers. I enjoyed the first day with Rory and Christian Hotus and even Edwina Rasmussen, despite her attitude problem. I also thought our own Birdman Brian Murphy's paper was terrific. But after that we were just kind of talking to ourselves. I was surprised that there weren't more experts, but I have a feeling a lot of them turned down invitations to speak because of Jasper. I think Edwina Rasmussen was a little surprised to find out it was just us Moaimaniacs. Maybe that explains why she's so crabby. Don't tell her I said that."

"Seth thinks someone called Anakena is trying to kill him," I ventured.

"The poor man," Susie said. "He seemed perfectly lucid when I was there."

"Maybe that's because he knows you aren't Anakena," I said.

As silly as it sounded, I did have to admit that two people who were part of an Internet chat group called the Moaimaniacs were dead, murdered. It had to be someone at the conference who was responsible, really, so some person who called themselves Anakena, but didn't want anybody to know who they were, made as much sense as a suspect as anybody else. And Seth had been absolutely lucid when he talked about the rongorongo tablet and even when he talked about Dave. Why wouldn't he also be lucid about this?

So who was Anakena? If anyone should know it was Brenda Butters, Avareipu, or whatever it was, the registrar of the congress. I went to find her.

"I don't have a lot of time to talk," she said in that breathless way she had. Life, it seemed to me, was one big emergency for people like Brenda. "The hotel is just chaos," she said. "The flights are starting to come in again and we're still here. They're blaming me, of course, as the person who did all the arrangements, but I don't see how they can blame me for people getting killed. Still, we are going to have to move a few of our people to the old wing, to free up a few air-conditioned rooms for arriving guests. People won't be happy, but I don't know what else to do.

"Who first had the idea for the congress? Was that your question? I really don't know," she said. "Jasper sent out a press release, that's all. He said something about how thrilled he was to be guest of honor at this event. Then, Kent Clarke also sent out a request through our Web group asking if anyone would be willing to act as volunteer registrar and if so to let her know what qualifications we had and so on. I emailed her and told her I had experience running training courses, booking the rooms, and everything. It's what I used to do before I retired. She said there was a free hotel room for every fifteen rooms taken, so I could have the first one if I'd agree to help out. I said sure. It's very expensive to get to Rapa Nui from New Jersey, believe me, so any help I could get would be fine. I'm retired, and so I had the time, and it's good to get involved, you know."

"So as registrar you would know the identity of all the Moaimaniacs?" I said.

"Not really," she replied. "We used aliases, you see. In some cases I knew who people were. Their names show up in their email addresses even if they sign on with an alias. I certainly knew Dave Maddox and Seth Connelly. Their

email addresses are their names, essentially, and they were
founding members of the chat group when it got going
three years ago. Dave used to sign on as Dave Maddox The
MoaiMan, so everyone knew him. I think that's why he
came out early to help out. Everybody in the group knew
him if not by sight, then by name. Terrible what happened.
But others, no. Yvonne, Hottie Matu'a, for example, used a
name which isn't the same as hers, her ex-husband's I think
she said. She hadn't got around to getting a new email address for her maiden name. I had no clue who she was. And
Poikeman already had that alias when he joined the group.
It already was his email address."

"So you were responsible for inviting everyone and dealing with the hotel and everything?"

"I was. Kent Clarke sent me a list, I emailed them, and
asked them to come. The list included the Moaimaniacs,
but also a number of others. I just posted the invitation to
the whole Moaimaniacs list. I attached a registration form,
which you could either fax to me with credit card information, or you could mail with your check. People registered
under their real names, not their aliases, of course.

"What about hotel arrangements?"

"I researched the hotels and picked this one, but with the
exception of the film team, everyone made their own reser-
vations directly with the hotel, or through their travel
agents," she said. "It was more work than I thought it
would be. I had to find special facilities for the film people,
a room where they could work with lots of electrical outlets
and stuff. They have tons of equipment with them. I booked
their rooms, although the cameraman lives here and didn't
need one, but I got them for the director and for Kent
Clarke and her daughter. Then we had to have the meeting
rooms all set up and everything and the AV equipment
everybody needed for their session all arranged. It kept me
busy, I'll tell you. I was always having to change the

arrangements I'd made. We held a block of rooms, for example, but we're actually quite a small group, so we had to release them as time went by. There wasn't the registration we originally expected. I'd thought originally we would have to billet people in other hotels or in bed-and-breakfast places, but we didn't."

"Why not, do you think?"

"The academics. We invited a lot of experts to come and speak. We even offered to pay for their accommodation once they got here. But most turned us down. Even Gordon Fairweather, who lives here, turned us down. Jasper is, was, a great man. They will come to realize that."

"You said two people canceled at the last minute," I said.

"Two of our speakers. I think they didn't want to have anything to do with Jasper, which I think is a shame. Academic arrogance of the worst sort."

"Did all the maniacs you expected turn up?" I asked.

"Everyone who said they were coming, with the exception of the two who canceled at the last minute, are here," she said.

"So Anakena is here," I said.

"I guess so," she said. "All the rooms were taken that were supposed to be and all the badges picked up."

"Do you have any idea who Anakena is?"

"No idea at all," she said.

So there I was back in line for the Internet. Question to Rob: *Is it possible to find out who people are and where they live when they use an alias on the Internet?*

Answer: *Possible, but often very difficult, especially if that person lives outside the U.S. and Canada and a few countries in Europe. Think of those hackers from Russia, for example. Internet is very hard to police. When are you coming home?*

Answer: *Soon I hope.*

So far this was going nowhere. The Moaimaniacs said

Avareipu invited them. Avareipu said Kent Clarke asked her to help out, but she didn't know where the idea for the congress originated. I supposed that meant I would now have to talk to Kent Clarke.

But I didn't get to that, at least not right away. I was just about to leave Brenda to her labors when Pablo Fuentes showed up. "Just the people I am looking for," he said. "Señora, your services as translator again, please. Señora Butters, would you please arrange for your group to be in the meeting room in ten minutes."

"Ten minutes!" Brenda exclaimed. I thought for a minute she was going to pass out at this addition to her responsibilities, but she rallied.

"Are you going to give me a preview of what I'm to translate?" I asked, as we walked over to the meeting room.

"I will be announcing that Gordon Fairweather has been apprehended and that I expect he will be charged shortly in the murder of Jasper Robinson," he said. My heart sank.

"The good news for your group is that once he has been charged, the rest of you will be asked to sign formal statements, and then you will be allowed to leave. The group will like you better this time, Señora. I think they blamed the translator last time, did they not?"

"A bit," I said.

"I trust they realized later that was unfair," he said.

"They certainly realized later that I knew nothing," I said. "I did get quite a few questions I was unable to answer."

He laughed. "This is a rather strange group of people," he said.

"Like Cassandra, for instance?"

"You know?" he said.

"Know what?" I said. "That Cassandra de Santiago isn't her real name? Anybody could guess that."

"That, too," he said, rather mysteriously, but he offered

nothing more. "Do you still believe that Dave Maddox was murdered?"

"I don't know," I said. I did, of course, but I also really wanted to go home. "Where did you apprehend Fairweather?" I asked.

"In a cave," Fuentes said. "We had a devil of a time getting him out of there."

"A cave?" I said, in my most innocent voice. "How did you find him?"

"We didn't exactly," Fuentes said. "He has got himself a high-priced lawyer from Santiago. The man took us to Fairweather and said that the reason he had not come in sooner was that he was injured conducting archaeological studies in a cave and had no idea we were looking for him!"

I liked the sound of this lawyer. It was all I could do not to smile. "Was Fairweather injured in this cave?"

"It is possible," Fuentes allowed. "He certainly had a very bad shoulder. We had to send someone down from the top of a cliff over the sea and then get him out that way because he couldn't make it the inland route. I am wondering, of course, how he survived. He said he had a little food with him and some water. We only found a couple of bottles of water, empty. He must have gotten rather hungry and thirsty if he was there the whole time. Personally, I think this is a complete fabrication, but we will have to deal with it."

"You know an academic argument, no matter how heated, does not seem to me to be a motive for murder," I said.

"Professional jealousy," Fuentes said. "I'm sure Dr. Fairweather does a fine job, but it is Jasper who was the great success. And Robinson humiliated Fairweather didn't he, that night when he made his presentation?"

"I'm told Gordon took it very well, that he was a gentleman," I said. "He didn't yell or anything."

"Perhaps because he had other plans for revenge," Fuentes said. "I saw the tape of the presentation, how Jasper

first quoted Fairweather and then flung his new discovery in
Fairweather's face. And showing a photograph of a potato! I
do not pretend to understand the arguments, but I have
some sense of how galling that must have been. It may
seem, to people like you and me, to be a tempest in an academic teapot, but I believe it was a lifetime of work and a
sterling academic career down the drain. Perhaps Fairweather lost all sense of perspective and in a fit of rage killed
the man. Perhaps he will get off with manslaughter. I do not
presume to speculate."

"Robinson also quoted Dr. Carlyle," I said. "You aren't
charging him, too, are you?"

"No, not yet, although he may be charged for helping
Fairweather escape if I can prove it," Fuentes said. "I do understand what you are saying though, and I agree with you
that academic disagreements in and of themselves do not
constitute motive. But my sense of it is that the disagreement between Fairweather and Robinson was very, very
personal."

The trouble was, he was right. Fairweather might say it
wasn't, but it seemed to me it was. The animosity between
the two men was palpable. Robinson had really rubbed
Fairweather's nose in it. Academic careers could be fickle
things. If you were hot, then grant money came your way. If
you weren't, if you were considered a has-been, or just plain
wrong about something, then you could languish for years
in some remote corner of academia. Even the cave might
seem preferable. Fairweather liked to be on Rapa Nui. He
liked living here and working here. But his income came
from a university in Australia, and it was that university and
the grants he got from various sources that enabled him to
be here.

"I still think an argument at the quarry is not enough evidence to convict Fairweather," I said.

"Why would you think that is the only evidence I have?"

Fuentes said. "And don't bother asking me what the other evidence is."

It wasn't ten, but it was only about twenty minutes later that the group was once again assembled, and indeed, as Fuentes had predicted, I was much more popular with the audience this time around. People even offered to treat me to pisco sours. I could have had as many as I wanted, all for free, and indeed I went and had a couple, just to get a sense of how the wind was blowing, as it were.

I was actually a bit surprised. I expected that the talk would be all about Fairweather and the fact he'd been charged, and there was some of that. Primarily, however, everyone was talking about how to get home. LanChile's lines were inundated by calls from all of us, and Albert disappeared immediately. He apparently grabbed a cab and went to the airport, but could find no one to talk to because the day's flight had already left. When the subject came up, the group was inclined to think Gordon was guilty, but I thought that was because they had never really met him or talked to him at any length.

What I did learn was that while I'd been languishing with a migraine, Robinson and Gordon had had another heated discussion, witnessed by Brian and Yvonne, that had ended with an actual scuffle: some pushing and shoving was the way Yvonne characterized it. I wondered if that was the additional evidence to which Fuentes had referred.

After two pisco sours, I realized I wasn't really in the mood for a celebration, and so I thought I'd just go to my room. Moira had taken it upon herself to deal with LanChile on our reservation. It would be a few days, actually, before everyone got out of there, given the limited availability of seats on the planes that time of year.

It occurred to me that from my vantage point on the stage as Fuentes's translator, I had not seen Seth at the meeting. If anyone would be thrilled at the prospect of getting out of here, that person would be Seth. He'd have his bags packed in nanoseconds, I was sure. Given he intended to go on to Tahiti, he might be more successful getting a seat on the next flight, although when that was, exactly, I didn't know. Remembering my promise to bring him something to eat, I asked the dining room to package up some dinner for Seth, then took it over to his room. The door was closed, and the guard, presumably no longer required, was gone. I knocked, then knocked again. I tried the door and found it locked.

"I have some good news for you," I said, through the door. "You can go home." Still nothing. "I'm getting the key, Seth," I said, loudly. "You might as well get up and let me in."

Getting the key took some doing. Hotel desks do not generally hand keys to people other than those who are paying for the room. I finally persuaded my friend Celia at reception that I was really worried about Seth and that she could come with me, to make sure I didn't steal anything. At last, she agreed.

The room was dark, and it took me a moment or two to get used to the gloom. I tried to turn the light on, but it didn't work. The room had been rearranged, the bed pushed against the far wall. At first I thought Seth was asleep in it, but when I went to shake him awake, I found only a jumble of blankets and pillows. I looked around. The bathroom door was closed and, like the outer door, locked. I knocked there, too, and called Seth's name, then put my ear to the door. I couldn't hear a sound, no water running, no sense of a presence behind the door. With a grave sense of foreboding, I threw my weight against the door. The lock immediately gave way.

Celia screamed and screamed. I just stood there for a second, stunned. Seth was hanging from the ceiling. I struggled to lift him, to ease the pressure on his neck, yelling at

Celia to stop screaming and help me. There was no question it was too late. He'd pinned a note to his shirt: *I'm sorry for what I did. I hope this will make amends*. In a gesture that struck me as incongruous, the note was actually signed: *Seth Connelly*.

9

THE QUESTION WAS, sorry for what? Making amends for what? Most people at the conference thought poor Seth was confessing to the murder of Jasper Robinson. One or two voiced the idea that he, too, had been murdered. Generally, however, that notion was pooh-poohed as soon as it was uttered. There was no question, however, that Seth's death and the note he left threw Fuentes Into a tizzy. Gordon's fancy lawyer was all over this one, and within a few hours, Gordon was back home, although his passport was still in the possession of the carabineros.

Seth had gone to a lot of trouble to kill himself. According to the guard who had been on duty at Seth's door until recalled after the meeting, Seth had closed and locked the door shortly after I left. The guard had knocked on the door to tell Seth that he was going off duty and that Seth was free to leave his room. Seth had not answered and it may well have been too late, even then.

It was not easy to hang yourself in that room. I would have thought it would be simpler to slash your wrists with a razor in the bathtub. But Seth was a tidy sort of man, and I suppose the idea of all that blood would have distressed him even more. You could tell that from his room, which was in sharp contrast to the mess that had once been Dave's.

He'd tried a couple of things, apparently. There was evidence he'd attempted to hang himself from the light fixture in the main room. The bed had been moved, and the light was half out of the ceiling, which explained why it hadn't worked when I flipped the switch. Somehow, though, he'd managed to rig something up in the bathroom. I had a feeling he'd stood on the edge of the bathtub and then stepped off.

I didn't think Seth had killed Jasper any more than Gordon had. I was very troubled by his death, much more so than the others. I had been the last one to have a conversation with him, and I felt I should have recognized the symptoms, the calm that had descended upon him when I'd said I thought Dave was murdered. In some way I had confirmed something for him, and then he'd taken his own life. I kept thinking that if Fuentes' meeting had just been a little sooner, then Seth would be alive. But maybe not. Perhaps knowing he no longer had police protection—albeit in the form of house arrest—had upset him so much he'd taken his own life. Seth, it seemed to me, had been frightened to death.

It was possible, I suppose, that he had been murdered, that this Anakena person had got into the room once the guard had left and strung him up. But there had been no sign of a struggle and, as Fuentes told me later, no sign of drugs in his blood.

Fuentes was in a snit about something else. His pathologist had finally issued a report and said that the blow to Dave's head had occurred after he'd died. The pathologist had not determined the actual cause of death. That meant that Fuentes might have to concede that Dave, too, had been murdered, which surely must have set a new record for Rapa Nui.

I didn't actually intend to go on looking into this Anakena business, but I inadvertently found myself right back into it as a result of a conversation I had with Kent Clarke. Kent and her daughter were in the midst of something of a dustup when I happened upon them. Brittany took one look at me and left.

"Sorry," I said. "I didn't mean to interrupt."

Kent threw up her hands. "Kids!" she said.

"She'll grow out of this phase," I said.

"I hope so," Kent said. "Do you have kids?"

"I have a stepdaughter of sorts. She was a teenager when I met her father."

"Then you know what having a teenage daughter is like. She wanted to get a tattoo. I said no. She got one anyway. I completely lost it. She said it was no big deal. I told her it was a question of trust. I'd asked her not to get one, and she'd gone behind my back. She went and had another one done. Shows pretty much what she thinks of my opinion. I'm afraid a tongue stud will be next."

"Either that or she'll run away to the circus," I said. I detected a hint of a smile.

"Did your stepdaughter do these annoying things?"

"Jennifer went through various phases. At one point she talked backwards," I said. "I don't mean whole conversations, or anything, but phrases. She was in this class for gifted kids, and her teacher thought this would be a good exercise for her. There'd be this pause while she thought through the answer to one of our questions that she didn't like, and then she'd come out with this gobbledygook, and between us we'd try to figure out what she'd just said to us. It was very annoying. We thought she'd never get through that period and that we certainly wouldn't. Her father kept threatening to go to the school and throttle the instructor."

Kent laughed. "You've cheered me up," she said. "Which is hard to do right now: my daughter with her tattoos and of course this documentary, with a director who drinks like a fish and a cameraman who is not only picking up the director's bad habits and who spends half his time making fun of me and the production, but also is the individual who persuaded my daughter to get a tattoo! Why don't you come to my office and sit for a few minutes. I could use some company right now, if you're free. You can watch me pack up."

"Lots of kids have them," I said as I followed her into the hotel. "Tattoos, I mean. They seem to be quite the rage. That and piercing."

"That's what she said. Her father is going to be livid. He already is. Did I mention my revolting ex? She lives with him. I get her for vacations and, when I'm in town, every second weekend. He would never have stood for this. I didn't intend to bring her down here, but when I saw the moai, Orongo, and all this magnificent history, I phoned her father and suggested he take her out of school for a week and put her on a plane. He agreed, much to my surprise. But now she's been here more than a week, and he's threatening to take me to court for kidnapping her or something ridiculous like that."

"That won't work," I said. "All you'd have to do is get a statement from the carabineros and that would be that."

"I know, but it would be a lot of trouble, and it wouldn't help with the tattoos. Welcome to the site office of Kent Clarke films, better known as the garden shed," she said. "It's where the manager used to keep that little tractor thing he uses to cut the lawn. But it has electricity, and it keeps us away from the hotel bar, important for reasons I believe I have already mentioned. Here, have a seat."

"This is rather impressive, all this equipment, although I'll grant you it's small," I said. "What's going to happen to the documentary now that Jasper is, well, dead?"

"Good question," she said.

"Whose idea was it to hold the Moai Congress?"

Her lip curled. "Jasper's, who else? At least he said it was, although it may actually have been one of us, now that I think about it. There isn't a good idea out there that Jasper hasn't claimed as his own. He was a great one for ideas on how to promote himself. Please tell me you didn't think some prestigious organization was behind this, inviting Jasper as their guest of honor, did you?"

"I guess not," I said. "Was it Jasper who suggested inviting the Moaimaniacs?"

"The what?" she said.

"The Internet group on Jasper's Web site."

"I guess so. He just handed me a list of email addresses and told me to make it so."

"I never did get to see the rongorongo tablet up close," I said. "I had a migraine and had to leave. I suppose I never will now, unless you finish the documentary, that is. Then I might see it on TV."

"I can't even think about that right this minute," she said. "There's footage of it here somewhere, but I'm not sure where, or I'd show it to you. I'm just the money person, you know."

"Did Jasper bring the rongorongo tablet with him?" I asked.

"Jasper?" she said. "Of course not. The man could barely tie his own shoelaces."

"So how, then?" I knew what Seth had said. It would be interesting to see what Kent did.

"Dave Maddox brought it. We—Jasper—needed some-one here early to help get everything set up as far as the ac-tual presentation was concerned."

"Do you know where it is now?"

"No idea," she said. "The last person to have it was Jasper, I think. That's what I told the police. He had it under his arm when he left with Gordon Fairweather."

"He left with Gordon Fairweather? I thought they weren't speaking."

"I wouldn't know about that," she said. "I'd like to get my hands on the tablet, though. I'd like to have it tested, by a real expert, by which I don't mean Jasper or Dave."

"You don't think it's authentic?"

"I don't know. This is hardly my area of expertise. But Dave came to see me and told me he thought it was authentic, but just not from Chile. He said he and that other fellow, the one who hanged himself . . ."

"Seth Connelly," I said. Seth obviously had not made a big impression other than by his death.

"Right," she said. "Dave said he and Seth thought it was authentic."

"Did you believe Dave?"

"I'm not sure," she said. "There was a lot of smoke and mirrors around Jasper. In my opinion, Jasper was the biggest fake of them all."

"Why would you say that?"

"He just was," she said. "He was an all around jerk, too. I'm pretty well ruined, you know."

"You filmed a lot of Jasper's adventures," I said. "I guess this pretty well ends it."

"It was over anyway," she said. "Even before he died. You put up your savings, you give up custody of your daughter so you can do something, and what happens? You get screwed."

"That's too bad," I said. I waited. She seemed to be in a confessional frame of mind.

"I've been with Jasper for years. Kent Clarke Films was

there in the early days, when he swam the Straits of Magellan," she said.

"Did he actually swim the Straits of Magellan?"

"In a manner of speaking," she said. "We just didn't show the time he spent in the boat."

"Seriously? He got out of the water and took a boat?"

"Yes and no," she said. "He had to be pulled out several times, warmed up and put back in the water."

"But that's fraud, really."

"Look, I was desperate. I was recently divorced, my husband wanted alimony, if you can believe it, and child support for Brittany. And it wasn't as if Jasper was the first person to swim the Straits. I might have had some qualms about faking that. I had a little film company, and Jasper helped make it a bigger film company. I've never made a lot of money on these expeditions of his, you understand. They are incredibly expensive to film. But I got something of a reputation and therefore other work. The thing was, Jasper started to believe his own publicity. He thought he was a real-life adventurer. He had a bit of amnesia where the early going was concerned. And perhaps because he came to believe in himself, things started happening for him. That fortress he found in northern Chile, for example. He did that. That was the real thing. Nothing like creating your own mythology, I suppose.

"And he did find the rongorongo tablet. I was there. I have it on film. I'll even show it to you if I can find it. And no, I didn't help him hide it. I thought this was the one, the one where I started to make decent money. Then Dave Maddox came to see me. He said that he'd had a good look at the thing, that he had a book on forgeries, and he was pretty sure that Jasper's rongorongo tablet wasn't one. I wasn't quite sure why he was telling me it was authentic. I thought maybe it was to make me feel better about it. Then he got to his second point, which was he was almost certain it hadn't come from Chile. Something about the wood."

"Didn't you just say you were there when Jasper found it, and you hadn't helped him bury it? Wouldn't that be a fairly elaborate fake for a guy who couldn't tie his own shoelaces, to hide it in a canyon in the Atacama Desert so you could find it on film?"

"For the man who faked swimming the Straits of Magellan?" she said, sourly.

"Point taken," I said. "What did you do when Dave told you about his concerns about the tablet's origins?"

She hesitated for a second before answering. "I told Jasper, of course."

"And what was the reaction?"

"He laughed. He said Dave had been a loser as long as he'd known him, 'a bloated bag of wind,' I believe the expression was. He said he'd talk to Dave."

"And did he?"

"I'm not sure, but I do know it didn't matter after that because Dave wasn't saying anything to anybody."

"Do you think it's possible Jasper killed Dave?"

"The idea did occur to me, but the police kept saying it was an accident. Apparently, if the gossip in the bar is right, they're not saying that anymore. But what does that mean? Let's assume for the moment that the tablet is a fake, or even that it's real, but didn't come from Chile. Then Jasper might kill Dave to keep him from telling anyone else. I have a feeling Jasper would be capable of it, to save his reputation, but Jasper died, too. Who killed him? Fairweather? That Seth person?"

"I don't know," I said. "Does the name Anakena mean anything to you?"

"Sure," she said. "It's a beach. I took my daughter there just before we were confined to barracks. You should go if you haven't been. There are actually palm trees there, several of them, rather refreshing after all this rock and grass."

"So is this the end of the documentary?"

"Yes, and it is also the end of Kent Clarke Films," she said. "I'll be filing for bankruptcy soon, unless a miracle occurs."

"You didn't make money on these escapades of Jasper's?"

"Far from it," she said. "We broke even on the last one, the one about the fortress in Chile. This one would have done it, I think. The trouble was it was going to be the last. Jasper was moving on. He said he'd had an offer from one of the large companies in California, and his next big adventure was going to be a feature film. He seemed to think an award of some kind was in the bag. He dropped that little detail on me when he got out here. I could have killed him."

Her face colored. "That would be a figure of speech," she said. "I didn't do it. I wasn't sorry when he died, though, far from it. I'd scrambled to find the money in the early days. He put up some, but not much. He wasn't for spending his own money, you see. I mortgaged my house because I believed in the jerk. Then when we finally started to get somewhere, he moves onwards and upwards. I still have to pay the director and the cameraman, even if they're losers."

"Why do you keep hiring them," I said, "if they are such a problem for you?"

"Fire them? Are you kidding? Believe me, I'm not in a position to do that as both of them very well know. We are all complicit, aren't we? We're irrevocably joined, tarnished by the myth of Jasper Robinson, an illusion we prostituted ourselves to create. It doesn't matter anyway. The point is that now that Jasper's dead, the project is dead, too. Too bad, because this was some of our best work."

"This may sound like an awful thing to say," I said. "But

is it not possible there would be more interest in this documentary now that he's dead?"

Perhaps in reply, Kent went searching about for a
minute, and then she pulled out a cassette and inserted it in
a VCR. "Here, be my guest. Have a look," she said. "It's a
bit rough still, but you'll get the general idea. I'll even cue
it up for you. It will never make it to air. Just press this button when you're done, and if you don't mind, make sure the
door is locked when you go." With that, rather mysteriously, she was gone. I pressed PLAY.

Kent Clarke had not been entirely forthcoming about
the videocassette she'd shown me. This was not a documentary. This was revenge. What appeared on the screen was
not *Rapa Nui: The Mystery Solved,* not by any stretch of the
imagination. Instead, it was the exposé of a con man, one of
the most vicious hatchet jobs I'd ever seen. And it was art-
fully done. It could have been used in a film studies pro-
gram to show what could be achieved with several hours of
footage and some careful editing.

For starters, there was the interview with Cassandra de
Santiago, who came across as a complete flake, emoting
about Lemuria and visitors from outer space. Jasper was
shown talking and smiling to her, and the way it was put together, it somehow implied he agreed with her outlandish
theories, that she was one of the people he consulted. The
scene with Gordon Fairweather at the quarry was edited in
such a way that Gordon did not come across as an aggres-
sive, to say nothing of arrogant, academic, but rather as
someone who knew enough about the subject to be able to
call what Jasper had to say horse manure.

During Jasper's presentation the evening he died, his
grand finale, I suppose you could call it, although swan song
might be more accurate, Rory was shown shaking his head
in despair as Jasper spoke. Rory's name and his credentials
appeared on the screen as he did so. When Jasper quoted

Rory and Gordon, rather than show Jasper, the camera had caught the two academics. Again their qualifications appeared on the screen. Jasper looked like a complete idiot.

The one straightforward interview, and the only one you could really call reasonable, was one that featured Rory. His opinion was that the rongorongo tablet needed more study, but that if it proved to be authentic, then this was a find of great significance.

"So what do you think?" a voice behind me said, and I jumped. Mike Sheppard was leaning against the door jamb.

"It's, um, interesting," I said.

"By which you mean vicious, libelous, what else?" he said. "Vindictive?"

"Pretty much," I said.

"You know what they say about a woman scorned," he said.

"Hell hath no fury?"

"Exactly," he said.

"Did you do this?" I said. "Edit it, I mean?"

"I did the actual work, I suppose," he replied. "With considerable direction from the producer, shall we say. I knew what she wanted, and I worked at it until it did just that."

"That must have taken some doing," I said. "You are very creative. I think there's a job for you teaching film editing."

He laughed. "It's just a matter of going over and over it, looking for the spots where one can cut. Choosing the angles. Once we knew what Kent wanted, I was able to direct Daniel's camera accordingly."

"Did you think it was fair?"

"It doesn't matter what I think," he said. "Kent pays the bills."

"So what now?" I asked. "Are you and Daniel out of work?"

"Temporarily," Mike said. "Kent's been very good about seeing we get paid for our time to this point, I'll say that for her. But there's lots of film work in New Zealand and Australia these days, so we'll be fine. I may actually try my hand at something different after this."

"So what do you think about the San Pedro tablet?" I said. "Is it real?"

"Haven't the foggiest," he said. "Not my area of expertise. J. R. must have gone to a lot of trouble to fake it if he did."

"That's what I was thinking," I said. "He'd have to hide it and then find it and look surprised. Kent said she was there and thought it was the real thing at the time."

"Ah, yes," he said. "Kent Clarke Films was on hand for the great event."

"Were you?"

"I was. What can I say? We're in this canyon in the middle of nowhere. The sun is blasting down on us. The air is a trifle thin. We're having trouble with filters to get the light right. But Jasper has found this mummy, a nasty little bundle that was once a person, and there's what I think is a stick of old wood with it, but Jasper is panting over it, and we have to capture the moment as it were."

"But was the tablet tested or anything?"

"I really don't know. Jasper said the mummy was."

"Surely that's not the same thing. You can't say two objects are the same age just because you found them together. You might assume they were the same age, but you wouldn't know for sure."

"I really can't recall if Jasper said anything about that. You could ask Daniel, next time you see him. He may recall."

"So Daniel was there, too?"

"The Kent Clarke Films team in its entirety was there, yes."

"Anybody else from this group here that was on site when the tablet was found?"

"I believe what's his name, Albert, was there," he said. "And that unpleasant woman who looks like Lotte Lenya as Rosa Klebb in the James Bond movie."

"Edwina Rasmussen," I said. I had to smile. "But not Dave Maddox?"

"Not Dave, no. Not when I was there, anyway."

"Kent thinks now that the tablet might be a fake," I said. "Or maybe not from Chile."

"She would, wouldn't she?" Mike said.

There was a lot to chew on, which might explain why I couldn't sleep that night. There was something really bothering me. For one thing, I knew the minute I went to sleep that Rob would be there telling me I was missing something really obvious. I did not recall Rob ever being that annoying in real life, which was just as well, because if he had been I would no longer be with him. In my dreams, however, he was persistent as can be.

What bothered me more than anything, though, was the thought that no matter how unwittingly, I had played some part in Seth's decision to kill himself. Rob had told me once that people would be much less likely to try hanging themselves if they knew that, unlike official hangings where the victim's neck is broken, those who step off chairs endure a slow death by strangulation, sometimes taking as long as half an hour to die. If Seth had stepped off the edge of the bathtub as I suspected he had, he could easily have swung himself back if he changed his mind, but he hadn't. It was a horrible thought.

The trouble was that none of this made sense. Dave told Kent he thought the San Pedro tablet was real, but not from Chile. Kent told Jasper. Given that the Chile connection was absolutely key to his theory, Jasper presumably went to talk to Dave, and it is possible he killed Dave to prevent him from telling the world. Then what? Jasper didn't bash his own head in. Seth decided Jasper had killed his friend

Dave and took his revenge? Seth had gone all quiet when I'd said I thought maybe Dave was murdered. He'd said he was sure he was. How could he be sure? Was it because he knew something the rest of us didn't? Was he not really sure at first, did he have doubts about killing Jasper in revenge, doubts that I had inadvertently assuaged?

Or maybe Jasper killed Dave, and Kent killed Jasper because he was leaving her for another film company. I thought she hadn't been truthful about her relationship with Jasper. I was willing to bet her marriage failed because she fell for her star in a very big way. It would certainly explain her willingness to help him fake his early adventures. She was paying alimony, and she'd lost custody of Brittany. That meant some court somewhere thought she was more at fault than her former husband.

There was always the possibility that Gordon killed Jasper, I suppose. Fuentes had been right when he said that Jasper had set out to deliberately embarrass Gordon and Rory. It would have been quite possible to present the San Pedro tablet without making it nearly so personal. But if Gordon had been humiliated, so had Rory. Was Gordon the suspect because he had a temper and Rory didn't? Perhaps Rory had an alibi and Gordon didn't. Kent said that Jasper and Gordon had gone off together, Jasper with the tablet under his arm. Was that the evidence—that Gordon was the last person to see Jasper alive? I very much doubted that Fuentes was going to discuss the case with me in this kind of detail.

And where exactly was this San Pedro tablet, fake or otherwise, and what was its place in all of this? I could see it as a reason for Dave to die, but Jasper? Gordon kills him because he faked a rongorongo tablet's find spot? Kent killed him because he faked a rongorongo tablet? Why? Why not let the truth come out, as Kent intended in her documentary, and let him suffer the public humiliation that would ensue?

What if it was a fake, start to finish? Just how did Jasper fake this thing, if indeed he did? I couldn't have done it, and I've read *The Art Forger's Handbook* from cover to cover. I could have found the wood, all right. I'd have done a better job on that, something native to northern Chile, some kind of tree that would have been there for a very long time. Algarrobo, maybe, although I'd have to do a little work on its particular properties. But I could find something. And I could age it, so to speak, put the little worm holes in it and so on. As someone who sold antique furniture, I knew what to look for in wood. The rongorongo, however, would have posed a major problem for me. From my visits to the shops and markets of Hanga Roa, I could see that lots of people carved rongorongo-type symbols onto their particular work. But Seth had said someone had gone a long way toward deciphering rongorongo, so it would not be enough to just carve a bunch of symbols; you'd have follow whatever conventions the ancient carvers had.

Did Jasper know enough about rongorongo to do that? Maybe. Maybe not. The man was a cypher to me, really. I hadn't been one of the women attracted to him like moths to his flame. I'd seen him in action a few times, up at Rano Raraku, and then at some sessions at the congress, and finally at his big announcement. He hadn't endeared himself to me any of those times. Maybe he paid someone to carve it for him. Seth might have been that person, and maybe it was one of the people of Rapa Nui. Did this mysterious person kill Jasper because he or she didn't get paid, or because he or she didn't realize that Jasper was going to present the work as authentic, and worse still from that perspective, from Chile?

Or maybe, and this was a different thought, Jasper had been the butt of a practical joke that had got out of hand. Maybe someone planted it deliberately to deceive him. If so, who? Albert or Edwina perhaps? They were there. None of

the other Moaimaniacs had been, as far as I knew. Maybe
Seth was a part of it, somehow, and that was what he was
sorry about, the deed for which he was trying to make
amends.

And maybe . . . if I didn't stop thinking so hard about all
these maybes, I was going to give myself another migraine.
At least Moira had a pharmucopia that she could put at my
disposal.

At the end of the day, the other disturbing aspect of this
was that on an island with three thousand plus inhabitants
and a congress with about forty attendees, there were two
murderers. It seemed statistically excessive, if nothing else.
What was also alarming was that in a group of eleven—or
was it twelve?—members of an Internet group on this island, three of them were dead.

What was it I wasn't noticing? All this thinking was
making me toss and turn, and at some point in the night
Moira asked me if I was okay. I realized I was keeping her
awake, too. So I lay very still until I knew she'd gone to
sleep, and then I pulled on my clothes and went out to look
at the stars.

I'd done this once before with painful result, when I'd
found poor old Dave. This time I saw no dead bodies. What
I did see, however, was a light in what had been until yesterday Seth Connelly's room. It was just a little light, a
flashlight most likely. I positioned myself so that I could see
the door, without, I hoped, being seen. It was a bit of a wait,
but eventually the light went out, the door opened, at first
just a crack, and then someone slipped out. That someone
looked a lot like Poikeman to me.

I intercepted him just before got to his room. "Taking an
evening stroll through a dead man's room, are we?" I said.
Lewis jumped about a foot at the sound of my voice.

"I guess I've been caught," he said.

"I guess so," I said. "I don't suppose you'd care to share

your reasons for this expedition while I consider whether or not to tell Pablo Fuentes about it."

"I would prefer you didn't," he said. I waited. I wasn't too nervous. He was in his underpants, and although he had his hands behind his back, I didn't think he was hiding a weapon.

"I lent Seth a book," he said. "And I figured I'd just go and get it before they cleared out his room. I thought if I asked for it, they wouldn't believe me."

"I see," I said. "Did you find it okay?"

"Yes," he said, showing me. He didn't tell me which book it was, but I knew anyway. *The Art Forger's Handbook* was making its way around the place pretty well. I wondered if the rongorongo tablet was, too.

"Albert was supposed to be on lookout duty. Not very good at it, is he?" Poikeman said. We found Albert in his candycane-stripe pajamas, seated on the ground, his back against a tree, snoring.

"I've been caught, Albert," Lewis said when we'd roused him. "We have to persuade this young lady not to rat me out."

"Would you two care to join me for a little libation?" Albert said. "I have some rather good cognac."

"Why not?" Lewis said. "We're up anyway."

Why not, indeed. We must have looked quite the picture, Lewis in his underwear, Albert in his outrageous pajamas, and me with jeans over my nightie. Albert reminisced about his life as a PR consultant in Washington, and he was hilarious.

"I have a question for you, Albert," I said, well into my second tumbler of cognac.

"Fire away, my dear young lady," he said.

"I'm wondering about this Moai Congress," I said. "I get the impression that Jasper Robinson himself came up with the idea for this event."

"Possibly. And your question is?"

"Is that normal? To create your own event when you have an announcement to make?"

"Where I come from it is," he said. "Long and dishonorable tradition. Suppose you're a congressman who wants to make an announcement of some sort. You could look around to see if there is an event in your neighborhood that would suit—a hospital opening, for example, if you wanted to talk about health care, let's say. So you get one of your staff, or in my case your PR consultant, to phone up the hospital and put out feelers out as to whether they'd like to have you attend, if there would be enough media there to suit you, if they would give you enough time to make a long-winded—to say nothing of self-serving—speech. Or, if you have something on them, if they need your client's support on a vote soon on their funding, for example, you tell them your man will attend. Or you could ask some supporters if the organizations they are involved with would like to host an event at which your client, the congressman could speak.

"But you might be a little nervous about that. Your opponents might show up, the hospital administrator might be thinking of running for your job, unbeknownst to you. You never know. So what do you do? You create your own event somewhere."

"Really?" I said. "How . . . ?"

"Disillusioning? You don't strike me as that naive," he said.

"I guess I just never thought about it," I said. "So Jasper wanted an event he could control to make this announcement of his."

"Perhaps," Albert said.

"Picked a good spot, if you ask me," Lewis said. "Thousands of miles out in the Pacific has got to get you some control."

"Except that he's dead," Albert said.

"Yes, and except that he came right to the lion's den, didn't he? Right where someone like Gordon Fairweather is sure to hear all about it."

"True," they agreed.

"Maybe Jasper's ego was such that he rather relished the battle," Lewis said.

"Now about your little excursion into Seth's room," I said.

"Oh dear," the muffin said.

"That would be *The Art Forger's Handbook* you went in to find, would it?"

"Caught in the act," Albert said. "It really is his book, though. He didn't steal something that didn't belong to him."

"And you brought the handbook to Rapa Nui because . . . ?"

"Just because it sounded interesting. I picked it up in a rare book shop a few months back, and this was the first chance I had to read it. After Jasper's presentation, Albert had his doubts about the tablet," Poikeman said. "We were hoping to get a close look at it."

"And did you?" I asked.

"I'm afraid not," Lewis replied.

"I think she's asking us if we stole the tablet," Albert said to his pal.

"I see. No, we didn't, but I did have a wee look around for it while I was in the room," Lewis said. "I rather thought that Seth was the most likely person to be hiding it. He was nuts about rongorongo. I figured he had to be the one who stole it. I was just taking a look to see if there was anything the police had missed. If I had found it, I'd have turned it over to the police right away, you understand."

I wasn't sure if that was what I understood or not. "You didn't happen to see a photograph lying about, did you?" I asked.

"A photograph? No," Lewis replied.

"Weren't you there when the tablet was found, Albert?" I asked. "You and Edwina?"

Albert paused for a moment before answering. "I was, dear girl. I was. It was a great moment."

"And he didn't even tell me about it," Lewis said, feigning indignation.

"We were sworn to secrecy. Not allowed to spoil Jasper's big moment. I think I may have mentioned that in my retirement years I volunteer at dig sites. I do whatever menial tasks they give me, but this was very exciting. Jasper was excavating what he thought was a tomb. We'd been working for several weeks, and then he found some mummy bundles, and lo and behold, this tablet that he pronounced to be rongorongo. Not often you get that kind of experience on these digs, you know."

"You do when you go with Jasper. He seems to have an unerring instinct for the spectacular finds," I said.

"Perhaps he's not weighed down by too much education," Lewis said, giggling.

"That does seem to be an issue," I said.

"You can't argue with success," Albert said.

"You can, if the tablet is fake," Lewis replied. "And you did say you thought it might be."

"Jasper was not the easiest person in the world to like," Albert said. "Perhaps my suspicions had more to do with that than the tablet itself. It just seemed very out of place there, I must say. Edwina, however, was enchanted by it, but then she shares Jasper's view of the world, about Rapa Nui anyway."

"Do either of you know who Anakena is?" I asked.

"I was hoping it would be you or your equally lovely friend, Moira," Albert said.

"I was sure you were, that first day on the bus to Rano Raraku," Lewis said.

I left the two of them there, swigging on the brandy, and slipped back into my room. They were both kind of cute, it had to be said, in their underwear and pajamas, but Albert had worked for years in a pretty cutthroat business. He couldn't be nearly as nice as he seemed, and they were, after all, breaking into a room.

The cognac had taken hold, however, and this time I slept. Rob was there as usual. "You're off your game, hon," he said. "It's that vacation thing. You don't do vacations. You have to look for links, for the unusual detail that will reveal the murderer. You have to see what both these murders and Gabriela have in common. You know what it is. It's that niggling detail."

I woke up and thought about it. Rob assumed I knew what this elusive whatever was. I didn't. I went back to sleep. This time Rob wasn't there. Instead I found myself being grabbed by Cassandra de Santiago and dragged along the ground. Someone with a hood over his or her face watched from a distance. "I am taking you to Hanga Roa to get a tattoo," she said, cackling like a wicked witch. "Anakena is going to give you a tattoo of a little bird."

"No!" I screamed, or at least I tried to. I was trying to get the attention of Moira and the others, but Moira was showing Rory her own tattoo and didn't seem to notice what was going on. The others were all standing with their backs to me, watching for an airplane. I knew with absolute certainty that if I went with Cassandra and got this tattoo, I'd be dead by morning.

"That's it," I yelled, sitting right up in bed.

"What? What happened? Did somebody else get killed?" Moira said, completely confused.

"There's only one murderer," I said.

"That's a relief, I'm sure," she said in a soothing tone. I think she thought I was talking in my sleep just like Seth a few nights earlier.

"I have to phone Rob," I said.

"It's the middle of the night," Moira said, but I was already trying to use the phone. The trouble was, it wouldn't allow me to make a long distance phone call to Canada. I pulled on shorts and a T-shirt and headed for the reception desk. There was no one there. The lights were dimmed and the phone, which I tried to use, was shut off.

"Where are the car keys?" I said, coming back to the room.

"You're crazy," Moira said, as I dashed out. I blasted into town, right up to Gordon and Victoria's door, which I started to pound on. A very sleepy-looking Victoria opened it.

"I've got to make a phone call to Canada," I said. "It's life or death."

Question to Rob: *Is it possible to poison someone with a tattoo needle?*

"Are you all right?" a very confused Rob said.

"I am," I said. "But I have a really important question for you."

"It's four in the morning here," Rob said.

"It's four in the morning here, too," I said.

"Okay, just so we have that straight. What's the question?" I told him. I heard Victoria gasp as I asked it.

"Yes, it's possible," Rob said. "There was a very high-profile case a few years back in which some guy claimed he'd been poisoned by someone poking him with an umbrella. Everyone thought he was nuts, but he died a while later, poisoned, and sure enough there was a puncture hole in his leg."

"Do you remember what the poison was?" I said.

"Not really," he said. "But I can find out. What are you up to, Lara?"

"I'll explain it all later, but I'm not planning to poison

anybody. Somebody here, three people in fact, have been poisoned. What I don't understand is why the pathologist or the doctors haven't figured this out. Don't they have machines now that tell you in minutes what's in a person's bloodstream?"

"You watch too much television," he said.

"Maybe," I agreed. "But I'm not off my game."

"Of course you aren't," he said in a somewhat mystified, but soothing, tone.

"Forget I said that," I said.

"I knew I should have gone with you on this trip," he said.

"I feel as if you've been with me all along," I said.

"I'm not sure what that means exactly."

"I'll explain later," I said.

"It sounds to me as if you'll have rather a lot of explaining to do later," he sighed. "Be careful."

"It's the tattoo," I said, hanging up and turning to Gordon. "There was some kind of poison in the tattoo. Dave had one, Jasper had one, and Gabriela has the start of one. She didn't die because she didn't get as much poison as the others. She must have managed to get away, or the killer was interrupted. You have to tell Gabriela's doctors right now. There's a pathologist working on what killed Jasper and Dave. Maybe he knows already, or maybe if the doctors tell him about Gabriela, he can piece it all together, figure out what it is."

Gordon was reaching for the telephone when Victoria put her hand on his arm. "Gordon," she said. "Think for a minute. If all three of these people are poisoned with the same thing, then it may well point to you, especially because of Gabriela. You are already a suspect, even if Fuentes had to let you go for now."

Surely Gabriela isn't that close a relative, I was thinking.

"She's my daughter, Victoria," he said. "I'd die for her."

"His daughter?" I said, as he dialed.

"I'll explain later," Victoria said. "But yes, Gabriela is his daughter."

I guess we all had some explaining to do.

10

"SNAKE VENOM," Fuentes said.

"Snake venom!" I exclaimed. "Are there poisonous snakes on this island?" I thought about the miles of long grass I'd put my sandaled feet through and the tons of rocks I'd climbed over.

"Apparently not," Fuentes said. "No snakes at all, in fact, which explains why snake venom was the last thing they were looking for in the señorita's case."

"Is there an antidote for this snake venom?"

"There is, I am happy to say, and it will be here tonight, or perhaps in the early hours of the morning. The question is whether or not there has already been too much damage to the señorita's internal organs."

"Where is the antidote coming from?"

"Australia, where the snake normally resides."

"Australia to Rapa Nui would be a long swim for a snake," I said.

"It would," Fuentes agreed. "Which is why I am operating under the assumption that someone had either the snake or the venom in a vial and brought it with them. I am told it is used in minute quantities to treat certain conditions, which ones I have no idea, but it means it is possible to obtain it."

"From Australia," I said.

"Yes," Fuentes said. "Which, as I'm sure you know, is where Gordon Fairweather lives at least part of the year and where he teaches."

"But poison his own daughter? I saw him when I told them last night. He knew it was a risk, and he made the phone call anyway."

"Yes," he said. "But there are, shall we say, issues regarding that daughter, and he would look more guilty if he did not make the phone call. I trust you would have told me all about the tattoo, if he didn't."

"Yes, I would have," I said. "I wouldn't let Gabriela die without doing something I knew might save her."

"I am most happy to hear that," he said. "Are you going to tell me what gave you the idea of poison in the tattoos?"

"If I told you, you'd think I was crazy," I said.

"Tell me anyway," he said.

"I dreamt it," I said.

"That's a relief," he said. "I was afraid you were going to tell me that your friend the Mountie knew it all along. A little professional jealousy, you see, even if I've never met him."

"That's your way of telling me this whole mess is about professional jealousy?" I said. "I have a question for you. Does Gordon Fairweather know how to do tattoos?"

"I don't know that," Fuentes said. "These tattoos were not particularly well done, I'm told, so perhaps not by an expert, like the cameraman's wife, Eroria, for example. We are having a little chat with her, right now. So far, I'm told she has been helpful about the tattoos."

"Her husband has been at this congress the whole time," I said.

"Yes, but does he know Gabriela, other than as a waitress at the hotel? Does he really know anyone but Jasper?" he said. "We must find someone with ties to all three victims and who has been to Australia recently, although that is not necessary in this day and age. One could purchase snake venom, I'm sure, from anywhere."

"It seems to me that lots of people on this island go to and from Australia," I said.

"It is interesting that you should say that. This observation of yours about the tattoos gives new direction to our investigation. There are several people here who have been to Australia in the last several months. There is only one, however, who knows all three victims."

"Fairweather," I said. Fuentes said nothing. "But Fairweather didn't know Dave Maddox, did he?" Again, Fuentes said nothing.

It was Gabriela who had thrown the spanner in the works, to use Jasper's term. Fairweather taught in Australia and knew Jasper and Gabriela, but there was no indication he knew Dave Maddox. The rest of the Moaimaniacs knew Dave and Jasper, but how on earth would they know Gabriela? There were very few people who knew all three of the victims: Moira and I and Cassandra de Santiago, who was a fake through and through if you asked me. I couldn't speak for Cassandra, but I knew neither Moira nor I had been to Australia. There was only one person I could think of that knew all three and who I knew for certain had been to Australia.

"Rory Carlyle," I said. Fuentes smiled. I took that to be a yes.

"Motive?" I said. "What could possibly be his motive? You'll say professional jealousy of Jasper, but that would hardly apply to Dave and most certainly not Gabriela."

"We're working on it," Fuentes said. "And by the way, should you be wondering where your friend Señora Meller is, she is being questioned at the station."

"What?! What possible reason could you have for questioning her?" I said, indignantly.

"I shouldn't tell you, but I will, given you have been helpful to me. You may need to see that she gets some legal assistance of some kind. I did not make the same mistake this time. When we went to talk to Dr. Carlyle, we had someone covering the back door. Your friend was caught going out that way."

"So what?" I said. "Visiting a friend is hardly a crime and leaving the back way because a police car pulls up at the front isn't necessarily, either."

"It is, if she takes the San Pedro rongorongo tablet with her when she leaves," he said.

"I don't believe it!" I said.

"Believe it," he said. "And yes, our case against Dr. Carlyle does hinge in some respects on his possession of the rongorongo tablet. I do not think your friend stole it in the first place, nor do I think she murdered anyone, you'll be happy to know. But there is no denying she was aiding and abetting, as it were, and she did have stolen property in her possession. It was you, was it not, who told me about this rongorongo tablet?"

Hadn't that been a brilliant idea? "I want to talk to her," I said.

"You will have that opportunity when we have finished questioning her," he said.

"Moira!" I said about three hours later. "How could you?" She looked exhausted and was swallowing some kind of medication when I was allowed to see her.

THE MOAI MURDERS   201

"How could I? This from the person who helped you-know-who get to you-know-where and then brought this same person food and water? You believed in him, and I believe in Rory. The difference is I got caught, and you didn't. When we saw all the police cars pull up at the guest house where he's staying, he had just shown me the tablet. It was right there. So I tried to get it out of the house because I thought it would look bad for him to have it."

"It does look bad for him to have it," I said.

"He says that Jasper agreed that in exchange for doing an interview for the documentary that was more positive than not, Rory could have it for a few hours to have a closer look. Rory did the interview, saying something reasonably nice, thinking that if he found that it was fake, then he would simply retract what he had said. But then he couldn't find Jasper in the morning to return it, and when Jasper ended up dead and obviously murdered, he didn't know what to do with it, and really in all the confusion, he simply forgot about it."

"I see," I said, pulling pen and paper out of my bag as I did so. *That is the official version,* I wrote, careful to shield the paper as I did so. *Where did he really get it?*

"You don't want to know," she murmured, looking toward the guard on the door.

"Yes, I do," I murmured back.

She took the pen. *Gordon F.* she wrote.

"I don't believe it," I said.

"I told you," she said. "You know what else?" She took the pen and paper again. *Rory thinks it's real,* she wrote.

"No kidding?" I said.

"No kidding," she said. "Here we are, right in the middle of this mess. I want to go home, Lara."

"Okay," I said. "I'm on this. I'll go talk to Gordon's lawyer and see if he'll take your case. Just hang in there. You don't look well."

"I'm fine," she said, but I knew she wasn't. I had this vision of all the times I'd seen her taking pills of some sort—sleeping pills, pills she told me were vitamins, but now I wasn't sure, pills for headache; pills for stomach upset. I suddenly realized, with absolute certainty, that Moira had not been entirely truthful about the state of her health. And now she was in police custody very far from home.

Up until now I had tried to keep telling myself that this was all none of my business. I'd let myself get drawn into it when, acting more on instinct than good sense, I'd helped Gordon get out the back door of his place, which I suppose was exactly what Moira had been trying to do for Rory. Once Gordon had his lawyer and was out of the cave, though, I'd gone back to my none-of-my-business mantra, however imperfectly. Now Moira was going to be spending a lot of time in Chile if it was found that Rory was guilty of murder. This was now very much my business.

I didn't think Rory had killed two people and tried to kill his friend Gordon's daughter. Nor had I changed my mind about Gordon, despite this latest revelation. Clearly what I had to do was find someone who had ties to all three, make that four, victims. I had to assume that Seth's suicide was tied into all of this. He'd said he was sorry, that he wanted to make amends. He obviously knew Dave and had told me Dave and Jasper went back a long way.

I could think of many people who had reason to hate Jasper and perhaps even be capable of killing him. Dave was more difficult, because the only person I could think of who could want to silence him was Jasper himself. There had to be something else going on here.

I went back to the hotel with a lot on my mind, grabbed a couple of things Moira wanted and dropped them off at the carabineros headquarters before going into town. I had decided there were several areas where my lack of knowledge was a serious impediment to figuring this all out. I made a list of them, and I gave myself twenty-four hours to find out what I had to do to get Moira out of jail.

At the top of the list was the small matter of the rongorongo tablet and Gordon's having had it in his possession, according to Rory. Second was the question of Gordon and Gabriela's relationship and where Gabriela had been found. I needed to talk to Victoria or Gordon about a lawyer for Moira, anyway, so I decided I could kill two birds with one stone by paying the Fairweather household a vist.

"It's simple, in a kind of complicated way," Victoria said, after I'd phoned the lawyer—who was unfortunately back in Santiago—and convinced him he needed to help Moira now. "Gordon and my sister were together for a number of years and had two daughters, Gabriela and Edith. Edith was born just about the time my sister and Gordon split up. I'm not able to have children and desperately wanted a child. This will sound very strange to you, but my mother insisted Edith be given to me when she was born. I was single, and I suppose I still am. Gordon is still legally married to my sister. No doubt this all sounds very incestuous to you. I hope you'll let me explain. My sister has many children. She had six before she married Gordon, two with him, and she has had two more since with her current partner. The women in this society are very strong. The men may head the families theoretically and hold public office like mayor, but believe me, the women make the major decisions for the families. My mother made the decision and insisted Edith be given to me. I love her as my own daughter.

"Gordon and I got together about five years ago, and

while my mother does not entirely approve of the arrangement, I think he and I will be together forever, and she approves enough that she lives part of the time with us. And now he has one of his daughters with him. Gabriela chose to stay with her mother. She was old enough to make that decision. Before this horrible poison business happened, though, she was at our place all the time."

"The serum is on its way," I said.

"I pray every minute that it gets here on time," she said. "I do not understand this, Lara. Why do this to a child? The carabineros say that whoever it was drugged her and then started to tattoo her. They think that someone interrupted the murderer before the tattoo was finished. Are the tattoos all little birds?"

"Yes, they are," I said.

"I wonder why," she said.

"Where was Gabriela found?" I said. "At her home?"

"At the hotel," she said. "We assumed she had gone back to see her friends there, or to pick up something she'd left. As I told you, she'd quit her job there. The manager was doing a walk around the property before he left the hotel, around midnight I think. He found her on the edge of the garden."

"Did he hear anything, or see anything?" I said.

"We never thought to ask," Victoria said. "Why would we? Who could even imagine something like this happening?"

"Maybe I'll talk to the manager," I said.

"Let us know what you find out and if we can help. Gordon hasn't heard yet about Rory. I'm sorry about Moira. We seem to keep drawing the two of you into this mess."

"Did Gordon know Rory had the San Pedro tablet?" I asked.

"If he did, he didn't mention it to me," she said.

"Where is Gordon now?" I said.

"Back up on Poike," she said. "With his students. He'll be back before dark."

I wasn't going to attempt to retrace the route to Poike by myself, and I decided I had many other things to do while I waited for Gordon to come back. It was difficult seeing where Gabriela fit into all of this, even if she was Gordon's daughter, and even if he was the one who'd stolen the rongorongo tablet. I had a feeling that if I could find her relationship to the others, I would have the answers to all my questions. With all the horrible events that had taken place since, I had forgotten about Gabriela's nasty engagement with Cassandra. It was not all that long after that that Gabriela had been found unconscious. I decided it was time to reopen that unpleasant subject.

I was roaring along the main street in the four-wheel-drive, hastening to get back to the hotel and find the vile Cassandra de Santiago, when a sign caught my eye: Eroria's Tattoos, it said. One of many huge gaps in my comprehension of what was going on here was the subject of tattoos. Moira hadn't said much about hers other than it hadn't hurt as much as she thought, and she couldn't go in the pool until it healed. How did these people get their tattoos? The trouble was, ever since I'd started dreaming about them, and since I'd seen dead people with them, I was terrified of the thought of having one. *Get over it,* I told myself. *How bad could it be?* After all, I'd seen Daniel and his wife, Eroria, at the police station while I waited to visit Moira, and she'd seemed a reasonable-looking person, not somebody who put snake venom in your tattoo. I parked and stood outside the place for a minute or two, summoning my courage. *Get on with it, Lara,* I told myself. *Just walk in there.* It took a couple of minutes, but at last my feet started to move.

"Hi," she said. "I'm Eroria. Are you here to book an appointment for a tattoo?"

"I guess so," I said, looking around.

"What did you have in mind?" she said.

"I'm not sure," I said. "Something discreet, small, somewhere nobody can see it."

"Nobody?" she said.

"Well, nobody who isn't really, really close," I said.

"Base of the spine? Something small on the bum?" she said.

"Did you do these?" I said, pointing to photographs on the walls.

"I did," she said.

"Some of them are beautiful," I said. "If you like tattoos, that is."

"Thank you, I think," she said.

"Does it hurt?" I said.

"A little," she said. "If you're worried about that, you're better to choose a part of your body that is, um, fleshy."

I didn't think in my case that narrowed it down much. "Okay," I said. "That doesn't sound too bad. Can I pick a design, or something?"

"Of course," she said. "I have stencils, or you can have a custom design."

"Will it take a long time?" I said. In other words, how long had it taken to tattoo Dave and Jasper and put a partial tattoo on Gabriela?

"Not for something very small and discreet," she said. "Maybe an hour. Are you sure you really want a tattoo?"

"Er, no. I mean yes," I said. "What I mean to say is that my friend Moira got one here, and she thinks it's terrific and that I should have one done, too. But it's not something I've ever considered, really. I suppose I had my ears pierced on a whim, and I haven't regretted that, but I don't know what my partner would think about this." *Stop babbling, Lara,* I thought. *You are making a fool of yourself. It's just a tattoo.*

"Moira, yes. She got a little hummingbird if I recall. Rory Carlyle brought her in."

"That's her," I said. "You can have them removed, right? Tattoos, I mean."

"Yes, you can," she said. "But it's more difficult and more expensive—a lot more expensive—than having it done in the first place."

"Oh," was all I managed to say.

"Would you like to come in and see the equipment?" she said. "I could explain the procedure to you better, and that might help you decide. I have someone coming in for a big job in about an hour, but I'll show you my setup, and you can think about it."

"That's good of you," I said. "That would be helpful." I didn't say helpful for what, but followed her into the back room. It was very nice and clean and professional-looking, for want of a better term—sort of like a dentist's office. It would have to be. It had, after all, passed the Meller Spa test.

"This is the tattoo machine I use," she said. "It's very carefully sterilized, and I'll open the package of needles right in front of you. I don't reuse the needles or anything, and the equipment is always sterilized before it's used again."

"A machine," I said.

"Yes," she agreed. "What did you think? A bone chisel or something? That hasn't been popular in a long time."

"You have to plug the machine in," I said.

"It's electric, right," she said. She was looking at me as if I was some nutbar, which maybe I was.

"I really didn't know that," I said. That certainly meant that Dave hadn't been tattooed on Tepano's Tomb, Jasper at Ahu Akivi, and Gabriela at the back of the hotel grounds. For Jasper in particular that would have required a longer extension cord than would normally be available.

"This machine has been around for more than a hundred years," she said, laughing. "An early version of it was invented in the late 1880s."

"But people got tattoos before that," I said.

"Oh, yes," she said. "There are Egyptian mummies with tattoos, and I've heard that people were tattooed in the Stone Age. In this part of the world, tattoos are very much a part of tradition. In the old days, both men and women here covered their bodies in tattoos. And people here still get them, only not quite as elaborate."

"I'll bet they didn't use this machine," I said.

"You've got that right," she said. She did not, however, volunteer what they did use.

"You look familiar to me," I said, feeling we were beginning to establish some rapport despite my babbling. "Did I see you at the police station with Daniel Striker, by any chance?"

"Yes," she said. "Daniel's my husband. The police asked me to come and help them with an investigation. I saw your friend Moira there, too, didn't I?"

"Yes," I said. "The police are questioning everybody at the hotel again, I guess. That's why I was there. Were they asking you about tattoos?"

"Yes," she said. "But how would you know that?"

"I found the body at the hotel," I said. "Dave Maddox. After that I was out at Ahu Akivi when the group found Jasper. I happened to notice they both had a similar tattoo."

"How awful for you," she said. "But those tattoos! That was the worst tattoo job I've seen in a long, long time."

"You saw them?"

"Photographs," she said. "The police showed them to me.

Looked as if they'd been done in a back alley somewhere."

"They didn't look anything like these," I said, gesturing again at the photos in the room.

"Most certainly not," she said. "To do a tattoo properly you need the right equipment, and if I may say so, a good deal of skill. This machine vibrates up to several hundred times a minute, moving the needle up and down, so you have to know what you're doing." This sounded unbelievably complicated to me and not a way to go about killing somebody.

"If I were giving you a tattoo," she said, "we'd decide on a design, I'd do an outline, either from a stencil, as I said, or freehand on your skin. Then I'd use the machine to redo the outline, permanently, I mean, with the needle. After that, we'd fill in the design, with color if that is what you wanted. The skill is in how well you use the machine. If the needles go too deep, there is excessive pain and bleeding, too shallow and the line will look kind of uneven when it's done. You have to get it just right. These tattoos on the dead bodies were done by a butcher, without a machine. Whoever did them simply used some sharp implement to scratch the skin surface, rather deep, too, I'm afraid. It would have hurt, but maybe they were dead at the time."

I knew, from the traces of blood on the tattoo, that they'd all been alive when it was done, but we could hope they were unconscious.

"Then the ink—and I'm not sure what was used for the color or whether or not it would be permanent—was just rubbed into the scratch." It was permanent, all right, for Jasper and Dave. I could only hope it wasn't for Gabriela.

"Horrible job, and really very, very unsanitary, I'm sure," she said. "This is the kind of tattoo procedure people in prisons use to give each other tattoos and kids try out on their friends. Very bad idea." Obviously the police had not bothered to mention the snake venom. That was about as unsanitary as it gets.

"So it's possible to do tattoos without this machine?" I said.

"Of course. Even now people use an empty pen into which they put a sharp wire of some kind, and they just use the ink you'd use in a fountain pen. I shouldn't have told you that," she said. "I've probably put you off. Really, people have been getting tattoos for thousands of years, and they are now very trendy. It's quite safe, and it hardly hurts at all. If you want something small and not too fancy, I can do it right now. You know what I'd suggest for you? I don't know if you've been to Ana Kai Tangata, the cave . . ."

"I have," I said. I was trying to remember to breathe and not have a complete nervous collapse at the thought of this tattoo.

"Then I'm sure you recall the wall paintings. There is a bird motif there that relates to the cult of the bird man. I could do that. It's pretty and it's discreet. It would be a good souvenir of your trip; and you never know, maybe having a little tattoo would make your life more exciting. Why don't you go for it?"

I managed to stop myself from commenting that finding three bodies so far on this trip was more excitement that I could stand and that right now a bird tattoo was out of the question.

"I guess if these tattoos were done in such a primitive fashion, it is difficult for the police to narrow down their search," I said.

"It is," she said. "I was able to tell them one thing, though. I'm almost certain the person who did this was left-handed."

"How would you know that?" I said.

"You draw an outline of the design you want on the skin

first, so you start at a point, and go in a direction, that prevents you from smudging the design. If you're right-handed, as I am, you will tend to start at the top and go around the design counterclockwise, and if you're left-handed you go clockwise."

"But if they're finished you can't tell. You're talking about Gabriela's, then."

"Yes," she said. "It wasn't finished, and the person who did it stopped in the middle of piercing the skin. I'm almost certain I'm right," she said. "Now, how about it? Maybe just a little bird?"

"Could I think about this overnight?" I said. "Maybe email my partner, Rob, for his opinion on this subject?"

"I'll bet he'd find something small and strategically placed rather interesting," she said.

"I suppose," I said. Apparently all that is necessary to make life both interesting and exciting is a little tattoo. I wondered if that is what Moira thought, a tattoo and a little fling with Rory.

Nonetheless, I was feeling positively euphoric that I had managed to get that much information without actually having to get a tattoo, even if I had proven to myself without a shadow of a doubt that I was the most boring person on the planet. No guts, either. Never mind: I now knew it was possible for someone to use something as simple as a ballpoint pen and a sharp piece of wire to do a tattoo. It was possible I was the only person in the world up until that moment who hadn't known this. The point was, now I did.

My second visit of the afternoon was to the hotel manager, one Celestino, by name. I managed to corner him in the garden, so that it would look like a chance meeting rather than my having to make an appointment. I casually introduced myself and commiserated with him about the

events unfolding at the hotel he managed. I told him I'd
been to see Gabriela in the hospital because I knew her father and stepmother and how appalled I'd been to hear
about the poison.

"I found her," he said. "Right over there. It was dreadful.
I live just down the street with my family, and I was doing a
last-minute check of the property before I left for the night.
I heard a moan, and there was some shuffling around. Her
body seemed to fall out of the hedge, although I must have
been imagining it. I thought at first someone had tossed her
there, but that couldn't be the case, could it?"

"I certainly hope not," I said, but of course it could. This
was probably the person who had inadvertently saved
Gabriela from instant death.

"I thought at first she was drunk, you know, so I didn't
call the police right away. But then, when I couldn't wake
her . . . I'll be glad when this is all over," he said. "I've
never seen anything like this in the ten years I've been
here."

"I'm sure we'll all be on our way very soon," I said. I sure
hoped I was right.

Cassandra proved more elusive. In fact I was beginning
to wonder if she was hiding out somewhere, but she did like
her food, and I eventually found her in the dining room. "I
need to talk to you," I said pulling up a chair without being
asked.

"I don't need to talk to you," she said.

"Fine," I said. "I was just coming to warn you. Have the
carabineros interviewed you yet?"

"Why would they want to do that?" she said, giving me
the evil eye.

"I guess you haven't heard," I said. "Gabriela, the young
woman from the hotel, was poisoned, deliberately, by someone. The police are treating it as attempted murder now."

The gypsy turned green. "Oh," she gasped.

"Yes," I said. "It would probably be best if you talked to them about that night before I do. What is your real name by the way? I'm sure they'll want to know that."

"Muriel," she said. "Muriel Jones. My friends call me Mu. That's how I got interested in the goddess Mu and Lemuria." She had completely dropped her pseudo-Hungarian gypsy accent. I'd say she was from the Midwest somewhere.

"Have you got any other names, like Anakena, maybe?"

"Anakena? No," she said. She looked as if she were going to throw up.

"Have you ever met this Anakena?" I said.

"I suppose I must have," she said. "Anakena is here."

"But you don't know Anakena for sure," I said.

"No. I don't know why all these questions about Anakena," she said. "It wasn't what you thought, you know, that night."

"How was it then, Muriel?" At least she wasn't trying to stick to her story that I was mistaken about seeing her with Gabriela.

"It was the cards. They predicted this."

"Oh, please," I said.

"It's true," she said. "I read her cards. It cost me a lot to get here, but given my years of study of Lemuria, I felt I couldn't pass up the opportunity to come. I rather needed a little spending money while I was here, though, so I started reading cards in my room for anyone who cared to pay me. A lot of the girls on staff came. There's nothing illegal in that."

"I'm not sufficiently familiar with the laws of Chile to comment," I said, rather acidly. She turned even greener, if that was possible.

"The thing about Gabriela was that bad news kept coming up. She came two or three times. Do you know the tarot cards?" Cassandra asked me. I shook my head. "I won't get into the technicalities, but Gabriela's cards were not good.

Death, number 13, showed its face every time I did them. That is not necessarily bad in the tarot, but it was in the context of the other cards. She got absolutely hysterical about it. I mean truly hysterical. It was during the filming of my interview. They were adjusting something or other, and so I went back to my room for a bathroom break. Gabriela was there, insisting I read her cards again. At this point, I wasn't charging her or anything. Then the tower, reversed, turned up, signifying unavoidable calamity. I tried to soft pedal it, but essentially the cards said that her chosen course would lead to someone's death. She went crazy. I think they are very superstitious people here."

And Cassandra, née Muriel, wasn't? "Go on," I said.

"She went out the back door, and I followed her. I was afraid she was going to pass out or something. I remembered hearing you should slap a person to bring them around. That's what I was doing when you saw me. Honest. You do believe me, don't you?"

"I'm not sure," I said. "Perhaps you should tell this story to the police rather than to me." Cassandra looked as if she was about to faint dead away. I didn't care. I did, however, believe her story, pathetic though it might be.

At ten that night I went back to the police station to pick up Moira, who was being permitted to go back to the hotel. I found her sitting with Rory in a room with bars on the windows.

"I'm going to wait with Rory," she said.

"No, you aren't," he said gently. "You are going with Lara. You're going to have a good night's sleep. I will be out of here in no time."

"I don't want to leave you here all by yourself," she said.

"I'll be fine. Get her out of here," Rory said to me.

"You can come back tomorrow, Moira," I said. "Right now, you're coming with me."

I wanted to ask Rory about the rongorongo tablet, but I knew doing so here was a very bad idea, and I also knew Moira needed some rest. I decided I was going to get her something to eat, then into bed, feed her one of those sleeping pills of hers, and get on with my job. I tried not to watch as they kissed each other good night.

II

THERE WAS NO kissing going on in the Fairweather household. In fact, Gordon and Victoria were in the midst of a rather heated discussion, by which I mean a rip-roaring argument, part of which I witnessed before they noticed me lurking on the porch outside their living room.

"I insist, Victoria," Gordon was saying as I walked up the steps. I was not eavesdropping. You could hear him in Alaska.

"I am staying here with you," she replied.

"Have I ever insisted on anything in our relationship?" he demanded. "I am asking now just once, please."

"I don't believe I'm in the habit of insisting either, Gordon," she said. "But I am now. I will not pack Edith up and take her to Melbourne. I will not leave Gabriela in hospital. That's that. When Gabriela's well and you can go to Melbourne, we'll all go to Melbourne. Not a minute before!"

"You must go," he said.

"This is my house, Gordon, my home. Have you forgotten? We live in my house here, your house in Melbourne. I will not leave my home."

"Victoria!" he said. "If I could leave this island, I would. I can't, so you must." My eye was caught by some movement over to one side of the room. It was Edith. She was sucking on her fist, and tears were running down her face. I don't think her parents realized she was there.

"I will not leave without you," Victoria said.

"Victoria, please," he said again. It was an anguished cry. "I am trying to tell you that you and Edith and Gabriela are not safe with me. You are both in danger as long as you are with me. We cannot stay together."

I stood rooted to the floor of the deck. He knows, I thought. He knows the same way that Seth did, that Dave did, maybe even Jasper. He knows where the danger lies, maybe not the specifics, but he knows what this is about. It wasn't about Gabriela. It was about him. That realization hit me so hard, I think I spoke aloud. The room inside went silent, and Gordon turned on the light and came to the door.

"It's you," he said.

"I'm sorry," I said. "I didn't mean to interrupt."

"We'll call this round a draw, shall we, Gordon?" Victoria said. "I think you want to speak to my husband, Lara. I'm not sure how much you heard, but we have a difference of opinion here. Gordon wants me to take Edith and go to Australia. I don't want to go until we get this mess straightened out. I'm going to check on Edith, and then I'm going to see how Gabriela is doing, Gordon. You talk to Lara."

"Edith was watching," I said.

"Oh, no!" Gordon said. He slumped into a chair as Victoria went to find and comfort the little girl.

I waited until he'd composed himself, and then I asked about the rongorongo tablet. "I hear that you had it," I said.

"Yes," he said.

"You got it from Jasper," I said.

"Yes," he said.

"Did you steal it from him?"

"No," he said.

"Look, Gordon, my friend Moira spent all day in jail because she was caught trying to get the rongorongo tablet out of Rory's place. I could use a little more than yes and no."

"Jasper asked me to take a look at it, to see if it was what he thought it was. I said I'd need to take it home with me, and he agreed. It's as simple as that. I had a look at it, and then I asked Rory to also look at it. I'm not entirely sure what happened to it after that. If you will recall, I was hiding out in a cave."

"So is it authentic?"

"Yes, it is," he said. "It just isn't from Chile, that's all."

"So where was it from?"

"Here, of course. Despite what Jasper tried to show, this is the only place you find rongorongo. If he'd thought about it, he'd have known that, too."

"Did Rory agree?"

"He thought it would need more testing," he said.

"You didn't?"

"No," he said. "It's real."

"How could you say that, just by looking at it?"

"I just know that it is," he replied.

"And you aren't going to tell me why," I said.

"No, I'm not," he said.

"I'm sitting here wondering why Jasper would consult you on this, Gordon. It seemed to me you weren't the best of friends."

"He had his reasons," Gordon said.

"Are you going to tell me what this is about, Gordon?" I said softly. He shook his head. At this moment Victoria arrived with a sobbing Edith. Gordon gathered the little girl up in his arms and sat down in a rocking chair, wincing as she grabbed his sore arm. "Go and see Gabriela, Victoria," he said quietly. "I'll stay here with Edith. We'll talk later. If you don't mind, Lara, I would like to spend some time alone with my daughter."

I turned back on the darkened porch and looked at him. He was sitting with his head back, eyes closed, stroking Edith's hair, and swaying slightly. Edith had wrapped her arms around his neck and was already falling asleep. I thought then how much I liked these people, Gordon and Victoria, but also Dave and Seth. I thought of the evening I'd spent with Seth while he told me all about rongorongo, how his enthusiasm for his subject had fired my imagination. Poor Dave had the social skills of a gnat, but he had a good heart, and I had liked him, too. Even Jasper, while I hadn't known him, had earned my grudging admiration for the way he had defied the established way of thinking and done some groundbreaking work. Somewhere out there, someone was destroying them. They were going down, one at a time, without uttering a word. Worse yet, they were taking others, like Gabriela, and even in some respects, Moira, with them.

So now I knew it was about the four men, Gordon, Jasper, Dave, and Seth. They must have had something in common, something they weren't talking about, something that had come to haunt them. What had Seth said? *We should never have come back.* If they had come back, when had they been here before? It was a question I realized I should have asked myself much sooner, but events, and a certain skepticism on my part where Seth's seemingly incoherent ramblings were concerned, had gotten in the way.

I thought it might be difficult, but it wasn't—just a few hours staring at a computer screen in a little Internet cafe in Hanga Roa the next day. Jasper was particularly easy to find. He had a very impressive Web site, music and all, had I been able to listen to it where I was. I chose the low-tech version from the home page and clicked on something that said *All about Jasper.*

Jasper's resumé went on and on about his great prowess, his huge discoveries, the immense contribution he'd made to our understanding of the history of the Americas, and so on. It was all a bit over the top. By contrast, the section on his education was a little sparse, as I suppose Gordon Fairweather could have told me. Indeed, he'd made the point rather loudly up at Rano Raraku. Jasper's resumé did say he attended college, but the word *graduate* did not come into it. It said he'd studied anthropology at Veritas College in Wisconsin. At least he hadn't faked a degree.

I then Googled Gordon Fairweather and found he was listed on the faculty at the University of Melbourne in Australia. It took a little fiddling around, but I did find his CV as well—Ph.D. in archaeology from the University of Southern California in 1982, as well as his master's degree in 1977. His undergraduate degree came from something called Veritas College in Wisconsin in 1975. My, my, Jasper and Fairweather did go back a long way, thirty years in fact.

I couldn't find anything about Dave Maddox specifically, but I did find his construction business in Orlando. I emailed them to say I was writing an article about him for the local Rapa Nui newspaper and wondered if they would mind sending me a copy of his CV. I could find nothing about Seth Connelly.

By late afternoon I was back at the Internet cafe, and lo and behold there was a lovely email from someone by the name of Dolores, who said they were all devastated by Dave's death, and she was happy to hear that someone was going to write something about him. She said he'd only rated a three-line obituary in Orlando, as well as a news squib about how a local man had died in the Easter Islands.

I didn't bother telling her there was only one lonely Easter Island in this part of the world.

Dave's CV listed at length all the projects he'd accomplished in his building days. The last line said he had a BA from Veritas College in Wisconsin in—wouldn't you know?—1975.

It seemed almost unnecessary at this point, but just to make sure, I turned my attention back to Seth. First, I tried rongorongo. There were a mere 9,270 entries on that subject, a rather daunting prospect, but then I keyed in his alias, "Rongoreader," and lo and behold, there he was. *Rongoreader explains rongorongo,* the brief description provided said. On the site itself there was a great deal of information, photographs and drawings of the script and so on. At the end there was a little blurb on the mysterious Rongoreader. *I've been interested in rongorongo for thirty years, ever since I visited Rapa Nui as a student in my junior year at college in Wisconsin,* the biography said. There was more, but that was all I needed to know.

Something had happened on Rapa Nui in 1975 when four men had been here as students. The problem was that three of them were dead, and the fourth wasn't talking. I tried a few more searches on archaeology on Easter Island. There was lots of material but nothing useful. I thought long and hard about how to get closer to this event, whatever it was, and also to narrow my search. Rapa Nui was a small island under normal circumstances, but it seemed rather large now.

I was back at the hotel, staring at the ocean and worrying this problem to death, when I realized I was looking at a potential solution—literally. Felipe Tepano, the man Rory said had been a key feature at archaeological projects for almost forty years, was working away on the grounds about fifteen yards from where I sat. I waited until he was finished and had packed up his truck, and then I followed him home.

Home for Felipe Tepano was a guest house on the far side of Hanga Roa, out past the museum. It was, I knew, Rory Carlyle's home while he worked there. I parked down the street and walked up to his door.

"Mr. Tepano," I said. "My name is Lara McClintoch."

"I know," he said. He didn't seem even remotely surprised to see me, but here was a man who evidently foresaw the future. I hoped he liked the look of mine.

"I would really like to talk to you," I said. He gestured toward a chair on the patio, and we sat looking at the sunset. His wife, a plump woman with a lovely smile who he introduced as Maria, brought us some fresh juice and sat down with us.

"This is Señora McClintoch," Felipe told his wife. "She helped Gordon Fairweather."

Maria smiled warmly. "I have heard about you, from Victoria and Rory and also my husband. I have also met your friend Moira when she was here with Rory."

Were they comparing tattoos? Now I had something else to fret about, but it would have to wait until later. "You've been working with Gordon and other archaeologists for many years, haven't you?" I said.

"Yes," he said. "Many years."

"Thirty-seven," his wife said proudly. "Gordon told me that we wouldn't know nearly as much about Rapa Nui as we do if it were not for Felipe."

"Mr. Tepano, I don't know a gentle way of putting this. What I want you to tell me is what happened here in 1975."

"A lot of things happened in 1975," Felipe said, choosing his words carefully. "Wasn't that the year we got electricity?" he said, turning to his wife.

"I think so," she said. "About then. You might have to narrow this down a bit," she said with what I took to be an encouraging smile.

"What happened at the Veritas College archæological project here in 1975?" I said. "In fact, what happened at Anakena in 1975?" It had to be that, didn't it?

Felipe Tepano rocked back and forth in his chair. "I know of nothing like that," he said finally. His wife shifted in her chair.

"Do you like Gordon Fairweather, Mr. Tepano?" I said.

"Yes," he replied. "Very much."

"I do, too," I said. I waited.

"Felipe," his wife said. He shook his head.

"Three people are already dead," I said. "I presume you have heard what happened to Gabriela as well."

Maria almost sobbed when I mentioned Gabriela's name. "Please, Felipe," she said.

"I gave my word," he said. "I will not break my pledge."

"Do you know who is killing these people?" I said.

He hesitated. "No, I do not," he said. "If I did, that I would tell you."

We chatted for a few minutes longer, but I knew it was hopeless. I thanked Maria for the juice and went back to my car, completely discouraged. I had to do a U-turn to go back because the only way I'd find my way to the hotel was to retrace my steps, and when I took the first corner on my way back to town, Maria was at the side of the road waving at me. She must have gone out the back door and across a neighbor's yard to get there.

As I pulled up beside her, she thrust an envelope into my hand. "I have made no such pledge," she said. "My husband has forbidden me to speak of it, but you look at this." In a second, she was gone.

I stared for a very long time at the envelope's contents. It was getting too dark to see properly, but I'd seen enough. I went back to the hotel and showed it to Moira. "This is something you need to see," I told her.

The colors of the photograph had deteriorated rather

badly, leaving the sky an unpleasant greenish yellow. But you could see the people—a tall, thin, distinguished man in shorts and a whitish shirt open at the collar, maybe fifty or so; a younger woman with reddish hair in a sun dress, cut straight across the top with wide straps and a big skirt and sandals. She was holding the hand of a little girl in a similar sun dress, with blonde, almost white, hair. There was something about the way the woman stood, a certain rigidity to her stance perhaps, and some anxiety in her expression, that made me think she was very tense. Beside them was a man of about forty in work boots and trousers, his chest bare. Five young people, late teens, early twenties, I'd say, clustered behind these four. The older man was holding something, and they were all smiling at the camera.

"Isn't this adorable? That has to be Jasper, and this one is almost certainly Dave. He looks the same only a bit younger. The tall one with all the hair must be Gordon, but I'm not sure about the rest of them, although the one with his head down looks familiar," she said.

"Seth Connelly," I said. "He often stood with his head like that. The man in the work boots is Felipe Tepano. I don't recognize these other two people, do you? I assume this is a couple with the child, even if there is a considerable difference in their ages. They look as if they belong together. I don't recognize this other young person. Is that a man or a woman?"

"Hard to say," she said. "It looks like a man, but the features are rather effeminate. I don't know the couple at all. However . . ." She peered at the photograph, then went to get something out of her bag. "I'm afraid I'm beginning to need this from time to time," she said, holding up a little magnifying glass. "This or longer arms."

"Alas, I know that very well," I said. "What are you peering at?"

"I believe I'm looking at the San Pedro rongorongo

tablet," she said after a pause in which she pressed the magnifying glass to the photograph.

"Are you sure?" I said.

"No, but I think it is. I've only seen one rongorongo tablet, and I think this is the one I've seen. As you know, I had a pretty good look at it yesterday."

"You recognize the rongorongo?" I said.

"No, I recognize this," she said, pointing to one end of the tablet. "The one I had in my hands was rotted away a bit on one end, just like this one. You see, it's kind of a V-shaped cut into this end, where it's broken off."

"I see," I said. "And you're saying that the San Pedro had the same cut."

"That is exactly what I'm saying," she said.

"That's what Gordon meant," I said.

"Are you going to explain this?" Moira said.

"Gordon said the San Pedro tablet was authentic. He was absolutely definitive about it, even though he admitted Rory wanted to do some testing on it. Gordon also said that it was not from Chile. It was from Rapa Nui. I asked him how he knew and he wouldn't say. If this tablet in the photo and the one Jasper presented at his talk are one and the same, then Gordon knew it was authentic because he was here when it was found. Isn't that what this photograph looks like to you? They're all having their photo taken because it's a special occasion, and obviously the tablet is front and center here. This picture is to mark the discovery of the tablet."

"That's what it looks like. When and where was this picture taken?" Moira asked.

"According to the note on the back, August 10, 1975. You know where it was taken. You've been there."

She peered at it. "It's Rory's guest house, Maria and Felipe Tepano's place. Where did you get this?"

"Maria gave it to me. I'm not sure her husband knows this, so if you're back there, mum's the word, okay?"

"Okay," she said. "What does this mean? If this is the same tablet, then Jasper was presenting something as coming from Chile, when it actually came from here."

"Yes," I said.

"Did he know he was doing that, or did someone play a trick on him? I mean who are these other people?"

I told her my fears, my belief that the deaths were tied to something that happened the summer the four men were here as students. I told her how I'd gone to see Felipe Tepano in hopes he would tell me, but that he wouldn't and that his wife had given me this photograph as a result of her husband's refusal. "She's trying to tell me something without disobeying her husband directly," I said.

"I have a feeling this photograph explains everything, if only I could understand it. I am also wondering if the missing photograph, the one Dave kept in his safety deposit box, is similar, maybe even a duplicate."

"There are two photographs?" she said. I told her about Seth's ramblings, at least that's what I'd thought they were at the time. "So Seth said he'd have destroyed the photograph and assumed someone else had?" she asked.

"Right," I said. "Is it too far-fetched to assume we may be looking at a copy of it? Maybe they all got one."

"I don't know," Moira said. "But it's all there is. Why don't I ask Rory if he knows anything? I'll go back and see if they'll let me see him again."

"Let's leave it until tomorrow," I said. "I want to think about this some more. You know what bothers me most about this? It is that whoever is doing this is prepared to kill someone like Gabriela, who could not possibly have anything to do with 1975. She wasn't even born then."

"That may mean this is about something else entirely," Moira said.

"Then why won't anyone tell me about the summer of 1975?" I said.

"Good point," she said.

The next morning, Moira headed for the police station to see Rory, and I went back to the Internet cafe. Being the technologically backward person that I am, I had to get help, but within a reasonable period of time I had scanned the photograph Maria had given me and had it on a CD. This I took back to my friend Brian Murphy. "Can I see this on the screen, bigger, I mean?" I asked him.

"Sure," he said. "An old photograph, I see. Is that Jasper Robinson?"

"I think it is," I said.

"Could that be Dave Maddox?" he asked.

"Yes, and that would be Seth, and that would be Gordon Fairweather."

"No kidding," he said. "They knew each other a long time."

"They did," I agreed.

"Who are these other people? Is it a man or a woman?"

"Now that I'm able to see the picture better," I said, putting my nose right up to the screen. "I believe it is Muriel Jones."

"I don't know her," he said.

Actually you do, I thought, but I kept that thought to myself.

"Here I am again, Cassandra, or Muriel, or whatever your name is," I said, approaching Cassandra a few minutes later.

"Leave me alone," she said.

"Not going to happen, Muriel," I said. "I want you to tell me about the summer of 1975."

"I don't know what you're talking about," she said.

"How about you have a look at this photograph?" I said. "I can show it to you blown up on Brian's computer screen if you like, in case you don't recognize yourself as a guy."

If Cassandra had gone green the last time we'd talked, I don't know how you'd describe the color he or she was now.

Her hands were trembling badly, and there was a little tick throbbing near one eye. "Are we going somewhere private?" she said.

"Okay. Let's go sit under that umbrella and look at the sunset," I said.

"You're going to kill me out there in front of everyone in the dining room?" she said.

"I don't kill people," I said. "I just want to talk to you."

"You can't tell anyone," she whispered.

"I can understand your concern. If someone recognized you, you might end up dead like the rest of them."

The gypsy slumped in her chair. "Please, don't," she said. "Let's go outside."

"Cassandra, Muriel, what is your name, anyway?" I said.

"Andrew Jones," he said.

"Okay, Andrew," I said. "Tell me what—"

"Please," he said. "Call me Cassandra."

"Cassandra, if you don't tell me what I want to know, right now, I'm going to make an announcement at dinner about who you really are."

"Why are you doing this to me?" he said.

"People are dying, in case you hadn't noticed. Other people's lives are at risk. Gordon Fairweather won't tell me, Felipe Tepano won't tell me, but believe me, you are going to."

"We should never have come back here," he said. "I don't know why we did."

"Would it surprise you to know that is exactly what Seth said before he died?"

"Please!" he said. "I didn't think anybody would recognize me. The more outrageous you look, the less people look at you. I know that, believe me. Can we go to my room so I can take this wig off? My head aches."

"No," I said. "Start talking. No one can hear you out here by the water."

"I can't," he said.

"Okay, then, it's back to the dining room for my announcement. I think just about everybody was in there, weren't they? Anakena would have to be there."

He groaned. I waited. "Do you know the story of Ana o Keke?" he said at last.

"I know it's a cave," I said. "Something to do with virgins. One of your Moaimaniac pals uses the name."

"Cave of the White Virgins is what a lot of people call it," he said. "But do you know what happened there in the 1860s?"

"No," I said. What the 1860s had to do with all this, I didn't know. It was 1975 I was interested in.

"The cave was used as part of the bird man rituals, tangata manu. Young girls, virgins, were highly valued, and they were sent to Ana o Keke for weeks, if not months, before the birds came. The cave is several yards down from the top of the cliff out on Poike. It is a rather hazardous place to get to and a very long way to fall. It would have been crowded, too, but it was a great honor to be chosen. The idea was that the girls were to become pale and fat. Their fathers brought them their food."

"Okay," I said. I could feel my impatience growing. "Is there a point to this?"

"In 1862 slavers came to Rapa Nui," he said, ignoring me. "The islanders came to the beach to greet the ship. The slavers threw trinkets down on the sand, and everyone scrambled around to get them. While they were down on the ground, the slavers grabbed as many able-bodied men as they could, tied them up, and took them away. They were taken to work the guano mines in the Chincha Islands. The conditions there were terrible, and many of them died. But then—"

"I know this," I said. "Your old friend Gordon Fairweather told me. The bishop of Tahiti intervened and insisted they all be sent back. They were, but they brought smallpox with them."

"Did he tell you about the girls?" he said.

"No," I said.

"I guess he wouldn't," he said. "Cuts a little too close to the bone."

"So, what happened to the girls?" I said.

"Almost everyone on the island came down with smallpox," he said. "Most of them died. There was no one to bring the little girls food and water."

"They starved!" I gasped.

"They did," he said.

"Tell me this is just a fable," I said.

"It may be, but the people here believe it to be true," he said. He turned his head away from me, and spoke so quietly I could barely hear him. "I don't imagine she'd starve in three days," he said. "Dehydration, though, or maybe just exposure."

I had this sense of impending disaster, a kind of tightening in my chest, and an intense desire to run away, not to listen to the rest of this. "Are we talking now about the 1860s?" I said, very quietly.

"No," he said, and a tiny rivulet of wet mascara ran down his cheek. "We are talking about little Flora Pedersen."

Please don't tell me a little girl died in a cave, I thought. *Please don't tell me that.*

He took a few moments to compose himself. "We came out from Valparaiso on a Chilean supply ship," he said, finally. "Five of us, all classmates at Veritas College—Gordon Fairweather, Dave Maddox, Jasper Robinson, Seth Connelly, and me. We'd all studied anthropology together, hung out together all semester, and when one of our professors was looking for students to assist with his work here, we volunteered. I was trying very hard to be one of the boys in those days, as futile as that may have been. I hadn't quite figured out why I felt the way I did.

"Jasper was especially keen on the trip. He'd read all of Thor Heyerdahl's books, and to go to the site of one of them was something he just had to do. The supply ship anchored off Anakena Beach, and we were taken in on a small boat with our sleeping bags and the rest of our gear. Jasper was over the moon, because Anakena was where Heyerdahl set up camp. Gordon and Jasper were the serious ones. For Dave and Seth and me, it was all a bit of a lark. While our classmates were waiting tables at resorts in Michigan, or something, we were on Rapa Nui looking for treasure.

"I don't mean we didn't take our work seriously. We did. Professor Pedersen worked us very hard, and we had some tremendous success. We found a cave on Poike and excavated there. There were some ritual carvings in it, a skeleton, too, and best of all, a rongorongo tablet. Those things are scarce as hen's teeth, but we found one."

"That wouldn't be the one that is now being called the San Pedro rongorongo tablet, would it?" I said.

"How would you know that?" he said. I pointed to the photograph. "I think they were one and the same. Seth and Dave did, too. In any event, we worked very hard, much harder than most of us expected, I think. Except Gordon, of course. He was really into it. We had fun, too. We drank ourselves silly every night, The others found themselves Rapa girlfriends. Pedersen and his wife kind of adopted us, made sure we ate, that sort of thing. We stayed in the same guest house they did. They lived in the main house, and the four of us shared a bunkie out the back. Mrs. Pedersen was really very kind. I'm sure she had a first name, but we called her Mrs. Pedersen, even though she wasn't that much older than we were. She was very much younger than her husband. These were more formal times. But then," he said and stopped.

"Then," I said.

"Something terrible happened," he said finally. "The Pedersens had a little girl. Her name was Flora, but the native workmen called her Tavake. Tavake is the name of a little bird on Rapa Nui, and she flitted around like one, I suppose. The name kind of stuck."

It would have had to be a little bird, wouldn't it?

"I think it was Felipe Tepano who actually gave her that name. He was the foreman on the project. I notice he's still around, but now he's making predictions of impending doom."

"True predictions," I said.

"Apparently."

"I take it you really don't believe in tarot cards and Lemuria?"

"Yes and no. It's all part of the act, literally. We should never have come back you know. Never. But at least I knew enough to come back as someone else. Do you know what I do for a living? I have a cabaret act that I perform in bars, the sort of place I don't expect you frequent. Men dressed up as women. It's a transvestite act. Queen Mu is the name I use. I'm very good at it."

"I can see that," I said. "But maybe you should stick to answering my question."

"We had Sundays off. The workmen all went to Mass, and we just hung out, usually drinking a whole lot of beer, and carousing with the girlfriends, those of us who had them. On that particular Sunday the Pedersens asked us if we would watch Tavake while they went to visit some people they'd met. We said yes, of course, but after a beer or two, we decided we wanted to go to the beach. We debated about it, but the Pedersens had said they wouldn't be back until dinner time, and we figured we'd be back by then, too. We took Tavake with us."

"By beach, you mean Anakena?" I said.

"Yes," he said. "The day went wrong, right from the start. We were drinking a lot of beer. We'd taken two trucks because we had Tavake with us. Dave took one and loaded up on beer. We drank all afternoon. Jasper and Gordon had a huge blowup. Gordon thought Jasper was sloppy and was going for the glory instead of doing the methodical work that we needed to do. He was right, of course, but Jasper has always been like that. He was then, and he is, or was, right up until the day he died. They never really got along, the two of them. Two strong personalities, I guess. Gordon was really meticulous about the work we were doing, and Jasper just wanted to go for the big find. You can't be slapdash in archaeology you know and Jasper may well have been. Gordon took the keys to one of the trucks and left in a huff.

"I had so much to drink that I did the unthinkable. I made a pass at Jasper. It was an eye-opener for both of us. Jasper was absolutely disgusted, and Dave and Seth were appalled, too, I know. These were the 1970s, and this was unheard of in his circles. He yelled at me, threw sand in my face, and told me to stay away from him. I was devastated. I didn't know why I had done it in the first place, of course. I remember I went and threw up. Jasper demanded that we go back.

"I don't know how it happened," he said. "Maybe we thought Gordon had taken Tavake with him, I don't know. I guess we had too much beer, but we just forgot about Tavake, all of us. One minute she was flitting around, the next she wasn't."

He stopped talking for at least a minute. I should have pressed him, but part of me didn't want to hear what he had to say.

"We forgot her," he said at last. There was a catch in his voice. "We packed up and were halfway back to the guest house before we remembered her. We went back, of course, and searched and searched, calling her name over and over.

Finally we realized we'd have to go to town for help. By then, it was dark. A search party was formed immediately, and the whole town came out, I swear, to look for her. They couldn't find her that night, nor the next day. The poor little thing had crawled into a cave, you know. I guess she was frightened, she must have been terrified of being alone in the dark. She was only four. They'd already looked in that cave, but she had crawled down a shaft they didn't see at first.

"Maybe she was playing hide-and-seek, you know. She loved that, and we always went along with it. We would pretend we couldn't see her behind the tree, and go looking for her while she giggled loud enough for us to hear her. They didn't find her for almost three days!" he said. "Three days!" He was almost shouting. "She was dead!" He began to weep uncontrollably.

"We were sent home," he said, finally, dabbing his eyes with the tissue I'd handed him. "Gordon was the only one who stayed in the field. He went to another university to complete his studies. I heard he was working in Peru, not here. But I guess eventually the siren call of Rapa Nui got him. Seth became a history teacher, Dave a builder, and Jasper, who dropped out of college before he graduated, made a fortune as a stockbroker before he retired to become an adventurer. My own career path, I've told you.

"I still dream about her, cold and frightened and abandoned in that cave. I've often wondered if that was why Jasper and Seth and Dave never had kids and why all my relationships end so badly. Dave got married, you know, but he never wanted kids. Seth didn't marry at all, and Jasper married every woman he slept with, as near as I can tell, but he never had kids either. We should never have come back."

"And why did you?" I said.

"I don't know, except that we were invited. No, I'm not being honest here. I came because I wanted to see Jasper again. Despite the way he treated me, there is still some feeling there. Dave and Seth had stayed in touch, although not regularly. I had stayed in touch in a way, I suppose, through the Internet, although I never identified myself to them that way. I never told them about my, well, you know. I told them I was an actor, which is true, after all. Seth and I talked maybe once every couple of years. Maybe not even that often. We stayed interested in Rapa Nui over all the years. You can laugh about Lemuria, but it is possible there is a sunken continent in the Pacific. Dave and Seth should have stayed in the field, too. They were good at it, especially Seth. Rongorongo, I mean. He told me he just kept working at it in his spare time. He set up an office in his garage. A terrible waste, really. Dave was the same. He told you, many times, no doubt," he said, with the hint of a smile, "how he was watching a TV show and an idea about how to move and raise the moai just came to him. Rapa Nui drew us, you know. We were still in its thrall.

"Dave emailed Seth and me to say he'd received an invitation to this Moai Congress. I had, too. We talked on the phone a couple of times. Dave thought maybe if we went we'd exorcize a few demons, you know. He said Jasper had emailed him and asked him to come, so maybe it was time we got together again. He said he'd persuaded Seth to go as well. They'd emailed Gordon, but he said he was too busy. He didn't suggest they come and visit or anything. Bad feelings still, I guess, between him and Jasper. That and the ghost of little Tavake.

"I told them I couldn't come, that I was in a show and couldn't leave it. At the last minute, though, I changed my mind. I came incognito. Seth recognized me, but respected my request for anonymity. The others didn't know me at all. I suppose that is what saved me. Dave brought Jasper's rongorongo tablet with him, as Jasper asked him to, and Dave and Seth both had a look at it. Dave must have suspected it was the one we'd found years ago, because he'd called Seth

at home and asked him to bring a copy of the photograph of
the group of us from that summer if he could find it, which
Seth did. Dave wanted to compare the tablet in the old
photo with Jasper's tablet. I think Dave and Seth were almost certain they were one and the same. They tried to persuade themselves otherwise, but I don't think they could.

"Seth said the tablet was a sign, a warning of what was to
come. Whoever is doing this wanted us to know. Jasper, being the kind of person he is, didn't seem to notice. He was
so intent on his big find in Chile that proved what he
wanted to prove that he didn't see the resemblance. Dave
was going to talk to him, to warn him, but I'm not sure he
did. He may have been killed before he could. Dave also
planned to tell everyone at the congress that it wasn't from
Chile. He thought that was a travesty, for Jasper to say such
a thing. If he did manage to talk to Jasper, then Jasper
didn't believe him or he wouldn't have gone on to make that
big announcement in front of everybody.

"In a way we got what we deserved, you know. We were
unbelievably self-absorbed, terribly careless. As a result, a
little girl died. If you make that announcement in the dining room, tell everyone who I really am, then maybe I'll pay
the price, too. Maybe this is as it should be."

"But not for Gabriela," I said. "She has done nothing to
deserve this."

"But her father has, hasn't he? He may be the least culpa-
ble. He left the beach first. But he is still paying, isn't he?
The rest of us have no children. It is Gordon who is to learn
what it is like to lose one.

"It was thirty years ago that it happened. Thirty years
ago! Life held such promise then. There was nothing we
couldn't do. It ruined our lives, I think. It ruined many
lives. The Pedersens divorced, I heard. As far as I know, Professor Pedersen never remarried. I don't know what hap-

pened to Tavake's mother, but I am sure she never completely got over it. How could she?

"For me, at times over that thirty years, days would go by when I wouldn't even think about it. But it was there, and when I came back here, it was as if it had just happened. I imagine the others felt the same."

"So who is Anakena?" I said.

"I don't know," he replied. "I'm just pathetically grateful it isn't you."

12

THE SHADOWY FIGURE I'd come to know as Anakena was very slowly beginning to take shape in my mind. Like the hooded individual in my nightmares, I didn't know if it was man or woman. I did know that this was a person of keen, if malignantly misdirected, intelligence, someone of almost infinite patience. This war of retribution had been devised down to the last detail, and it had been planned for a very long time, each piece of the strategy carefully put into place over a period of at least three years and in such a way as not to raise any alarm.

It had to come down to the Internet group. There were others at the congress, certainly. Several Chilean experts had flown in to present papers, a fellow from CONAF, the Chilean national park service, had come to present a paper on efforts to reforest the island, for example, but he had come and gone, in one day and out the next. Other Chilean archaeologists had done the same. The people who had stayed for the whole event and who hadn't been able to leave were the Moaimaniacs, Kent Clarke Films, Moira, and me. I knew who all the members of the group were, with the exception of Anakena. Technically that should have meant that none of the people whose aliases I knew were Anakena, but I didn't think I could count on that. It would have been easy enough for any one of them to have a second alias.

Andrew and I had talked for a long time after he told me about Flora Pedersen. He told me that he regularly checked Jasper Robinson's Web site out of sheer curiosity about his former schoolmate's exploits, even if that schoolmate had rejected him in such a harsh fashion so many years before. He'd signed up for the Moaimaniacs the moment the notice appeared on the Web site, about three years before. The anonymity it afforded was very appealing to Andrew, and he'd been pleased, he said, when he realized that both Dave and Seth were members.

I could see the hand of Anakena everywhere now. Was it Anakena who had suggested the idea of the group in the first place? Kent had said that there was no good idea that Jasper wasn't prepared to steal. Had the killer suggested the Internet group, then later suggested the congress? Was that person close to Jasper, trusted by him, whispering ideas in his ear like some scheming Iago? Did Anakena know Jasper so well as to be able to predict what he would do? His overweening vanity? His blindness to anything that didn't further his theories, enhance his reputation?

Physically, Anakena had to be strong enough to drag unconscious bodies to their resting places—Dave to the tomb, Jasper to Ahu Akivi, or at least to some kind of vehicle that would carry him there. Did that mean it had to be a man? Could I have dragged the rather rotund Dave Maddox from his room, say, to Tepano's tomb? I thought it would be difficult, but possible if sufficiently motivated.

Anakena had to be bold, as well, to carry out these murders on the grounds of a hotel. I also knew, thanks to Eroria, that Anakena was very probably left-handed.

As for the vehicle, assuming that Jasper hadn't gone to Ahu Akivi in the middle of the night of his own volition, almost all of us at some point had rented a car of some sort. Enrique, I know, had done so and squired Yvonne around the island. Lewis and his wife, Judith, had, too. Jasper had died before the keys had been taken away from all of us.

Who was left from that fateful time in 1975? I went back to the Internet cafe and checked on Professor Pedersen. I couldn't find him listed on the college faculty, but I did find a scholarship in his name—a memorial scholarship. Professor Pedersen, who had been at least fifty, I'd say, in 1975, was now deceased. He'd been dead for five years.

Flora's mother, however, could be very much alive. She had been considerably younger, early thirties, I'd say, at that time. She would have remarried, perhaps, and changed her name, and she would now be in her sixties. I asked Andrew if he thought he would recognize her thirty years later, and he said he thought he would, and he didn't think she was there. Even so, it was a possibility. Yvonne was way too young, as was Kent. Brenda Butters was the right age, and Susie Scace was close. Edwina Rasmussen certainly had a bitterness of outlook that might be attributed to personal tragedy, but she was too short to be Flora's mother unless the camera had done something strange to perspective. Brenda and Susie, however, were about the right height. Susie was also blonde, but when I really looked at the photograph, I couldn't see any resemblance. On the fringes of the group there was Judith, doctor and wife of the muffin. She was about the right age, seemed very strong to me, the right height, and while not a member of the Internet group, she was related by marriage. If Anakena was not a second alias, then she was a definite possibility. Were any of them left-handed? I tried to picture them eating, but I couldn't recall.

I picked up my email, the usual spam, the daily question from Clive and one from Rob. *Something has been bothering me about those photos of the ground where that fellow Dave was found,* the message said. *I had them enlarged and a couple of us have had a look. I think I told you that horseshoes are unique, made to fit an individual horse. You can see quite distinct shapes and also maybe markings. All of the prints that I can see well enough to comment on are made by exactly the same horseshoe. There's a little notch on the right side of it. If you look at your photos, you'll see. I don't think you're looking for a horse. I think you're looking for a horseshoe. Be careful.*

What on earth did that mean? That somebody, a left-handed somebody at that, had a horseshoe and was making marks on the ground around Dave to make it look as if a horse had trampled him? Wasn't that a little bizarre? It had been very effective, though, now that I thought about it. Fuentes had maintained for days that Dave had had an unfortunate encounter with a horse. The appearance of an accident would also have the benefit of not overly alarming the next victims. After Jasper's death, the implications must have been clear to the others, but by then it didn't matter. We were all here for the duration. Horseshoes and tattoos: Anakena possessed a creative mind as well.

How important was the San Pedro rongorongo tablet to the plan? It tied the person, whoever it was, to that summer of 1975, most certainly. The staff of the museum in town, who should know these things, said they had never heard of the San Pedro tablet. Therefore, one of the people associated with its original find most likely had had it in their possession all this time until it was planted for Jasper to find. It was too much to expect that it had turned up in the window of an antique shop like mine, somewhere where Anakena just happened to be wandering by.

Seth and Andrew considered it to be a sign, a shot across the bow, as it were. Was it a necessary one? It was, insofar as it was instrumental in luring all of them to Rapa Nui. It was to release it on an unsuspecting world that the Moai Congress had been set up. If Anakena was trying to convince Jasper to hold the conference, then the tablet would be an incentive. Who was in Chile when the tablet was discovered? Kent Clarke Films, Albert Morris, and Edwina Rasmussen. That was unless the tablet was a mere frill.

Who was doing this? Who was this frighteningly intelligent, endlessly patient and creative person carrying out this plan? I emailed the college and asked if they might have an email address for the former Mrs. Pedersen. I didn't expect a quick response, but at this point, anything was worth a try.

Who else had been devastated by the death of little Flora? Felipe Tepano, it seemed to me, most certainly qualified. Had he predicted the death on the mound of dirt in order to divert suspicion from himself? Surely that wouldn't work. Was it rather not more likely to point to him as a potential killer? Was it a coincidence, then? Did he really foresee a death? And if he wasn't involved in the deaths, did Anakena view the prediction as a serendipitous event that added an element of almost supernatural intensity to what was to follow? If so, then Anakena was adaptable and responsive to a changing situation.

I drove to the Tepano's guest house. Felipe wasn't at home, but Maria was. "Thank you for the photograph," I said. "I now know about Flora Pedersen."

"That didn't take long," she said. "You won't tell my husband, will you?"

"No, and I've brought it back. I made a copy."

"How did you find out?"

"I'm afraid I can't tell you that," I said. "I just did."

"There aren't many people anymore that could tell you," she said. I hoped I hadn't betrayed Andrew's confidence.

"She was the loveliest little girl, our Tavake," she said. "So pale and pretty, and very sweet. We all adored her. All of the people working at the dig site helped to look for her, all of us. We searched into the night. I remember the Pedersens sat on the beach all night and well into the next day. Everyone's first thought was that she had drowned, of course. I guess after a while they thought the tide might bring her body in. But Felipe had one of his visions, you know. He said she was in a cave. We all searched the caves, but we missed her. She had climbed into a very small lava tube and perhaps had fallen. She may have been unconscious, because we called and called her name."

"Did you ever hear from the Pedersens after that?" I said.

"Sometimes," she said. "At first there was a letter maybe once a year, but then they stopped. One of the archaeologists working here later told us that the Pedersens had divorced and that she had moved away. She never recovered, though. She was—I'm not sure how to put this—she was very nervous all the time. She was not strong, you know, in the way she dealt with things that happened. I remember a dish was stolen from our house, and there was much crying. It was a dish and nothing special. She seemed to feel everything much more deeply than the rest of us. She was also much younger than her husband. They seemed to be in love. I think she was not strong enough, in her head, I mean, to deal with what happened to little Tavake."

"Do you know where she is now?"

"In heaven, I hope," Maria said. "She died maybe ten years later. I don't know why. She would still have been young. I think what happened killed her. It just took some time to do it."

Another theory down. "What was her name?" I asked.

"Margaret," Maria said.

"How did you feel towards those young men? It was a terrible mistake to make."

"I was very angry at first," she said. "But accidents happen, mistakes are made. We Rapa Nui tend to be more accepting of these kinds of things than perhaps you would be. Perhaps it is our tragic history. I have tried very hard to forgive."

"Has Felipe forgiven them?"

"That, I cannot say," she said. "I think so. He did love little Tavake. We lost a little girl a year or so before the Pedersens arrived here. She got very sick and died before we could get her to Santiago for medical help. I think Felipe saw something of his daughter in Tavake. Gordon, yes, I think he has forgiven. The others, I don't know. I know he never liked Jasper. None of us did."

I went back to the hotel yet again, and took a good look at the photograph, which Brian had very kindly printed off for me. There were nine people in that photograph, six of whom were dead. That left Andrew, who was obviously terrified he would be next, and Gordon, whose daughter was already a victim, and Felipe Tepano. He might be in his early seventies, but he was one tough seventy-something-year-old. I'd seen him haul stuff around the grounds of the hotel that would give me pause. I didn't think a body or two would even slow him down. Still, I didn't think he was the killer, any more than the other two were. So that was the whole group. I didn't know where to go from there.

And then I had one of those forehead-slapping moments when you wonder how you could possibly be so obtuse. Of course there had been someone else there, the someone who had taken the photograph! It was possible, of course, that the camera had a timer, but I didn't think so. I needed another person, and the photographer was that person.

I phoned the Tepano guesthouse. The phone rang and rang. Not only was there no answer, but there was no answering machine or voicemail.

I had been looking for people over the age of fifty or

sixty. I needed to expand the age range. I had assumed that Flora was an only child. Maybe she was their only child. Maybe either or both of them had been married before. There could be a sibling. Flora was four. The sibling, if from a previous marriage, would have to be older obviously, perhaps much older, if Professor Pedersen's child. Flora would have been about thirty-four if she'd lived. So who got pulled into the circle if I said forty-something or older?

Rory Carlyle? If there was a connection there, I didn't know what it was. He didn't like Jasper, but despite what Fuentes thought, his connection to Seth and Dave seemed to be pretty remote. He was in his forties, though, and therefore stayed on the list. Brian, however, was way too young.

Yvonne and Enrique might qualify, but it would be close. This person, whoever it was, had to be old enough to take a decent photograph. Kent Clarke would be back in the running again, too. My list of suspects was growing longer. This was not the way I wanted it to go.

When I thought about it, I decided that Gabriela was the key. She really was the odd victim out. She lived on Rapa Nui; she did not need to be lured here. She worked at the hotel, but she didn't stay, and she wasn't attending the congress. She had come to get her belongings, and she'd been upset, but I now knew why.

It was her cards, which Andrew/Cassandra had had the bad taste to tell her about. Celestino, the hotel manager, had said there was some commotion, which is why he'd found her in the hedge. What had happened to her after she got her things? Did she leave the hotel, only to be brought back? Not likely. Perhaps it was the scene of the crime, not the photograph, that would tell me what I now needed to know.

The sun was hot, even with the ocean breeze, and several of the Moaimaniacs were out by the pool. Moira was outside talking to Gordon, who had obviously driven her back to the hotel from her visit to Rory. They waved as I walked by. I walked along from Tepano's Tomb, past one row of rooms, and into the garden where Gabriela had been found.

I looked at the row of rooms by the sea. Jasper had stayed there. Dave had stayed elsewhere, in another building, but he'd been found on Tepano's Tomb, which was well within my view. Standing where I was in the garden, I could see Jasper's room, Dave's final resting place, and the place by the hedge where Gabriela had been found. I very slowly looked around.

It was so obvious: the garden shed, also known as the site office of Kent Clarke Films. I ran up to it, flung open the door, only to find it empty, except for a bare table, and a horseshoe on a nail over the door.

I was back outside and on my way to call Pablo Fuentes when what I suppose was either the culmination of Anakena's plan, or a last-ditch effort to wreak havoc and death before we all left the island, began to unfold. In my mind it was this frightening tableau, a scene that seemed to move in slow motion. To one side of the picture, Moira and Gordon were saying goodbye, with Moira turning back toward our room and Gordon heading the opposite way toward the main building, passing Cassandra as he did so. Edith was playing with a cat on the far side of the drive from Moira. The Kent Clarke van was slowly moving up the drive. As it approached Edith's position, it stopped, the door opened, and Edith walked toward it.

"Gordon," I yelled as loud as I could. "Edith! Get Edith! Edith, run away!"

It was too late. The little girl was in the van, and it was starting to move. Moira, who had heard me and turned to see what had happened, grabbed the passenger door, wrenched it open, and climbed in as the van sped away. It swerved at the gate, but kept going.

Gordon, realizing at last what had happened, ran to his truck and started after them. My car was at least fifty yards away. "Andrew," I yelled, and he too started to run. We got into the Suzuki, but we were very far behind.

"Where?" I said.

"Anakena," he said, grimly. "Go!"

It was fortunate I'd been there before and could find the way. The fastest route to Anakena from the hotel hugged the airport runway before setting a diagonal course right through the middle of the island. I drove as fast as I could, and on occasion we could see Gordon's truck way ahead. When we got close to the beach there was a choice of roads. "Which way?" I said.

"I don't remember," he said. "It's not the same as it was. Just get me to the beach. I need to get my bearings on the beach."

I picked the road that led to the parking area. I couldn't see either Gordon's truck or the Kent Clarke van. "We've come the wrong way," I said, but Andrew was already out of the car and heading for the water.

Anakena Beach is a horseshoe-shaped ring of white coral sand, a strange oasis in an essentially rocky coast. The ground starts to rise gradually as you leave the sea. There are two hills, large mounds really, nearby, and I could see a cave near the top of one of them. But Andrew didn't go that way. He stood, his back to the water for a moment, looking left and right, before he started running across the sand. I followed. The surface was soft and very hard to run through, my feet sinking into the burning sand. I wasn't dressed for this and neither was Andrew.

He began shedding his garb as he ran, clothes flying everywhere, first the wig, then the long skirt, the jacket and then the blouse, until he was down to running shoes and his boxer shorts.

All these clothes presented an obstacle course to me, and

I kept getting farther and farther behind. We ran past the ahu with its moai and away from the beach. I was gasping with the effort of making my way through the sand. I followed him as best I could, and when I rounded a mound nearly ran into the van and truck. I kept going past that, trying to see where Andrew had gone. After a minute or two, I realized I was completely alone. I couldn't believe it. Not five minutes away was a beach filled with dozens of bathers and now nothing. There was no road here, just some trails leading off somewhere, I had no idea where.

I figured that Andrew had been about two hundred yards ahead of me at most when I'd lost him. But I could see over that distance and he simply wasn't there That had to mean the cave was somewhere close.

The terrain was rocky now, with grassy patches as well. I couldn't see a cave, at least not like the one I'd taken Gordon to, where the mouth was quite obvious in the rock. That said to me it was subterranean. I had to find the entrance. I was running, stumbling, trying not to break my ankle, when I saw something gleam in the sunlight. It was a pile of silver bracelets. Andrew was showing me the way. At first it looked as if he'd simply left them on a rock, but on closer examination I could see a small opening down about four feet in what looked to be simply a pile of stones interspersed with tufts of yellow grass.

I stood for a minute thinking about this. I had no idea what lay on the other side, but I was reasonably sure that pushing through that opening was not going to do much for anybody. I could go back to the beach and try and get help, but we were still going to go in there one at a time, and if Edith and Moira were being held hostage, as they most certainly were, that wouldn't help either.

I'd had experience with only one cave, although I had been told the island, being volcanic rock, was riddled with them. The one cave I did know, however, had two ways in, one of them on the cliff face over the water. This part of the coast did not have the high cliffs of Poike or Orongo, rather it was a series of rocky outcrops. I ran to the shore and picked my way along it, keeping the pile of rocks inland as my reference point. At last I found a cave, just a few feet up from the shoreline and in relatively the right spot. I decided it was worth a try.

The problem was that if the cave was exactly the same as Gordon's, then when I stepped into the cave, I would block the light and be immediately seen. Or, it could be a cave that went nowhere near where I wanted to go. I tried to listen carefully to see if I heard anything that would tell me someone was in there, but the wind was the only sound that was audible. I counted to ten and crawled up and into the opening. At first it looked to be a simple cave with no other chambers, but when I went to the back, I found another tunnel, a lava tube. It looked almost man-made, although it couldn't have been. I got down on my hands and knees and started in.

The cave was rock, but it might just as well have been broken glass. It cut through the knees of my pants within a minute or two. My hands were scraped and bleeding. I still had the light behind me, though, and knew I was keeping a reasonably straight course in the right direction and could, if necessary, find my way out. Then the shaft turned upward. I pulled myself along for a few yards in almost complete darkness.

I decided I couldn't go any farther, and stopped. The air was bad now that the shaft had changed direction. It was hot, and the shaft seemed to me to be getting narrower. I didn't know what to do.

It was then I heard the sound of voices. Not only that, but I thought I saw a pinprick of light above me. I hauled myself up the shaft and into a more open area, but not high enough to stand up in, lit from below. I peered as carefully as I could over the edge. I had been right about the other entranceway. I could see it and Gordon, Andrew, and Moira standing to one side of it, just far enough away, in fact, that they'd never make it if they made a run for it. The light that was focused on them, a powerful flashlight, cast huge shadows on the wall behind them. I couldn't see Edith, but I could see her shadow. She was behind them.

"Look," Gordon was saying. "It's me that you want. Not my daughter, not Moira. They have nothing to do with this. Please let them go. I will stay."

"I also will stay," Andrew said. "My name is Andrew Jones. I am another that you want."

"Andrew Jones! What a pleasant surprise," a voice that seemed to be right beneath me said. "I thought I wasn't going to be able to find you. This is very noble of you, I'm sure, but you are all going to die."

"You are very sick," Andrew said.

The voice beneath me laughed. "I've been told that many times, by people much more qualified than you. Runs in the family," the voice said. "My mother spent the last four years of her life staring at the wall and picking imaginary lint off her sweater. Can't imagine what drove her over the edge, can you? Could it have been the death of her daughter? I adored both of them, you know. I spent what should have been the best years of my life looking after my mother. She had to be spoon-fed, and she had to wear diapers. What do you think of that?"

"I'm sorry," Gordon said.

"I'll bet you are," the voice said. "You don't even remember me, do you? You were off in your own little world, oblivious to anyone but yourselves, and your petty wants."

"I remember you very well now," Andrew said. "You

were an obnoxious kid who resented your little sister, and all the attention she got." Perhaps Andrew thought he would provoke the killer into doing something stupid, but this killer was made of ice.

"You have no idea how I felt," the voice said. "I think this scintillating conversation needs to come to an end. Which of you would like to go first?"

"I will," Andrew said. His voice cracked.

"Nervous, are we?" the voice said. "Think how frightened Flora must have been, all alone in the dark. Your lipstick is smudged, by the way."

I couldn't see exactly where the killer was, although, given the angle of the light and the direction the others were looking, I was reasonably sure it was straight down, perhaps under the lip of the ledge on which I was now lying. Deadly tattoos were no longer the weapon of choice, I would assume, given the crowd in the cave. That probably meant that the killer didn't have a knife, either. Three adults could probably overtake one person with a knife. Anakena had to have a gun, so really the element of surprise was the only hope left. There was a large rock on the ledge, and I did the only thing I could think to do. I tried to push it off. It wouldn't budge. As quietly as I could, I turned and, bracing my back against the side of the bubble, I put my feet against the rock and pushed again.

I'm not exactly sure what happened then, except that I was falling. The ledge had given way. A shot rang out, and I hit the floor of the cave facedown. I tried to take a breath, but I couldn't. There seemed to be blood around me, and I was trying very hard not to pass out. I looked up to see Andrew holding his arm. Blood poured through his fingers, but he was still on his feet. Moira was hunched over what I took to be Edith. Gordon was just standing there, stunned.

I wondered why I wasn't dead. I had to have fallen ten

feet onto sheer rock. To my surprise, it wasn't as hard as I thought it would be. I tried to sit up, but could only just raise my head.

"Is everybody more or less all right?" I gasped.

"I think so," Gordon said. Andrew nodded.

"Are you?" Moira said, unfolding herself from around Edith, who ran to her father and grabbed his hand.

"I guess so," I replied. "Where's . . . ?" It was then I noticed that I was spread-eagled on top of the decidedly unconscious Mike Sheppard.

"Good of you to drop by," Andrew said.

EPILOGUE

I HAVE COME to regard Rapa Nui, a tiny island in a huge ocean of water, as a metaphor for our planet, a similar speck in the ocean of space. Against all odds, isolated for perhaps a thousand years or more, the people of Rapa Nui created a civilization. It is all there, the hopes and aspirations of all of us, for our children, for ourselves. In the extraordinary voyages of the people who went there first, we can see the curiosity and courage that impels the human race onwards. In their rituals, we can see our own longing for the existence of some power beyond us. In their history we can see man's inhumanity to man writ large in the ravages of imperialism, and more than anything, on that windswept isle bereft of trees, we can see the inevitable result of our casual disregard for the land and water on which we find ourselves. And I suppose, on a more personal level, in its human tragedies, we can see our own.

I know I will remember for the rest of my life the damaged souls I met on Rapa Nui, those men whose lives had been torn apart by a terrible mistake. Seth who'd spent his whole life after Anakena in his garage trying to read rongorongo, and Dave who was all hail fellow well met but who didn't seem to me to have any real friends, and who had a brother who would rather send money than come to his funeral. Then there was Jasper who had to go on proving himself over and over, and Andrew who went through life in disguise. Only Gordon, it seemed to me, had obstinately clung to some form of normalcy, no matter how deep his guilt. I hope he and Andrew both found some peace at Anakena at last.

Most of all there was Mike, his soul corroded by obsession and revenge. I don't like to think that human beings are irretrievable, but if they are, then Mike is one who is. He pleading insanity, of course, and it may work. His life was a series of horrendous losses—a father who left when Mike was a baby; an adored stepsister who died tragically; a stepfather who also left him after his stepsister's death and the divorce, never to be heard from again; and a mother, fragile at the best of times, who descended into acute depression and who eventually took her own life.

Perhaps people survive the best they can, and in Mike's case, it was the desire for revenge that kept him going. He had a checkered career as a film director and editor, given his substance abuse problem, but he managed to hold it together until he happened to get a job with Kent Clarke Films on a documentary featuring Jasper Robinson. Jasper was arrogant and fast and loose with the truth, but hugely successful, and it was all too much for Mike. It was then, perhaps, that his descent into what surely must be madness began, as he methodically and patiently began to plan and then execute his revenge.

Fate has dealt a better hand to some of the others. Kent Clarke took the footage she had of Rapa Nui and persuaded

Rory to be her on-camera expert. The resulting documentary, considerably more accurate than the one she would have done with Jasper, won a prize at some film festival, and Kent Clarke Films continues to be a growing concern. Her next documentary is going to feature Andrew Jones. He did a farewell performance for a rather select audience—the last remaining delegates to the Moai Congress—the night before we left and stunned everyone with his talent.

Before we left Rapa Nui, Moira and I went back to the cemetery we'd visited our first day. Victoria Pakarati was there, too, tending a grave. It was a simple white cross like the others, and it said only *Flora Pedersen, July 3, 1971– August 18, 1975.* Above that was a drawing of a little bird. A rosebush grew on the grave.

"Gordon told me about Flora," Victoria said. "I've decided that I will look after this grave from now on. Felipe and Maria Tepano have done it for years, but it's too hard for them. I will tend the others, as well, for Dave and Seth. I don't think they have any family that cares. I suppose it's right that they should be here together, the two of them and little Flora. Maybe Gordon will be here someday, too, in the far distant future, I hope."

"How is Gabriela?" Moira said.

"She's going to be fine," Victoria said. "I know words are inadequate, but thank you."

It was a long and exhausting flight home, especially for Moira. I could tell there was something she wanted to say to me, and I just waited until she got around to it. "About Rory," she said, finally.

"It doesn't matter," I said. "I won't say anything to anybody, including Clive. Wild horses, if you'll forgive the expression, wouldn't drag it out of me."

"There's nothing to tell," she said. "Honestly. I won't say I didn't think about it, or that I didn't find Rory attractive. But I love Clive. It was just a little interlude, that midlife crisis you accused me of having before we left, and nothing of any substance happened."

"Okay," I said. I just couldn't think of anything to say that would be appropriate.

"You're thinking that I kissed him a couple of times," she said.

"No, I'm not," I said. I was, of course.

"Yes, you are, but that was as far as it went. I suppose I've been feeling a bit . . . I don't know, as if life may have passed me by," she said.

"It hasn't," I said.

"I wasn't entirely truthful about my medical results," she said.

"I figured that out," I said.

"Of course you did," she said. "You figure everything out, eventually, bless your heart. The prognosis is good. I'm not making that up, but the chemo starts next week."

"Anything you need, Moira, I'll be there."

"I was hoping you might check the spa from time to time. I have a good manager, but I'd feel happier knowing she could call someone like you if she needed help. She would, too. She likes you."

"Any time," I said. "And I'll take care of McClintoch and Swain. You and Clive can just leave these things to me. Does Clive know?"

"Yes, he does," she said. "I wasn't entirely fair to him, when I said he wasn't dealing well with my illness. He has actually been terrific, once he got used to the idea. He's the one who suggested that you and I go to Rapa Nui, to have some time just the two of us, together again."

"I may have underestimated Clive," I said.

"Yes, you have," she said. "I appreciate your offer about the shop, because I'd like to have some time with Clive, too."

"The shop and your spa will be fine. Everything is going to be fine, Moira," I said.

"Yes, it is," she replied. "I wouldn't have missed this trip for anything. Despite everything that happened, I found it life-affirming in some undefinable way."

"You were very brave to get into that van with Edith."

"It was instinct. I didn't think I cared what happened to me, but when it came right down to it, I did. I'm very glad you showed up. Gordon and Andrew were wonderful. I think they meant it when they said to let us go and they would stay."

"I think everyone acquitted themselves rather well," I said.

"I think we did, too. The whole business made me realize that I am determined to get well. I will beat this, you know."

"Yes, you will," I said.

"When you came after us, did you know it was going to be Mike? Or just one of the people from Kent Clarke Films?"

"Once I realized the garden shed was the scene of the crime, I knew it was Mike," I replied. "He always sat at the end of the bar. As a left-hander, he sat where there couldn't be a right-handed person next to him. I guess, given his alcohol problem, he didn't want to spill a drop."

"As I said, you figure everything out eventually," she said. "He was poor little Flora's stepbrother, right? Margaret Pedersen's child by a previous marriage?"

"Right," I said.

"Did he shoot the horse on the shore?"

"I have no idea," I replied. "Maybe just seeing a dead horse gave him the idea. He was very creative, wasn't he? He planned everything just so, but he also took advantage of opportunities as they presented themselves. It's unfortunate he used his talents for such terrible ends."

"Where do you figure he got the snake venom?"

"A snake farm, apparently. He worked on a documentary at one, according to Pablo Fuentes."

"And the gun? How did he get that into the country?"

"Fuentes says it was probably in with all the film equipment."

"I guess Jasper was too self-absorbed to realize that the tablet he found in Chile was the one the group had found thirty years ago on Rapa Nui," she said. "Did Mike have the tablet all those years?"

"There is no record of it in any collection, so I suspect that when Flora died, the Pedersens packed up and left the island in disarray, for obvious reasons. The tablet would have gone with them, and with both parents dead, it ended up with Mike."

"But Seth and Dave recognized it?"

"Eventually," I said. "Dave brought it to Rapa Nui at Jasper's request, and he was clearly suspicious. He called Seth and asked him to bring a photo of the group taken when the tablet was found, I assume to make the comparison. The photograph went missing when Dave died, as did his paper. I don't think Dave would have let Jasper get away with presenting the tablet as coming from Chile, once he realized it didn't. Dave talked to Kent Clarke about his concerns, and Kent told Jasper, but by then it was too late for both Jasper and Dave, too late for all of them, in fact."

"Mike must have realized when he grabbed Edith that he'd be caught eventually. There was no way he was going to get off the island," she said.

"I don't think he cared at that point," I said. "It seems to me that Flora's death had become a symbol for him of all that was wrong in his life, and all he cared about was revenge."

"It is so sad," Moira said. "All of it, really."

Rob came to meet me at the airport. I've tried to train him not to do that, but every now and then he just does. He looked very nice in a chocolate-brown suede jacket I'd given him for Christmas. Clive was there to meet Moira as well.

He looked kind of tired and pale, but I could see from the set of his mouth that he was going to get himself and Moira through whatever the next few months held.

"Moira isn't . . ." I started to say when we'd waved good-bye to them, but I wasn't sure how to finish the sentence.

"I know," Rob said. "Clive told me."

"I've suggested Clive take lots of time off to be with her. I can manage the store okay, and I'm going to keep an eye on the spa, starting tomorrow." I was happy to have a job to do, something I knew I was good at, something I knew would really help.

"I had a feeling you'd say that. I've talked to Alex Stewart," Rob said. "He says to tell you that he'll be at the shop when it opens tomorrow, and he'll come in as long as you and Clive want him to."

"Isn't he wonderful? He should just be enjoying his retirement, but no, he keeps helping me out when I need him. Did you retire, by the way?"

"No. I'm going to open a restaurant instead," he said.

"You aren't a bad cook," I said. "Since when did you know anything about how to run a restaurant though?"

"Since I started taking a course."

"This has something to do with catching bad guys, doesn't it?" I said, after a moment's contemplation.

"Money laundering," he agreed.

"And you complain about the way I get into trouble," I sighed.

"Think of the bright side. Tomorrow night I'm coming to your place to cook you dinner. We'll eat at the dining room table, beautifully set. I'll be chef and waiter. Duck à l'orange, I'm thinking."

"Bacon and eggs in the kitchen would be fine," I said. "If I had a kitchen, that is."

"I am the bearer of good news on that score," he said. "I

am here to tell you that due to my tenacity, courage, and all the negotiating techniques I learned at the police academy, your kitchen is finished!"

"Promise me you aren't just toying with me!"

"It's true. It looks really nice, I have to admit, so much so that I'm thinking of moving in with you."

"Rob, I own the smallest house on the planet. You know we can barely manage a weekend together at my place."

"Which is why, when it came on the market a few days ago, I made an offer on the equally small townhouse right next to yours. It's similar, if not absolutely identical to yours. I have until midnight to up my offer." We both looked at our watches. It was eight p.m.

"I'm thinking that the only big part of your house and the one next to it, is the backyard. If we took down the fence between them, we'd have a huge yard. Maybe we could even get a dog. It's up to you, but it could work out well. We'd both have our own space, which I know means a lot to you, and best of all, when we have a fight I wouldn't have so far to walk home."

I had to laugh. "Okay," I said.

"Okay? You aren't toying with me now, are you?"

"No. I think it would work out well."

"All right! Let's get going. I have an offer to sign back."

"I got a tattoo," I said in as close to a conversational tone as I could muster.

"A tattoo!" he said. "That sounds interesting."

"It's small and discreet and only you will get to see it."

"Is it a heart with the word Rob across the middle?"

"No, it isn't," I said.

"Hedging your bets, I see," he said, but he was smiling.

"It's just that I had this little tattoo phobia to get over."

"Most of us could just ignore a tattoo phobia," Rob said.

"Not me."

"I know," he sighed. "I hear you apprehended the bad guy."

"I didn't so much apprehend him as squash him." I tried to laugh, but I couldn't. It must have showed, because Rob stopped right there in the parking lot and gave me a hug.

"I brought you a present," I said into the brown jacket.

"That's nice."

"Not really. It's a flowered shirt."

"Flowers," he said.

"You'll never wear it."

He smiled. "You never know."

"I know."

"I got you a present, too," he said.

"A present?" I said.

"I know you don't want to get married, but I wanted to mark our relationship in some way. It's a ring."

"A ring."

"With your birthstone, and maybe a couple of very small and discreet diamonds," he added. "Only you will be able to see them."

"Diamonds," I said.

"You'll never wear it."

Carpe diem, I thought. "You never know," I said.

LYN HAMILTON

ARCHAEOLOGICAL MYSTERIES

"Hamilton's archaeological mysteries [are] sure
to have armchair travelers on the edge of their
settees. At once erudite and entertaining."
—*New York Times Book Review*

The Xibalba Murders	0-425-15722-9
The Maltese Goddess	0-425-16240-0
The Moche Warrior	0-425-17308-9
The Celtic Riddle	0-425-17775-0
The African Quest	0-425-18313-0
The Etruscan Chimera	0-425-18463-3
The Thai Amulet	0-425-19487-6

Available wherever books are sold or at
penguin.com

C.J. Box

The mystery series about Joe Pickett, a Wyoming game warden trying to keep the wilderness—and the family he loves—safe from danger.

OPEN SEASON
0-425-18546-X

SAVAGE RUN
0-425-18924-4

WINTER KILL
0-425-19595-3

TROPHY HUNT
0-425-20293-3

THE JOE PICKETT NOVELS ARE:

"Muscular." —*New York Times*

"Heartfelt." —*Washington Post*

"Fascinating." —*USA Today*

"Suspenseful." —*New York Daily News*

Available wherever books are sold or at
penguin.com